IN DREAMS THE MINOTAUR APPEARS LAST

ADAM CRAIG

Published by Cinnamon Press,
Meirion House
Tanygrisiau
Blaenau Ffestiniog
Gwynedd
LL41 3SU
www.cinnamonpress.com

The right of Adam Craig to be identified as the author of this work has been asserted by him in accordance with the Copyright, Designs and Patent Act, 1988. © 2018 Adam Craig.
ISBN 978-1-78864-003-9
British Library Cataloguing in Publication Data. A CIP record for this book can be obtained from the British Library.
All rights reserved. No part of this publication may be reproduced, stored in a retrieval system, or transmitted in any form or by any means, electronic, mechanical, photocopying, recording or otherwise without the prior written permission of the publishers. This book may not be lent, hired out, resold or otherwise disposed of by way of trade in any form of binding or cover other than that in which it is published, without the prior consent of the publishers.

Designed and typeset in Garamond by Cinnamon Press. Cover design by Adam Craig © Adam Craig.

Cinnamon Press is represented by Inpress
and by the Welsh Books Council in Wales.

The publisher gratefully acknowledges the financial support of the The Welsh Books Council.

Printed in Poland.

Nothing is True. Everything is Permitted.
Hassan-i Sabbah

This is for

Jan, always
&
Cottia and Seth,
because imagination is the greatest magic
&
Merlin, to keep for another day.

In Dreams the Minotaur Appears Last

cold persistent, chill in the pavement flags, crack-faced and familiarly unfamiliar, ice in fingers splayed, hands leading blindly, through darkness that was not quite dark, pre-dawn bleeding into dawn, next turn a suggestion hanging in the murk, next turn after likewise, feet hesitant, hands reading Braille of ice, air and shade, incomprehensible no matter how hard she tried, wall angling sharply, bringing another turn sooner than expected, a second and a third before the wall, dropping away, left her stranded, stumbling, grabbing at nothing, the feeling persisting that she could see a wall and its twin opposite in each echo's step, although she walked softly, self-conscious and afraid of noise, of making noise, yet still there was step and echo-step and turning sharply revealed nothing, because that which followed behind might as easily be waiting in front, waiting in the space between each step and echo-step, and so   pausing, hesitating a moment, an agonising hour, this instant filled with uncertainty, every breath threatening to break silence, break into scream that would bring   she did not know, or refused to admit, fingers outstretched, little by little, until they met the nearest wall and, reading its surface rough and chill and signalling the next corner, the memory of making another turn just like this another turning just like this another turn just like this returned and, returning, reminded her of tightness between shoulder blades, skin crawling in expectation of the touch, the hand that might make contact at any moment, expected any second, unable to stop herself turning at the constant pressure, turning and looking into darkness that was not quite dark, turning back as quickly, memory and expectation binding tighter, next step-echo-step keeping close   chasing close   shadowing, need to run hard to resist, fear of making noise, attracting attention, holding her back through turn and alley-curve, alley narrowing, alley widening, sharply doubling-back, branching, next step-echo-step begging expectation, taking one fork, stumbling and feeling it was too late to turn back, thinking it might be there, she might see what was behind, the dead-end makes her gasp and turn and hurry and stumble into the mouth of a side-turning, stomach a knot of water threatening to burst, scream a third companion keeping step but straining to break free, break nerve with it and run, run break-neck pell-mell head-long, wildly into the wind, wind nothing more than a breath against neck and she knows, fear shrieking, fear mumbling, whispering to her calmly, that it will be after the next turning, or the one beyond that, but soon: a hole in the darkness, head huge, spread like open arms, its ears twitching, the hole waiting as she turns the final corner, or turns away from the final corner to find it waiting, inevitably, behind her, an infinite darkness within the blackness of air and alley and yet she will be able to see its eyes, their liquid blackness, body an absence that will reveal itself to her in greys and smudges of umber and in suspicion and in sharpness and she will stand waiting as its mouth opens as if to speak, stood waiting for it to speak, eyes large and obsidian and alive and finding hers but never speaking, may never speak, never yet spoke, never getting beyond opening its mouth, shoulders swelling with first breath, with foretaste of words, the first word, whatever that might be, whatever it was going to say, if only it would—*cusez-moi, madame, mais parlez vous anglais? Madame?*'

Minnette managed to turn towards the voice. Aware of the shop. The man's clothes, accented French. 'Yes.' Middle-aged, gaunt not from hunger but from obsessive dieting and exercise, muscles around the eyes and forehead tight, caught between alarm and outrage. 'Yes, I speak English. How can I help you?'

No direct request. She had been expecting that, he looked the type. Probably something in technology rather than finance or any of the other things affluent, middle-aged people found to fill their time and pockets these days. This one sidled up to what he was after.

She glanced at the ornate clock standing next to the till, escapement hoisted into the air by two brass-coloured demons, cabbalistic signs and open books of Wisdom and alembics and magical paraphernalia lying in a jumble at their feet. Glanced again, wondering if the battery needed changing, wanting to be sure she remembered what it had read the last time she had looked at it, position of the sun outside no help, this part of the Rue St Jacques getting little direct sunlight during the early autumn, the shade cast by the buildings on the other side of the road giving nothing away.

'I see.' She nodded, too distracted to have listened closely to what the American had been saying. 'Well, you could try browsing this section—' walking around the counter, gesturing towards a floor-to-ceiling bookcase facing the front door— 'where we have a very wide selection of independently published works—' words faltering when she saw the arthritic bulge of her outstretched fingers, conscious of pain in her hands, faint though it was today, not as bad as her hip, both sharper now she was thinking about them.

Minnette put her hands behind her back. Continued:

'We have pamphlets, monographs, even very rare, mimeographed booklets from the—' just the faintest of catch in her voice, hard not to stumble and feel a little affected whenever she said this— 'the middle of the last century, together with items from around the turn of the Nineteenth. Works on Numerology, Cabbala, Earth Mysteries—'

'Er, no.'

No. She knew this wasn't what the American was after. Knew she couldn't simply tell him, admit that she knew. That wasn't how this was supposed to be played out.

'I guess… Well, y' know…' He fiddled with a dog-eared first-paperback-edition of Bergier and Pauwels' *The Morning of the Magicians* resting on the small, Discounted Specials stand next to the till, the same edition likely to be on the stalls along the Quai Bonaparte for at most two-thirds what the shop's owner was charging. 'I mean, I read Crowley at college and that, y' know, that made an impression and I've been, y' know, searching ever since so…'

Minnette stared at him, one hand gripping the reading specs hanging from a cord around her neck. Until she willed herself to stop.

'Do you know his later works? They reach a maturity that is startling.' She knew this was not what the customer was here for. Knew and hoped anyway he might be interested. Might genuinely be searching. 'And those who came after him, Spare, of course, you're probably familiar with Spare, but—'

'I'm sorry, Madame, I don't think…' Frown deepening, eyes tracking: the bookshelves on each wall, the ones standing down the middle of the shop, resting on the carrousel of booklets and yellowing magazines by the front door, lingering on the floor. 'A guy, friend of a friend, he's been here. I know it's not, y' know, not exactly advertised, not on the net or, y' know, but I understand, I mean this guy, friend of a friend, told me—'

'Of course.' Hard not to sag. Or snarl. Face straight and pleasant and understanding and only too pleased to help, she called out: '*Pascal, es tu occupé?*' Adding: 'My colleague will be able to help you, sir,' to the American. Pretending not to watch as Pascal led him through the rear of the bookshop and up the stairs to the windowless room where the 'special collection' was kept. And feeling a defeat. Or at least a sadness, and that muted as her mind turned over again the question of how long the American had been standing there before she had noticed him. How long she had been lost in thought. In memories.

That sadness, the small defeat, came back as she left the bookshop on the Rue St Jacques that evening. Forgotten until then, familiar-seeming on its return, yet enough to bring a sour flash to her stomach, which in turn made her consider limping uphill to the bistro on the Rue de la Montagne Sainte Geneviève, just beneath Le Panthéon. The place was too far to go for lunch. Or an evening meal, for that matter, trek enough make her bad hip chafe and ensure a sleepless, fractious night. But, between the sourness of defeat and the sourness of an empty stomach, the walk seemed less foolhardy. And there was no appeal in drinking alone in her apartment. Not tonight. No reason for that. None she could name. Tonight she deserved to dine out. For surviving another day at the bookshop. If nothing else. Minnette kept that in mind as she limped along Rue des Écoles, kept all other thoughts out of sight, all disappointments and defeats covered with thoughts of a meal, a bottle of wine, a liqueur afterwards. No need to think yet again that the only hidden knowledge she had found in the bookshop was the going rate for a particular kind of vintage pornography.

There had never been a plan. None she could recall with clarity, none she could admit. Working in bookshops had seemed to make sense: she liked books anyway and, so she thought, working in a bookshop would make it easier to find the kinds of books she wanted to read. It had worked out differently. And yet she continued. Because. Idealism, perhaps. Once. Stubbornness, certainly, yes. Perhaps. Maybe that. Maybe. And yet she continued. Habit. Call it habit. Call it that, wasn't worth the bother, anyway, and that was the—

The clock on Le Panthéon struck the quarter hour.

Minnette pulled the café door shut behind her. Hip twinging, beginning to throb. Footway uneven. Making her think again of carrying a walking stick, once in a while. Making her decide not to give in to the pain. Almost stumbling and blaming that on the wine. Street lights too widely spaced along this stretch. Which made her think. A petition. Or she could write to a newspaper. Road bending as it sloped downwards. Which made her think. Think that she should think of something else, time later than she had realised and still a way to go before the nearest métro station. Minnette watching her step as she passed under a street light, into the twilight on the other side, concentrating on that, trying to ignore other thoughts that, conjured, were unwilling to leave. Fixing on the bookshop. On having to buy food. And toilet cleaner.

She needed to buy toilet cleaner and kept forgetting that she needed to buy— A shade, a texture under each thought, because once it had surfaced, it was impossible to dismiss any thought so easily, even a memory that should be almost happenstance after all this time: the memory of walking uphill, up a hill, in the dark, in the cold. Minnette began compiling a shopping list, reciting it again with each new item added. And still the memory unpeeled, in the gaps between items. Not words. A sensation of memory. Familiar. Often recalled, turned over: walking up a winding lane— Minnette paused, looked for traffic that wasn't there, crossed to the other side of the street, street old and winding and she was going down and not up and yet: the familiar memory of the lane winding up and up. An old street in an old part of a town. Remembrance a familiar undercurrent, no power left in it. But it wouldn't leave her, not now it had been conjured, lane winding through the cold of a late, later afternoon, sure she would get to the top soon. Nothing else. Just that. Under, in the spaces. Not a word, or a sentence of description. Just a sensation, a feeling without words. Old as the street she had climbed— Minnette paused, looking for traffic that wasn't there, crossed to the other side of the street, street lights widely spaced here and, yes, perhaps she should write to the paper or to someone and complain about this street, which prompted memory only because it was old and on a hill and winding a little, just a little and

and it could be any street, in darkness, small-hours still— she might find herself walking, walking in darkness, along a street, a backstreet like this, narrow and quiet, buildings anonymous, footsteps chasing out of the shadows, walking just behind her as they had, forty years and a thousand kilometres ago, in twilight, in darkness, so, in sleep, she might find herself wandering an anyplace, one hand stretching out, air cold to the touch, wall dark, rough when she finds it, wandering a narrow lane, a backstreet nagging in its familiarity even if she knew, felt she knew, she had not been here before, bricks rough-faced and faceless and small-hours still but unyielding to the press of fingers, like the flagstones, the cobbles underfoot under darkness, footsteps darting away to come back under a sky touched by a trace of colour, not aware of fatigue or bad hip, simply walking, as she had before in dreams, old dreams that had become filled with running and the drive to keep running, running until she woke, running until she had therapy, until they faded and stopped, those dreams nothing like these dreams, where she walked in silence but for the sound of her footsteps following—and pausing at that, at this corner, listening for the distant sounds of traffic, refusing to walk on, not straight away, despite a tingling between the shoulder blades, an irrational fear, an anxiety like the ones that had made her run in her sleep, run nowhere, simply run with nothing at the end, not— not that she was going to worry about that, dreams of walking in darkness late at night, not when she was walking late at night, and not when there was an end to that walk: walking back to the apartment, ready to go to bed, not already in—she would know and think otherwise each time she walked home late at night, city quite, Paris never sleeps, city relatively quite and streets deserted but for her, but for footsteps and thoughts, Paris never sleeps, telling herself that, that she was walking home and not walking in a—place, this place, not an anyplace, she knew this place, it was familiar, vaguely, walked, surely, a dozen, a hundred times, always quiet even if Paris never sleeps, and simply not fixed clearly in mind because she had been distracted, had been thinking of walking in darkness late at night, or the shop, or another time forty years and a million kilometres away and that proved nothing, nothing, because she knew she knew the difference, between waking and dream, and this—didn't matter, because dreams didn't mean anything, of that she was certain, dreams, dreams meant—

Minnette stopped. Aware of the city's stillness. Aware of the ache from her bad hip stretching towards her knee. A tightness in the stomach. Tension across shoulders, neck. Pressure in the bladder. Of shadows clotting doorways, masking the windows of each building lining the street. Forming pools. Darkness that could be hiding —

Minnette stopped walking and waited.
Waited.

She startled when the hand appeared.
'You're going to buy this?'
The hand tilted the cover into view. She snatched the paperback away.
'I'm not—' Minnette dropped the book and turned away sharply, almost walking into a tourist. Grunting an apology in afterthought, limp worsening as she tried to walk faster, muttering under her breath. Notre-Dame reared over the opposite bank. Wooden bookstalls lined the parapet wall, casual browsers and tourists choking the pavement and making it hard to walk fast enough. Hip protesting, she stopped and gazed at the traffic along the Quai Voltaire in hope of getting across and back to the Rue St Jacques.
Began walking again. Unwilling to wait.
'You forgot your book.' He held it in front of her, easily keeping pace.
'I don't want it.'
'A present.' His expression hard to read, too easy to guess, one eye filled with silver, sky and dull sunlight reflecting from the monocle he always wore in public these days.
'Don't want any presents.'
He lengthened his stride, blocking her path and holding out the paperback. 'I bought it especially for you.' He smiled. Goading her, of course. Choice between stopping or walking into him, Minnette stopped, glowering as his smile never flickered, taking a little comfort in the wrinkles around his eyes, the lines folded deeply into cheeks and high forehead; in grey hair gone wispy, no longer full and dark. Refusing to meet his gaze, or take the book.

'Keep it, Guillaume. It's more your sort of thing.' Trying to put as much inflection in her voice as possible, hoping to hurt.

Guillaume shrugged, seeming not to notice. 'You seemed so engrossed...'

Thrusting the book and his hand away. 'I wasn't engrossed, I was—' re-reading the title, *Wisdom of the Ancients: A Practical Guide for Magicians, Witches & Warlocks*, giving the lurid, 1970s cover a dismissive sneer— 'I was curious. Contemptuous.'

'A-ha?' Nodding, Guillaume leaned forward as if waiting for her to say more.

Minnette turned, going back the way she had come. 'Piss off, Guillaume.'

'No, really—' he walked beside her, stride effortless when she knew she was close to having to stop, pain good for making her angrier if nothing else, anger allowing her to walk a little faster— 'it's a present—' and he held out the book.

'I told you—' stopping— 'I don't want the fucking book—' still avoiding his gaze, avoiding the eye made wide by the monocle, monocle she knew he had no need of, eyesight better than her's even though he was a year older, monocle an affectation like his bow ties and English blazers, like— 'it's a stupid book, it's books like that that —'

She shut her mouth. Took a breath. 'This is a stupid business.' Anger making her throat tight; hating herself for displaying so much emotion.

'Stupid,' she repeated, more quietly, wishing he would go, stop this.

Guillaume lowered the paperback. 'You should know as well as anyone, Minnette, this isn't a business. It's a passion, an avocation.'

He nodded goodbye, stepping around her.

'I'm...' Minnette almost held him back. 'I'm not exactly sure what this is any more.' Sure her voice wouldn't carry. But Guillaume paused, half-turning towards her.

'Then perhaps...'

Minnette waited, a few moments, long enough to become self-conscious, but Guillaume Boucaya did not look back again, did not finish what he had started.

There was a box of old pamphlets and a note waiting beside the till. No sign of Pascal. Or customers. The shop felt small, air close and filled with dust, the smell of ageing paper. Minnette pulled a face, a twinge of acid flaring across her stomach. She had not eaten lunch. Nothing to do with Guillaume. She had lingered too long over the bookstalls.

The ornate clock next to the till ticked, ticked, ticked.

Ignoring it. Holding her reading specs up to skim over the note from the shop's owner. Thinking: she didn't have to re-open the shop for another twenty minutes or so, she should buy food on the way home, clean the apartment, the kitchen. Thinking she should at least tidy up a little, thoughts meandering and not one word of the owner's note lodging although, reading it again, all it amounted to was: 'Sort these pamphlets.'

They were awful, the pamphlets. Badly printed. Badly bound. Badly written. Barely thought out.

Sighing. Muttering.

Charlatans.

All of them. All of these pamphleteers, every one. As bad as Guillaume.

Minnette flipped through one of the booklets. A word. A sentence. Reading a paragraph at random. Feeling the acid in her stomach grow sharper.

He had admitted it. More or less. Too late. And the admission had changed nothing. Hadn't harmed him at all: too many books by then, too many articles and too often on radio, even TV. All of it nonsense, rubbish, drivel, all of it—

A betrayal.

The box of pamphlets was still on the counter when Pascal came back from lunch. Lay untouched until he quietly gathered up those strewn across the counter, floor, put them back into the box and told her, since business was slow, he could manage if she wanted to go early.

mumbling. Two voices. A strain to separate them, words indistinguishable. More a buzzing. Hearing's edge. Sitting up straighter, book slithering from her lap, falling unnoticed. Disturbed by the voices even though she had explained them. Explanation not quite easing the fright of waking, of looking at the over-full living room and being sure for an instant it was part of a dream, dream already nothing but this fading adrenaline surge making her heart thump.

The voices stopped.

Minnette picked up the book, place lost.

It had seemed as though what they had been saying was important, words flowing on top of each other, voices seeping through the walls, very clear even as they buzzed, blurred, became tangled with the bricks that, between their hidden faces, contained corners and branching passages burrowing deeper into the wall as they folded one over the next, words walking along them, making sense of their twists, the words' twists, the passages', the overlapping buzz of a voice that explained, a voice that questioned, a voice softer as if deepened with age, a voice hoarse, gruff, having trouble shaping words, better at other sounds, but talking through the walls, winding, winding another, winding another thread around and through and under her sleep, her dream—

Until she woke. Gasp not quite a scream. Too quiet, too choked. Too aware of the buzzing voices.

The flat silent.

She took the book she had been reading before she had fallen asleep, her notebook and pen from the table beside the chair, standing, intending to go straight to bed.

The flat remained silent.

Minnette shook herself, 'This is ridiculous', dismissing dream, words flowing through, words gone, and only the memory they had been wondrous, or significant somehow, had made so much sense as they had flowed, been profound, somehow, only that somehow remaining.

They must have gone to sleep next door.

One lamp on.

Only one light on in the apartment, shadows hiding the face of the clock on the wall but presumably it was late, from the tiredness becoming an itch in every muscle, a weight in each joint, grating with each blink; from the stillness of the building as Minnette turned on the kitchen light, slotting her empty mug into the dish washer, debating whether to make hot milk, camomile tea, deciding to go straight to bed. Fingers brushed against the mirror hanging in the hallway, other hand finding the frame of the portrait hanging opposite, working down the corridor by touch alone, corridor completely lightless. Finding the end of the wall, the sharp radius of the corner, the wall's return. Pausing. Face of the clock in darkness. Picking up book, notebook, making her way down the corridor by touch alone, wall cool, each bump in the plaster, crack in the wall, seeming large, walking by touch alone until the wall turned, became a corner, making her way, wall cool, fingers moving over, other hand reaching out, falling, hand falling through empty space, rising, taking another step, moving slowly down the corridor, sure she was going to find

M. Jacotey sucked air through his dentures.

'I'm inclined not to agree. Don't you think?'

'U-huh.' Opening the last of the morning's post, junk mail joining the pile at the end of the counter.

'Yes, yes.' He nodded, mottled skin pink under the sparse white hair combed very precisely across his scalp. 'Yes, I agree, the chances of any sort of—shall we say "cosmic"?—cosmic convergence taking place—'

'Remote.' Glancing up again at the two young people —students maybe, probably from the Sorbonne, maybe, probably—drifting between Secret Societies and Auras & Astral Travelling.

'Quite so, remote.' M. Jacotey frowned, rummaging in the pockets of his shapeless canvas jacket, stooped shoulders hunching further. He produced a tin of throat pastilles, frown deliquescing to leave the vaguely serene expression he usually wore. 'Would you care...?'

Shaking her head, calling for Pascal.

'I admit, I'm not convinced,' M. Jacotey continued, pastille moving from one side of his mouth to the other, 'by the evidence I've seen, I'm afraid. No.' He shook his head, sorry to be feeling doubt at all.

The students glanced towards them. Minnette pretended not to notice.

'I've amassed a little evidence myself.' M. Jacotey stopped sucking on the sweet, the admission seeming to take him a little by surprise. 'Nothing—shall we say, "extensive"?—I couldn't say that...'

Scooping junk mail into the plastic waste paper bin under the counter and glancing again at the two students. Both pretended not to notice. Which made her less certain they were going to steal something. They might be curious after all. Or saw themselves as would-be adepts. Nodding at whatever M. Jacotey was saying. Calling for Pascal to take the remainder of the post into the rear office. And wondering whether it was her turn to deal with the bills and book orders today, after all.

'Which is why I've been working on this new interpretation or—dare I?—"theory", if you see what I mean.'

The pause caught her attention. Trying to remember what M. Jacotey had been saying. Gaze, unseeing, resting on the students. Unintentional stare enough to make one of them persuade the other to leave.

'That sounds interesting.' Hoping her smile did appear interested instead of confused. 'Oh, and of course, yes— I'd love to look at your theory, sometime. Bring it by the shop—'

There was a slight freeze in his expression. 'My notes aren't...' He rested a hand on the counter-top, blunt fingers stained with ink from the cheap ballpoints crowding the jacket's breast pocket, knuckles bent, raw. *At least ten years older than me*, she thought, trying not to dwell on the prospect. 'That is, they're still a little rough, scattered—'

'Next week—' regretting it as she said it— 'one evening some—' seeing him shrink and quickly altering this to: 'or tomorrow—' hating herself for yielding to an evening of crank theorising— 'I could come to your flat tomorrow night, if you like.'

'That would be so kind.' He picked lint from the jacket's sleeve. 'So kind—' the tilt of his head unmistakable— 'but tomorrow is the night of my meeting, you see, and—'

'Don't worry about it.' Trying to smooth over his embarrassment, ignore her own relief. 'Next week it is—'

'Would you like to come? To the meeting?'

'That's...' She had no idea what it was, aside from the conviction it was something she wouldn't want to do. 'I wouldn't like to intrude,' she managed, hoping it would be enough, imagining an evening of earnest people talking about Atlantis and the aetheric. 'Although I appreciate the offer. Really.'

'It wouldn't be an intrusion. We meet once a month, usually. Talk, exchange ideas, a small group, you see —"intimate", shall we say?—you'd enjoy—'

'I'm sure but all the same, I'd feel, simply turning up would be—'

'Oh, we have discussed inviting you before, but you often seem so busy, so—'

'I suppose I am—' as disconcerted by feeling anything as by being caught between hurt and flattery— 'but I'd feel like a gatecrasher even so, such short notice and—'

'Not at all. As M. Boucaya was saying only—'

'Guillaume? Guillaume's part of your group?'

'Yes. Yes, he is.' M. Jacotey had stepped back from the counter. She realised she had snapped out the question.

'Sorry.' Gathering up the remaining post, envelopes slipping from her hands. 'Sorry but I really have to get back to work.'

'Of course, and I, ah, I have things I should—' M. Jacotey retreated towards the door. 'Sorry to have taken up so much—'

'Don't worry about it.' Moderating her voice, trying again: 'It was no trouble at all.' Dumping the post and crossing the room. Opening the door for him. Repeating that he hadn't disturbed her, adding that they should sort out a time for next week. Thinking of leaving it at that, before adding: 'Enjoy your meeting.'

M. Jacotey, one foot out on the street, turned back, pulling a fold of paper from an inside pocket and pushing it into her hands.

'In case you change your mind.'

A web address. Underneath: a username and password. Lettering shaky, the handwriting of someone whose arthritis was just beginning to become a burden, but legible.

Minnette dropped it in the bin.

Thinking, *Charlatan*, as she left the shop, struggling to get the umbrella open, rain waiting until now to start and, regardless, deciding she had no choice but to wander up and down Boulevard Saint-Germain, the thought of staying in the shop for the whole lunch break not in the least bit depressing, not in the least, but she had to get some air, no matter how heavy the rain was coming down
—

Thinking, *Bastard*, as she tried to concentrate on a customer, handing the woman over to Pascal, sure there was no point in being angry any longer and sure it was habit and getting angry at him again for putting her through this—

Thinking, *Pointless*, as she fished the crumpled web address out of the waste paper bin before going home that evening.

The young man made the mountain bike rear up on its hind wheel, guiding it between disinterested stares and half-scowls and projecting knees and a shopping bag prolapsed at an overweight man's feet, alarm sounding. Doors closed, floor lurching. The young man seeming to see nothing but the bike's sinuous path between commuters standing, middle-aged women perched on the edge of seats, an art student's portfolio. Reaching the open area by the second set of doors. Finding insufficient space and setting off again, down the path between the seats, wheeling the bike deeper into the carriage.

Minnette watched, his hands gripping the handlebars, handlebars reminding her of the horns of a bull—which was a piece of art seen in a book, random memory that anyone might think of... Minnette looked at the floor of the Métro carriage. Remembering another train. Image hazy. Although the buttons on his denim jacket were clear enough. And his hair. Cropped short, very short for those times. Remembering sitting with the duffle bag on the seat beside her. Sitting, worrying the pages of a book. Nervous, too excited to read, any distraction welcome, noticing the boy, the youth wheeling a bike down the gangway. And wondering if he had just come out of the army, his hair so short, if he was on leave, Jimi Hendrix catching her eye, making her look at the other button badges pinned to his denim jacket, Che Guevara staring out the window, other badges colourful enough for her to remember them even if the slogans and band names were gone.

She had been on her way to Paris to start university.

Her father had wanted her to go to secretarial college. Go to church, get married, have children, be responsible. Minnette had never wanted that. Glancing at the youth with the mountain bike, bike and boy swaying with the motion of the train rattling through the tunnel. Thoughts turning to a memory of school. A friend with an older sister already at university—'67 or 1968; must've been '68 —books she had left behind, books leafed through instead of doing homework, friend moaning over and over how boring the books were and why was Minnette even curious and how crazy her sister was and Minnette should put them back. And Minnette putting down Jung, picking up *Meetings with Remarkable Men*, lingering over a phrase or a sentence, frowning, turning back to the cover and staring at the author's name; wondering how 'Gurdjieff' was pronounced. Both books had seemed illicit. Remembering those books on the train as the boy with short hair had wheeled his bicycle down the gangway. Remembering how positive she had been that there was more to the world than Father, church, marriage, children.

There had to be.

A third eye watched from over the squat's front door. The ground floor staircase swirled, spirals resolving into a mandala on the landing; becoming sagging gig posters on the next flight; water stains and patches of bare lath by the top floor.

Mostly she stayed in her tiny attic room: books, hand-me-down posters, a couple of LPs unplayed because there was no stereo, hot plate only source of warmth, October wind finding a finger-hold on every crack, every chink in window-frame, roof, mattress heaped with all the clothing she owned, flanked by steadily-growing ranks of empty wine bottles. Reading, studying, thinking; going out for lectures, still self-conscious about being in the city but wanting to do well; staying late in one library or another, reading the latest journals, making sense of them, some of the articles, sure it must make sense soon, wandering along the shelves, until, sometimes until, closing time.

A third eye watched over the doorway to the communal kitchen. Mostly she stayed in her room.

'It's, like, amazingly important to get that about it all: this is, like, a stage and other planes and states of being—' pausing to sip the dregs from the cup, holding it out without looking until someone refilled it from the pot on the stove— 'intersect here, see? This is the centre of—' another sip, a shrug— 'everything, kind of. Yeah?'

It was warm enough in the kitchen that she could shed a jacket, a jumper. Coffee mug cradled in both hands a hot coal against her palms, a tiny trickle of clear mucous set free by the heat and threatening to drip. She sniffed. Nodded.

'I never knew...'

'It's there, man, it's in Blavatasky, Ouspensky, it's in Crowley.' He scratched his beard, running the hand through his long hair in practically the same motion. It was hard to guess his age, easily fifteen years older than she, he and his wife—not really his wife and he sometimes stayed with another woman in another house a few streets away—the first people to move into the building. 'You dig Crowley?'

'Of course.' She nodded, some of the others around the table nodding too, which made her smile, a sense of belonging, lifting her mug to her lips because she was self-conscious, smiling more when one of the other women gently took the mug, refilled it without asking.

'It all comes from him,' someone added and she listened, needing to stay here longer, not simply the fractions of a moment it took to make dinner, wanting to put off the long climb to the attic.

Couple of minutes later and she had to admit she knew very little about Aleister Crowley, had yet to read any of his books.

'I'll lend you some, man,' was all the guy who had started the squat said.

As easy as that.

The physics student living in the ground-floor front room almost never came out except to go to lectures.

He began finding excuses to come into the hallway when she was leaving, coming back.

Minnette convinced herself it was coincidence.

'What are you reading?' he stammered. It had rained all afternoon, downpour penetrating, frigid and dour. She told herself what she wanted most was to get changed, burrow into bed.

'Sociology.' Standing in the middle of the entrance hall, rain dripping off her, making no move for the stairs.

'Oh.'

Somewhere overhead a stereo began to pound, guitars chasing away the sound of the rain. 'It's important, isn't it? Understanding people, society.'

'I guess. But everything comes from physical laws, from physics. In the end, I mean. Electricity, magnetism. How atoms interact. We're all physics.'

She said she had never thought of it like that.

The physics student found more excuses to come out of his room. Showing her text books. Articles. Giving her an introductory book on physics. 'It was in a sale, practically giving it away—' Going red, stammering that that had not come out right.

She tried the introductory book. Refused to give up so easily.

The physics student turned away, casually asking if she had had chance to read that book he had given her.

'A little. I've been so busy with a big essay they want before the Christmas vacation. I want to get back to it soon,' she assured him, thinking he might never ask her out if she never finished the book, at least got beyond the first few pages.

The wife of the man who had founded the squat taught her her first tarot spread. They found a second in a magazine.

Ground floor hallway dark, sound of movement from the floor above, laughter drifting down from higher in the building, squat quiet enough she thought she could hear snoring from the physics student's room.

She had never seriously considered knocking on his door. It had just been a fancy, something to think about while she came down all those flights.

Minnette had not noticed the candlelight filtering under the kitchen door, apologised, was backing out as the squat's founder waved her in, offered her whisky, a toke, a seat. A moment's awkwardness—the man alone for once, no crowd around the table—vying with embarrassment: she could not remember his name, wanted to say 'Sebastian' and suspicious it might be 'Patrice' after all.

She sat.

'Can't sleep?' Sebastian/Patrice took back the joint, relighting it.

'Trying to work on an essay.'

'Heavy?' Question an indrawn breath, smoke spilling from nostrils moments later.

Minnette thought, settling for: 'Harder than I thought it would be' and had an image of the physics student's door appear in her mind.

She took a mouthful of whisky.

Sebastian/Patrice poured them both another drink. Spoke about his time in university. About meeting Burroughs. Hearing Ginsberg read once, getting high with Leary. About the important thing being experience.

'Read loads, man. Think. That's what they don't want you to do.'

He was right, of course. She supposed he was right. 'I've been reading those books you leant me—' blushing a little, reminded of the physics student's questions, not wanting to sound gauche, provincial, topping up his glass, her own, and finding more words to say, turn over, carried along by the whisky, the thrill of being here, alone, with this man, all thought of the physics student carefully forgotten.

They talked until almost sun-up. Mostly Sebastian/Patrice talked. Minnette listened.

The physics student told her: 'I've been reading some sociology books. It's interesting. The theories and... that.'

'I guess.' Minnette was too cold to talk. She had no idea it could be so cold here in November.

Sebastian/Patrice stood in the doorway for a long time. It seemed like a long time before he came in.

He brought a book with him next day. It made her nervous, standing in the middle of her attic room, turning over the book to look at the front cover again, book feeling like a pretext, a change she had not been expecting, something she did not want.

Sebastian/Patrice dropped on to her mattress. 'You know this guy?' She took his outstretched hand, allowed herself to be pulled down. 'He's worth the effort, you know?'

Minnette stumbled again over the author's name as she said: 'No, I've never heard of Gurdjieff before.'

It was not her idea.

Everyone seemed to know everyone else but her. Minnette, sure her face was red, cheeks prickling and fingers clammy against the bowl of the wine glass, walked through the party, determined not to take refuge in a corner or against a wall and longing for at least that much security, that much chance of being inconspicuous.

'I always think a new decade should feel different to the old. From the first day, which is—'

'But the '80s have been—'

'They got off to a slow start.'

'You mean Reagan?'

'Or that bloody woman the English—'

Taking another confection of puff pastry and salmon from a tray—she would ask for the recipe if she saw either of the couple hosting the party, pretend she really would have a go at making them, that she was grateful they had persuaded her to come—drifting past another knot of conversation—'Well, I didn't think I'd live to see the Berlin Wall come down.'— questioning the expectation that everyone would be angry if she did try to join in and knowing she shouldn't forget that she didn't have enough worth saying in the first place.

'... reach our full potential if we use both sides of the brain to their fullest...'

Minnette took two steps, almost content to keep walking. She turned.

'I don't think that's true—that most of our brains are dormant, unused—I think that's a misinterpretation scientists have disproved.'

He didn't get angry at being corrected. Asking instead why the error was still accepted so widely.

'Because—' a gulp of wine, self-conscious in a different way because the small group he was talking to all seemed interested, perhaps sceptical some of them, but interested— 'because I think it's easier. To believe that, instead of what really, what I think is really—we hobble ourselves, you see, sometimes, you see, through boredom or fear of failure, not having enough belief, confidence, enough confidence that we can do... whatever it might be.' Falling silent. Worried she sounded like some New Age self-helper, that she was boring them, that she wasn't articulating properly ideas she hadn't thought about, had avoided, in a long while.

The woman on her right frowned. 'Boredom?'

'Oh—' finding her glass empty, concentrating on that instead of looking at the woman, aware of the man she had interrupted watching her— 'I meant how we stop paying attention, become acclimatised—to the journey to the work, say, or the street we live in, the person we live—' trying again to drink from the empty glass— 'we stop noticing. Don't you think? Like sleepwalkers.' Looking at the small group around her: an all-encompassing glance that met no gaze directly, offering no challenge: a habit hard to break.

Mumbling: 'We're all sleepwalkers, sometimes.'

The man laughed. 'Some more than others.'

The others joined in. And, although she searched hard, there seemed only humour in the laughter. Minnette took a breath. Admitted: 'Actually, the idea isn't mine. Others have said it before.'

'Have you heard of the Fourth Way?'

He got more wine afterwards, found a place near the Christmas tree where they could sit, asked her if she had had enough to eat, excused himself before filling a plate, didn't mind at all when, after he sat down again, she admitted she was hungry.

His name was Nicolas.

'Was your husband interested? In mysticism, esotericism?'

Minnette shook her head—*He hated*—explaining: 'I'd given it up by the time we met, so...' and glad when Nicolas nodded, began speaking:

'I always dismissed it. Out of hand.' His wife—ex-wife—had been something of a hippy in her youth. 'I found a box of books, was going to throw them out after she said she didn't want them... I had insomnia, began reading anything to hand.' He became fascinated. 'How about you? Were you into the occult at university?'

'I guess I was a bit of a hippy, too.' And, not sure what else she should say, asked him about his interests, the areas that caught his imagination.

But Nicolas kept coming back to her, her fascination with magic and the occult. 'What made you loose interest? You talk like there's still something that attracts you. Was it your husband—'

'No.'

'Sorry. I shouldn't—'

She apologised, told Nicolas it was fine, he wasn't prying, that she had simply lost interest, moved on: job, career, marriage. Magic seemed... 'less important,' Minnette finished, words feeling off as she said them, a silence opening between them as they looked at almost empty plates, empty glasses, Nicolas' cigarette smouldering in the ashtray between them, Minnette uncomfortable with the silence's weight, saying: 'But I think I'd like to go back to it,' and surprising herself with how true this was.

They had been seeing each other a little over a month when the man she was going to marry had said something about religion, and God, that God and religion were the same thing, or that you couldn't have one without the other, Minnette was never sure afterwards why her saying that they could be separate or weren't exactly the same, whatever it was, could have made him so angry, not that she realised at first, thinking his persistence was, at worst, a stubbornness she had not noticed in the past weeks, realising his returning to the same points, his tightening voice, his interrupting her, was nothing of the sort just before he began shouting, Minnette struggling to say a couple of words before his voice over-rode her again, her heart thumping, face warm, growing warmer as she felt herself trapped, every placation or concession a dead-end, bewildered by the way the conversation had turned, instinct vying with his physical presence, head thrust forward, hand jerking, up or out or away, swinging back so it was difficult not to flinch, sure, this time, he might hit her, and desperate to tell him to shut up, to stop, to tell him he could think what he liked but that didn't mean she had to listen, unable to speak, too intimidated and too aware that she liked and wanted to like this man she hardly knew, insecure enough not to want to jeopardise that through being too aggressive, because it might be a long time until she met anyone else, and because—but there was no time to think of the scars on her arms, fading but still visible, not that this man had ever remarked on them and she was touched by this discretion, liking him for that, for other reasons that spilled out when she was alone, more down than usual, those times when it was easier to talk to herself—certainly no chance to think of such things as his anger became strident—*'Trying to rub my nose in it, that I haven't read as much as you'*—no chance to reflect at all, only agree—*'I don't know much about this sort of thing, not really'*—apologise for trying to push her opinions on him, telling herself—then and later, even more so later—that she was only saying it to calm him, that she didn't mean it and that she wouldn't put up with anything like this again, never. Never.

They were engaged two weeks later; married seven weeks after that. A small wedding, mostly his friends, his family. She saw little of the guests over subsequent years. Of those she met, some said very little. But a few remembered the wedding. Remembered him shouting at her to get out of her own reception.

'And do you still use astrology to predict winning horses?'

Married almost a year. A chance meeting. In spite of claims of too little time to spare, it became coffee and mostly one-sided reminiscences.

'That was you, Yves. I never gambled.'

'You didn't?' Ordering his third pastry as he gave her a look of innocent confusion, Minnette unsure as she often had been whether he was teasing or genuinely confused, trying not to stare, how chubby he was, unlike the image in her head of a slim young man borrowing books and sometimes remembering to give them back, feeling... awkward... drawn... nostalgic?... a little out of place, talking to him again. After so long.

'No, that's right, it was me. You were like Boucaya, very... intense.' Laughing, washing down a mouthful of *mille-feuille*, wiping his mouth before asking: 'Do you see much of him?'

After so much.

'Not for ages.' Minnette drained her coffee, searched for money.

'Me neither.' Yves swallowed the last of his dessert. 'Except his picture, now and then.' Frowning. 'Is it ten years?' He stood, not waiting for an answer. 'I'll get this.'

Tempting to argue, if only for the sake of not being seen to give in too quickly. Gratefully, Minnette put her share of the bill back in her purse.

'How is married life?'

They stood on the street outside the café, seemingly reluctant to part, or unsure how to go about it.

'Like I said the other four times you asked, Yves: I like it. Being settled is good. You should try it.'

'Nah. Not for me. I like—' he swept his arms across some imagined horizon. 'And—' he asked after a moment where they both checked watches, made passing mention of the places they should be getting to— 'and magic? Are you still studying?'

Minnette shook her head.

'Not for years.'

Her therapist frowned.

The young man with the mountain bike must have got off the Métro without her noticing; no sign of him when the train reached her stop.

It still felt like an omen. Of some sort.

Assuming she wanted to believe in omens. Assuming she could make sense of it if she did.

She had enough trouble interpreting the past.

Nicolas looked dejected so she apologised, pressing a hand flat on the face of the book lying on the table beside her plate, wrapping slowly unfurling, flowering only to fall to the restaurant's floor.

'It's wonderful. Really. Just the surprise of it, so unexpected.'

'You keep saying you want to get more into it again, so I thought... Do you really like it?'

'Yes.' Minnette flicked through the book, an introductory guide to ritual magic. 'It's wonderful,' she said again and wished she had thought of another word. She smiled, squeezed his hand to cover her embarrassment.

'Oh, good. Great.' Nicolas sipped his wine. 'I thought we could read it together, learn together.'

'Wonderful.' Minnette smiled.

Silly.

'It's silly, I suppose, still feeling uncomfortable about it. After so long, nearly ten years.'

Therapist nodding. 'Strong emotions...'

Silly. 'It still seems...' Minnette shrugged.

'Did Nicolas remind you of your husband?'

He reminded me... 'They weren't the same at all. No.' Minnette took a sip of water, trying to put the glass back on the low table with as little noise as possible.

'Did you worry he might turn out to be? Is that why you didn't say anything about the present, thinking the book—'

'The book was sweet—' *it reminded me*— 'a sweet idea and that's why I didn't want to hurt Nicolas.'

'Not because you were worried he would get angry? Your husband—'

'I honestly don't think that I thought Nicolas was another version of my husband.' *I thought he was like...*

Minnette sat forward, clutching one knee, jeans crisp under her palms, denim new, wearing flairs for the time in twenty-five, twenty-three years, hard to believe so much time had passed, painfully aware next instant that *I look awkward*, pose saying as much as any answer she had given so far.

Minnette sat back. Tried to appear relaxed.

'I suppose, yes, I do regret how it ended between us—' *but he wasn't alike enough...* 'And, yes, I wasn't ready for another relationship, not so soon after my divorce, but it's still one of those things you wish you could go back... back and change. Isn't it?'

The therapist wrote something in her notebook before raising her head again, asking gently: 'And was this when you had the first series of running dreams?'

'Oh—' pausing, giving the appearance of thinking, setting the years straight— 'no, no. I think they started later.'

Paris deserted   war scares   poster hoardings peeling words torn   ink streaked   letters smudged   glimpsed *Gas   ttac !*   *u lear T rror*   *Saddam: other of All   a s!*   feeling Scud missiles circling behind the grey clouds   hijacked aircraft diving having to outrun them   these terrors   perched on the black roofs   wings twitching   terrors' wings coarse as torn cloth on the wind   voices convulsing with rust-edged harshness   mobbing sour clouds   desolate sky   black as bruise   sallow   as open wound   terrors *spurring*   road long stretching without turning without end without choice   *spurring* next corner next street next step next stride no turning back no end only on without stopping   *spurring* breathless no breath running through air filled with miasma   *sarin anthrax dirty bomb*   no junctions no turnings   but turning   but running   but turning but running faster but turn but run   *spurred impelled prodded*   but running on the spot street scrolling past   feet moving arms moving breath no breath never enough to scream chasing safety   ahead running   running from whatever is above is behind is chasing is coming is rotting her stomach is not what she is running from

   stumbling into the bookshop on the Rue de la Parcheminerie   missiles crowding at the narrow doorway jammed together   enough time to run down the first aisle   take a turning take a turning take a turning take a turning   running   taking a turning taking a turning taking the first book out of the parcel reading it as the second came out of the parcel   drawing a magic circle on the floor in front of the till   counter-top laid out as an altar   Nicolas reflected in the mirror behind the altar   there is no mirror behind the counter he is not in the shop   shop and circle gone
   running

The manager of the bookshop on the Rue de la Parcheminerie found Minnette surrounded by books, Biography in the midst of being moved to a different part of the shop.

   'You look miles away. Whatever's wrong?'

   Minnette took a moment to answer, climbing to her feet, dusting off her hands. 'Nothing. I didn't sleep much. A nightmare.'

'Warm milk,' the manager suggested. 'It always works for me when I have trouble sleeping.'

Minnette pointed to the books the manager was carrying.

'I'm guessing they're the ones you ordered.' The manager craned forward as Minnette paged through the first, lingered over the index of the second. 'That looks... abstruse.' The manager frowned over a complex cabalistic diagram. 'A bit more advanced than what we usually stock, isn't it?'

'A little.' Minnette closed the book, thanking the manager, seeing the question in the other woman's expression.

'For my boyfriend.' Assuring herself it was a white lie only, that it was wrong to boast about her studies, a danger to be avoided if she was going to keep improving. Keep searching.

Nodding, her new friend carefully rested her joint against the side of the saucer they were using as an ashtray and crawled across the floor on hands and knees to the hi-fi on the low window ledge.

'That's it. That's exactly how it happens.' She paused, slipping *The Hangman's Beautiful Daughter* back into its sleeve.

'Yeah, it's what—' Minnette paused long enough to review what she had been about to say— 'it's what a guy I used to know, it's what he said... Then, then I found this fantastic book.'

'Yeah?'

The girl helped out at a mystical study group that met a few times each week in rooms above a tabac on the corner of the Rue de Baigneur, in Montmartre. Minnette, twenty-four, feeling weary and old, began attending sessions at least once a week, unable to decide at first if she came to scoff or from a misguided sense of nostalgia, ready to drop it and leave at the first sign her fears, unnamed, might prove real. Feeling nervous in case this girl, eighteen, nineteen, surely no more than twenty and so young, in case this girl was being polite, wasn't interested in becoming friends, this despite her suspicion that she shouldn't be having friends, they were a crutch, or a hindrance, or something, suspicious of this need in her to reach out for someone, sure it was something she should work to erase, through therapy or… or something.

'I guess it's kind of—' the girl slipped out another record, holding it up so Minnette could see the weird engraving on the sleeve— 'well documented now, isn't it?' Placing the needle on the start of The Third Ear Band's *Alchemy*, the girl sat down, took another hit off the joint and handed it to Minnette.

'You've read Blavatsky, yeah?'

Minnette nodded.

'I'm always hoping, you kno—' the girl pulled a huge, Persian-patterned cushion closer and lay across it— 'hoping that I'll meet one, one of the Masters, that they'll come in a dream or a vision. Like in Blavatsky.'

'Yeah.' Minnette took another short drag on the joint, passing it back. The music on the hi-fi was hypnotic, strange; music that sounded like it came from another age, another physical plane. 'Only, my… this guy… I… knew—' sniffing, rubbing her eyes with the heel of her hands before continuing— 'this guy I used to know, he said it wasn't always like that.'

'But if you're worthy—'

'Sure, but—' Pausing again, telling herself it was the grass making her emotional. 'You see, they appear in different forms, if they appear, and it might be in dreams but it's just as likely to be, like, say a kid working in a supermarket or a dealer, say, as likely that as an old guy working in a junk shop that just happens to have the one book you need to find the ritual you're after… Or whatever.'

'But that happens, right?' The young girl waved the glowing end of the joint so its smoke mixed with the incense sticks smouldering on the table. 'You read about it a lot.'

'Oh, of course. Definitely.' Minnette oddly excited, passion welling so that a deeper feeling could remain masked. 'But, it's all a test. Always a test. They come, in different forms, or variations of the same one, see? The Masters come when you're ready and give you a chance.'

Silence as both listened to the music. Silence as the passion was already spent. But that was the grass, she was sure. Grass always made her tired. In the end.

'But,' the young girl asked in the space between one track and the next, 'what happens if you blow it? Is that it?'

'It's a test.' Minnette's head heavy enough she thought her neck would not be able to lift it to nod, so she repeated: 'It's a test.' Adding: 'Get it right or blow it. Never get another chance. Never.'

Going over it again, memories pushing, repeating, words spoken. Unspoken. Looking out of the window. Searching for distraction in the blur and slip-slip-slip of fields and buildings, telegraph poles there and gone, sky static, horizon unreeling. Turning. To look around the carriage, at other passengers. Voices and words and events jumbling. Static. Unreeling. Replayed and changing a little or a lot, same outcome, more or less, *that* had to be the same, reminding herself *that* shouldn't change at least, but Nicolas might have looked relieved or Nicolas might have looked upset but understanding and that might—she could hear him, in her mind he was saying that, of course, she had to follow her heart, be happy, do what was going to make her happiest, they would stay in touch and later, in time, they might... He understood and believed she should follow this path. The path to the mountain that separates the Lovers on the tarot card. Image passing through her mind. Associations unreeling, thinking: it must have taken them a day, longer, days to get this far, seven of them crammed into a Renault camper van, camper van unsure where it was going other than towards the ocean, getting this far south in days, short winter days, the train covering the same distance, a different journey but the same distance, in hours, a few hours.

Slowing, passing through another station, nameplate gone before she registered it, sky opening as the train accelerated away, sunlight furnace-bright through scratched windows. Minnette opened the book on her lap. Determined to read. And turning over the break-up with Nicolas again.

Too hard to concentrate after Perpignan.

'You have to wonder what was going on in his head, causing all this.'

The woman who had got on at Perpignan rustled her newspaper.

'Is he a nutter, d'you think? 'Course he is. Saddam's nuts, in't he?'

Minnette pretended to read.

'All them Muslims are nutters. Look at the Ay'toller. He was nuts, weren't he?' The newspaper rustled again. Woman pausing. Waiting for a reply.

Minnette shrugged. Her husband had hated when she shrugged, refused to be drawn. He got louder, more insistent. Badgering. She had tried not to respond, tried to learn to keep quiet.

'They say it's him, Saddam, behind that airplane what was blown up in Scotland a couple of years ago.'

Minnette frowned. Wiped the frown away. Remembered she was divorced now. And hesitating even so before asking: 'I thought that was supposed to be Gaddafi?'

The woman seemed not hear. 'We'll be invading soon, you'll see. We'll sort Saddam out.'

She sounded authoritative. Minnette wondered if the woman who had got on at Perpignan had a son or a nephew out there. Pictures in every newspaper of ranks of soldiers, huge transport planes disgorging yet more tanks into the desert.

'I've got second sight.'

The woman sounded completely matter-of-fact, like she had seen it on television.

'I've seen the allies taking back Kuwait.'

Minnette sat very still.

'And they'll take back Baghdad, as well. You'll see. Saddam's going to be put on trial and hung and they'll be pulling down his statues, just like they've been pulling down all them of Lenin and that in Russia. You'll see: next year. Early next year, before the desert gets too hot.'

The woman found the puzzle page in the paper, began hunting for a pen.

'It's fine if you don't believe me.'

Sure this was a joke and finding nothing to suggest it was, Minnette had no idea what to say. Conscious her mouth was hanging open.

'I see things.' The woman turned a page. Matter of fact. 'People try to explain them away but I know.

The words were there, waiting for Minnette to say them aloud: *I think I saw something, once.* She closed her mouth. *I think I saw...*

In Toledo.

It became easier. The conflict. The wanting to have help and the reluctance to be helped. The sense, unspoken, that she couldn't be helped, or didn't deserve to be helped, or simply could manage without, motives confused, unacknowledged, and besides the feeling of being trapped was much more dominant: trapped by her therapist, by herself for undertaking treatment. Working helped. Hard to begin again after so long, hard not reflect how much less of a struggle it had been thirty years ago. Tempted to give up: meditation, visualisation, the Work. Encouraged as it got easier to concentrate and believe and feel and, in the feeling, believe and, in the belief, feel, so when the therapist returned again to September, 1990, building the suspicion the therapist must sense there was something there, Minnette could say, without blushing or wondering if she gave anything away: 'I needed some time to think after I broke up with Nicolas. I needed to get away from

Paris, too. So I went on holiday. Just a week away.' Minnette could let her therapist ask her why she had chosen that particular place and, sensing her therapist might think there was something that was not being said, make herself believe that there wasn't anything to it when she replied: 'Oh, I think I saw it in a film. And the name. It sounds romantic, somehow, don't you think? And it was easy to get to. That's why I went to Toledo after breaking up with Nicolas.'

Why she had broken up with Nicolas was a question she side-stepped, saying only that she hadn't been ready, that it hadn't been fair to Nicolas to be with him, not with memories of marriage and divorce so fresh. Which was true, to a point, and matched the memories that came to her in March, 2000, thinking back to those days in 1990, Minnette no longer remembering Nicolas saying:
> *you say it's not me, not us, but you keep saying that you've needed to do this since we've met, that meeting me has made you... I don't understand, Minnette...*

any more than she could remember herself, in the late summer of 1971, saying:
> *no, that's right, I don't get it... Yes, I heard you the first — No, I won't fucking lower my voice... That's it? University, friends, the people who— Everything just gets dumped so you can fuck off... Enlightenment? Knowledge? So all that about the wondrous and the numinous just as likely to be here, right here, that's... It fucking is what you're saying, you shit. Ah, fuck it. Go. Alright?... Ah, fuck off, Guillaume. I never realised what a selfish shit you—*

The apartment smelled of Indian food and old books. Shelves along one side of the cramped hallway bowed under the weight of notebooks, magazines, tatty photocopies, mimeographed pamphlets and monographs; the contents of the bookcase under the mirror overflowing into the small living room and adjoining kitchenette. Tottering piles of books flanked the dowdy two-seater sofa, threatened to overwhelm the table under the window where the ageing purple iMac clung on amid scrap paper and scattered jottings. More notes, notebooks and scribbled memoranda lay around the room, across the floor, sprouted from the cushions of the armchair where she read and worked and thought.

Minnette took out M. Jacotey's piece of paper. Stared at URL, login details.

The apartment smelt stale, felt enclosed.

'Fuck it.'

But she changed her mind again, fishing the wadded note from the waste-paper basket. Setting the iMac to downloading the day's batch of spam as she looked at the crumpled sheet of paper. Indecisive.

Deciding to eat instead.

Reheating dhal, dropping naan bread in the toaster. Opening one of the books lying on the work surface to a page marked with a spoon. Reading. Tutting. Saying aloud: 'This is bullshit—' and pushing aside the book to massage her bad hip, pain throbbing towards her knee. Making her think: *You're just cranky because of this bloody hip*, before picking up the book again, telling herself it was time she pulled together an article or two, perhaps self-publish a monograph—*At least M. Jacotey would buy it*—pouring herself wine, water for pain killers, blood pressure pills, vitamins…

Leaving everything to drift back towards the iMac. The piece of crumpled paper.

The toaster popped.

Looking across the kitchenette. Steam rising from the bubbling dahl.

Stirring to swallow tablets, draining the glass of water and intending to have another. Remembering there was an open bottle of wine to be finished. Sitting. Watching steam rising from the pot.

Synchronicity: significant events occurring in close proximity without any obvious causal connection.

'No.' Glancing across the room: table, computer, crumpled paper visible where it lay against the keyboard.

She saw Guillaume more often than she liked, once a year at least, so him bothering her at the stall wasn't significant. And he always liked to be the centre of things, everything, so being involved in some cranky discussion group—
With M. Jacotey? Surely Guillaume wasn't that—
But the boy.
'There are lots of boy with bikes in Paris.'
So forget it?
Spooning dhal, swallowing too quickly, mouthful of wine making her splutter, tears squeezed from the corner of each eye. Turning towards the book lying open on the work surface. Thinking about finally writing something. Thinking of anything instead of submitting to the urge to swivel the other way, towards iMac, piece of paper. She could sell her books, her collection of periodicals, send all her notes away for recycling. She would give it up for good, do something else while there was time.
Time to... what?
To admit defeat.

The timetable left no choice but an overnight stop at Barcelona. Her hotel room was very neat, very clean, and far too confining. Striking off at random, Minnette walked, taking turnings or not, until she saw she was almost back at the hotel. She crossed the road, not yet ready to sit in bed waiting for tomorrow to finally arrive. Lingering outside a restaurant, place busy but not crowded, table lamps giving a comforting russet sheen to everything except the small TV behind the bar, screen crowded by soldiers, desert, maps of places she had not given much thought to until the last few weeks.
Remembering the woman on the train.
Finding a place with no TV, with hardly any patrons, took time, should have ensured she was ravenous. Pushing food around the plate, the few mouthfuls attempted seemingly tasteless, no recollection anyway of what she had ordered. Thinking she should have brought something to read. Knowing she would not be able to

concentrate. Almost wishing for someone to talk to. Feeling it better to be alone with her thoughts. Only one thing on her mind. Thinking only of Toledo.

Toledo.

Most of the autumn term of her second year passed in a blur of denial, grief always present no matter how much she refused to acknowledge it.

Yves eventually told her it was time she did something useful.

Something that would make her face the world again.

Dragging her from the squat, where she occupied the ground floor front room, physics student gone or graduated, lost somewhere in the spring and summer past.

Ignoring her complaints.

First a café. Night sharply dank, threatening rain, cold enough, surely, for snow. Which meant they needed fortifying. Insulating.

Two bars followed. Another café.

And then shopping. Provisions: one bar of chocolate; some stunning Turkish weed; a half-gramme of cocaine; two bottles of rum, four of *vin ordinaire*.

Before hitting the first end-of-term party Yves managed to find. Gatecrashing, as it turned out.

Escaping that drag.

Weaving a route between two bars, cocaine and half the rum gone, a steady dent growing in the wine as they braved the winter's night in search of excitement, experience, a leavening of the appalling boredom of Paris just before Christmas, and finding a café, beating a hasty retreat from a third when their fits of hysterics, weed similarly becoming depleted, made the *patron* give them a none-too-friendly glower...

Until chance—synchronicity, they both agreed—led to a party being thrown by one of Yves' friends from his anthropology course.

'It's kind of spontaneous, like critical mass: people just started turning up,' the friend explained as they shared the last of the weed, the three of them jammed into a corner, shouting over the soundtrack to *More* on the stereo, Yves' friend's eyes nearly all pupil, so Minnette thought the night had slithered into his skull, was using him like a space probe, observing what it was like to be human, to spend each evening in the light instead of wrapped in shadows... Pausing to wonder if there was something in her drink other than rum and orange juice... Deciding she didn't care.

She wandered. Rum gone, opting for whisky straight from a fresh bottle and so leaving no doubt what kinds of drugs were in her glass. Sidestepping a pass from a very stoned guy she vaguely recognised as one of Yves' tutors. Half-heartedly taking part in a discussion on the place of Maoism in critical theory. Listening to an aggressive young Scandinavian woman in her mid-twenties bemoaning the philosophy department, how neither her tutors nor the other junior lecturers understood what she was doing, how it was sexism, cultural philistinism, envy because— Wandering away at that point, thoughts of suggesting, maybe, the problem lay not with the department but elsewhere, like, maybe, the aggressive young Scandinavian woman herself, swallowed, secondary to the search for more booze, the desire to get thoroughly smashed. Because it was end of term. Because it was Christmas. Because... Finding vodka, more weed, a little more cocaine. Back of her head vibrating, tightening, tightness finding echo in the pit of her stomach. Tightness settling somewhere around her solar plexus. Chilling. Sobering. She knew, no matter how hard she tried, she was not going to get as smashed or as stoned as she wanted, never become numb, to forget for at least a while.

It was after midnight when someone from Yves' course mentioned that she and her boyfriend had decided to drive to Spain: 'Spend Christmas by the sea. It's got to be warmer than here.'

Minnette sat on the periphery of the conversation, working through a large glass of brandy, headache growing over her eyes and feeling as though it was the hangover to a drunkenness she had never experienced.

'Better than going home to all the shit parents do every year, right?' The young woman nodded in reply to her own question.

'We'll come.' Yves pointed to himself, Minnette.

Minnette lurched forward, almost spilling from the bean bag she was sitting on. Thoughts of going back to her parents' house—north of Paris, provincial, a world away, which should have held some appeal in spite of the boredom, the friction, the certainty her father and his opinions would drive her to spend most of the vacation in her old bedroom, alone—clashing with thoughts of staying in the squat—place dank, filled with unwelcome associations and sure to be practically deserted so she would spend the whole vacation alone—both appalling in their way, neither something she wanted and yet she was positive the last thing she wanted was to be stuck in the back of a car with people she hardly knew.

'I'm not going.' Icy rain making pavements slick, boot-heels skate.

Yves kept pace. Weaving a little. Shoes slipping, slapping hard against a shallow rain puddle, breath coming in clouds that wove around the smoke rising from the cigarette hanging from his mouth.

'You are.'

Wanting to walk faster. Balance on the edge of going. Street and rain and city and Yves and her quavering. Easy to say it was only the booze and drugs. Feeling queasy, stomach roiling, falling still. Waving Yves away and wanting legs to be longer, pavements drier, steps firmer.

'I told you.'

Yves slipped, swore. Cigarette bounced, pinwheeling to the gutter. Minnette slowed, beginning to reach out to help and making herself walk away, use the chance to put space between them.

'You are.'

Yves caught up. Refusing to let her go.

Unlike some people…

'Fuck off, will you?' Wishing she could run, could fly.

Street-light smeared across the pavement ahead. Rain pitching harder, worming down her neck, runnels the cold fingers of a blind man trying to know her face, know her from the set of her features.

Minnette sobbed.

Effort of walking, almost-running, making her sob. Tears nothing more than the rain. Pain only her bad stomach or because she was adrift. No, falling. Always almost falling.

Yves clutched her arm, holding tight as he slowed her.

'He'll be back.'

Minnette stared at him. 'I don't care what he does. It's his life, isn't it?' Sniffing hard, wishing there was something more to drink, to smoke. Wishing she could run, could fly. 'I don't care. I hope he finds what he's looking for. Enlightenment. Or wisdom. Or an Ascended Master to tell him the secrets of the universe. Whatever shit he wants to happen.' Turning and walking away. Only, instead of letting her go as she had expected, Yves kept pace, one hand on her arm, Minnette not thinking, simply holding on to his arm, hugging him close. 'It's not like we were anything, is it? Friends. We were friends.'

'You could have gone with him.' Yves' voice sounds like the rain. Was the rain talking to her. 'Taken a year off.'

'I—' and it was like talking to herself, the rain simply repeating what was in her head, turning round things she had turned over, refused to think about, said to herself in darkness even so— 'I'm not sure there's anything out there to find. I read some of the books he lent me and maybe some of it makes sense—Jung, Gurdjieff, some of it—but so does Laing, kind of; so does Mao, a bit; so do plenty…'

Only the sound of the rain. Water running down her face mostly cold. Becoming cold. Becoming thoughts that is was better to stay, to hold on to what she had, that she had managed to get away from her father and that small, closed, tight, shrivelled up life her parents had, and that getting away and having what she had was enough. Better this than becoming a frayed, acid shadow of someone else, never willing to say what she felt for fear it might upset the other person's view of the world. Better this than silence.

'I'm glad he's gone. Good luck to him.' Letting go of the rain's arm. Nodding away all the noise inside. Making sure not to slip as she walked. In one direction or another, it made no difference so long as she walked confidently. Voice firm. Loud enough to swamp anything else that was trying to speak. 'Good luck, Guillaume.' She waved to the night, sketching benedictions to each cardinal point. Allowing that internal voice to affirm: *I never want to see you again*. Before turning around, shaking her head, hands on hips. 'And I'm not spending Christmas jammed into a rusty old banger with you and a bunch of people I don't know.'

It was a Renault camper van. There was, she found, a fair amount of leg room if she sat on the back seat.

and later, other things were said, some lingering, some leaving nothing, or nothing more than the sense that something had been said, even if she could no longer be sure what…

> In 1973, he had said: 'I will call down the angel Hanael. I will. *We* will.' Unsure, feeling more afraid than she wanted to admit, she had laughed, laughter stopping when he had looked long and hard into her eyes, holding her head between his warm, firm hands. Asking: 'Don't you believe?' Staring so intently, she noticed flecks of green around each pupil for the first time, a trace of cerulean elsewhere in the otherwise cobalt blue of his eyes. Unable to look away as he added: 'I do' and waited for her reply…
>
> In 1975, her new friend, the young girl who helped out at the study group, black hair tied back with a leather thong and jeans patched and frayed but always clean, had told her: 'Oh, but I

know Atlantis exists. On another plane, this whole other parallel Earth...'

In 1978, the German had paused in showing her the collection of books he had bought cheap after the War, books that he had been assured had been owned by members of the Ahnenerbe, the occultists who secretly controlled the Nazis, had turned towards the window of his flat on the outskirts of Düsseldorf, looking out but not focussing on the traffic nosing along the street below, and said: 'You know, they say there are tunnels near here. I have met people who have seen their entrance. The Nazis never managed to go much more than eight, eleven hundred metres into them before they were turned back. So the story goes, the Green Monks—you know of them?—they wouldn't allow it. You see, my dear, those tunnels go all the way to Tibet, to Shambhala, the secret Capital of the World.' He had gestured, one pink, liver-spotted hand taking in street, blocks of flats, the supermarket on the corner. 'Do you believe that is so, my dear...?'

In 1981, the magician in the crumbling council house, last in a row that was surrounded by fields of rubble—all that remained of streets and streets of terraced houses—had pulled on a black robe and, Yorkshire accent making his French almost unintelligible, said: 'You will believe...'
and she had nodded each time. Said...

'I've been having running dreams.
   'Again.'
Two weeks earlier: A post-Millennium party thrown by a journalist friend. Overhearing someone asking, 'Do you do dream therapy?' And sitting on the edge of the sofa for almost an hour. Wondering whether to speak, waiting for a gap in the conversation. Unsure whether she wanted a second to come along when reticence made her miss the

first. Quandary pushing her, in the end, into the midst of a debate on the connections between Surrealism and the Occult, temper short, so she was shorter, sharper than she usually allowed herself to be in dismantling the idea there was any hidden symbolism encoded in the works of Lautréamont, the automatic writings of Desnos, wishing she had not pushed herself so firmly into the midst of the debate as it spiralled and sprawled into a broader discussion of esotericism, the structure of reality, the forces driving nature and the knowledge of them which was beginning to suffuse a great deal of Western culture, no comfort in a discussion as shallow as it was broad, thread and thrust of the talk moving too fast, too slowly, for her to extricate herself easily, thread and thrust holding her back from seizing any chance of talking with this psychiatrist, sure she should at least mention her problems, sure she would. If only the flow of the conversation would give her chance. The party was winding down when the wife of her friend introduced them, Minnette having spent the previous hour sitting in the kitchen lamenting how tired she was these days. The psychiatrist sipped his coffee, happy to talk, to draw out her problems as she doggedly denied having any to speak of, offering to put her in touch with a therapist who could be helpful.

'If you want to go down the route of therapy, of course,' he had finished.

Minnette sat back, trying to relax.

The therapist was very sympathetic, a gentle, middle-aged woman who did her best to make Minnette comfortable, feel safe to talk.

Minnette tried to relax.

'Can you tell me about your dreams?'

'Oh. Well, I'm running. Obviously. And it's like I can't stop.' Fishing a tissue from her bag, wiping her nose. 'And then I wake up.'

Of course, but did she think there was anything during the preceding day that was feeding into the dreams, did she run in the same place, did she feel any strong emotions, was there anything ahead of her, anything behind?

What, the therapist asked, are your dreams like, Minnette?

And Minnette, standing in the hallway leading to the therapist's office, replied: They start without—

But there was no time to say 'warning'.

I see, said the therapist, from somewhere. Behind, from somewhere behind. I think I—

The word 'understand' became a bend in the corridor already gone by, Minnette's feet pounding along Aztec-patterned carpet tiles, feet striking hard without any pain, corridor propelling her down its length, its length measureless and endless and endlessly becoming a boulevard, trees shadows in the darkness, darkness at 12:15 in the afternoon, this first session squeezed into her lunch-break, day otherwise full, day otherwise blue-grey, overcast shading blue-grey into night-shadows cast by the sun behind the clouds, clouds drifting behind the sun, sun wearing the moon's face, moon's face asking Minnette if she felt anything, if there was anything behind anything

you recognise? the therapist's voice stepping from behind a heavy wrought iron plant-holder outside an apartment house, planter and house no longer there, turn made without slowing without noticing, running arms pumping running legs striking tarmac, tarmac cracked sloping, an uphill slope making the running harder road lined with buildings that wound with the road's winding road looking flat and level feeling uphill, slope steeper-growing-steeper the further she ran, air growing colder—December cold, Minnette? but this is January—frosty, tarmac cracking hillside opening out on the left and the street so flat and steep, buildings watching her, therapist's voice nearby: can you describe this, Minnette? buildings falling back and away back and away, falling almost on top of her has she ran, road becoming a wide valley that folded around her road becoming a narrow passage back-alley lined by buildings leaning over her as they tell me, Minnette... therapist's voice keeping pace: not sound only chill, goose-flesh rising; legs churning no progress no progress ever enough never enough progress, voice a fingernail trailing up the spine heart pounding therapist's voice just behind her, whispering: tell

me what you see, Minnette, and Minnette saw:

a house run fingers down its façade, opening itself, exposing not floors and furniture but Minnette in 1991 talking to her sister, the pair never close not least because Minnette was almost eleven years the younger, her sister saying: do you still collect those books on magic? and Minnette shaking her head: I sold them all got rid of them, and Minnette shaking her head to her sister's next question: no, I did it because I needed the money, I—

that house gone, running to get away from that house, unable to stop herself running towards a bistro unfurling to project images of Minnette walking out of a shop in 1983 or 1984, a year or two into her marriage, Minnette walking out and almost bumping into a woman in her mid-twenties, Minnette apologising turning to walk away, and the young woman calling catching up with Minnette, asking Minnette if she remembers her and Minnette running to outpace the bistro's visions and the visions keeping pace, forcing her to look into the other woman's face, recognising her friend from the study group in Montmartre young woman asking: how have you been what are you doing now? and Minnette mumbling, reply stilted, amounting to: I don't want to think of those times... I don't want to know y—

gone by to leave the walls of an office block on which her face was projected, lips a dozen stories high, mouthing —gone, likewise, Minnette needing more speed, to get through the arch ahead arch closing forming an 'O' a mouth: Minnette's mouth, lips shaping—and running past a boutique, glass walls mirrors, every window in the floors above merging mirrors reflecting another memory, or the ghost of a memory what might be a memory Minnette not caring wanting only to run, can you tell me? therapist whispering, breath dank, a sharp finger caressing the nape of her neck, can you describe what you are seeing, Minnette? and wanting to scream and not having any breath eyes closed visions playing across the undersides of her eyelids, chasing, driving. Lingering ahead. Around the next turning. Surging from behind. From behind the next turning. Waiting beyond the slow-slowly opening door at the end of an otherwise blank wall wall a hillside a road upsloping, and turning back to point, moon a setting sun, sun a face, face her own: head shaking mouth working words inaudible no breath words enunciated clearly screaming to block them out, head and mouth and words not the thing driving her   thinking this allowing her to sleep   thinking otherwise meaning a lifetime of barren nights   head and mouth and words neither meaningful nor her own   this must be so and   being so meant   thankfully   that these dreams were random meaningless despite how it seemed in those first moments of waking   waking in the early hours   sweating or cringing   knotted bedclothes   a strait-jacket   a shroud a place to hide   watch daylight reluctantly build and dislodge the slough of dreams until   minutes after the alarm finally sounded   she could look forward to coffee strong and bitter   to being awake   to not being a victim of recurring dreams   those few she did have and remember simply   meaningless   head and mouth and words growing   pressing   driving   head a falling hammer   mouth about to split   words neither thorns nor barbs nor a feverish hand clamped over her face but nothing but air and sound and gone the moment they were spoken, and still they clung and crawled and slithered out of the air as she ran   ran ran   ran   ran ran into the choking words swallowing   feeling them squirm   feeling them

Minnette woke, throat locked so there was no scream. Only a sound of choking.

'No,' she told her therapist at their first session, 'I don't think I can describe the dreams. They're so vague, you see. I just know I run.'

> turning away from Leeds in 1981...
>
> running into Nicolas in October, 1990, mumbling through an awkward exchange and calling back to him before finally walking away, putting distance between them, face hot and heart pounding, calling back: 'Don't you see? Clinging to this nonsense... It's a delusion. All of it. A delusion...'
>
> giving her friend the journalist an *I told you so* look when he finished reading out an interview with Guillaume Boucaya in which Guillaume admitted he had exaggerated a great deal in his early books, that most of what he wrote about was very probably wrong. That was in 1998, just before her friend began writing sensationalist articles about the Millennium, articles that made her feel vindicated, made her say—a month or so later, her journalist friend and some mutual acquaintances watching from around the restaurant table, Millennium fever building, *The X-Files* still spawning interest in the paranormal, *The Da Vinci Code* a few years ahead, ready to take over, keep people wanting more—made her say and shrug: 'Of course I don't believe any of this nonsense' and mean more than UFO conspiracies and end-of-the-world cults and crystal skulls and Atlantis rising from the seas at the stroke of midnight on 1st January, 2000, happy she had finally seen the sense of this and, once and for all, got all this idiocy out of her system...

Four nights later, the running dreams returned for the first time in almost nine years.

There was no denying the dreams came less frequently.

'I do feel like our talks are helping.'

The therapist smiled. 'That's good. And you'll think about those things we spoke of? Your father, the other issues we discussed?'

'Of course.' Putting on her coat, the therapist showing her out of the treatment room, through the little reception area beyond. 'Honestly, I thought I'd come to terms with all those things years ago.'

'Old pains can come back when we least expect them. It only takes a small trauma, a tension that isn't properly resolved.'

'Yes. My marriage...' Stepping into the corridor, promising to begin work on an action plan, think about finding a more satisfying job. 'Thank you, so much,' Minnette said as the therapist waved goodbye, closing the door.

She had watched the tree outside the therapist's office change. From bare to filled with blossom. Dusk was coming earlier again, leaves becoming orange, drier, turning in the air as they fell. It was a cool evening, air nipping her face, first street lights glowing, headlights spilling over the gutters. Thinking the sessions were definitely helping, helping her through her conflicts. She would remember this—saying goodbye, walking past the tree, Métro station around the next block, thinking how these sessions had helped her find perspective, make a fresh beginning—memory coming back over subsequent years, one of those moments that never quite fade.

The tree's shadow swept towards her, the hands of a clock, vanishing, to reappear with the next car.

Remembering thinking how much the sessions were helping.

Air nipping forehead, cheekbones smarting, hands thrust deep into pockets.

Walking away from the door.

Remembering thinking.

Métro station around the next block, tree's shadow brushing over her like hands remembering a shortcut by the feel of one particular stone in an otherwise blank wall. This street lined by a wall of sandstone blocks, faces weathered and cold under her trailing fingers. Métro station a block away. Hesitating only a moment at the next junction, fingers trailing over the face of the wall because the leaves underfoot were slippery, remembering she had been going to wear shoes with low heels. Shortcut swept by headlights, light wind nipping her face as she ducked under a swaying tree, its branches bare and silent. Traffic growing heavier, headlights masking some of the cars, hiding their drivers, slithering over the leaves on the pavement, the shops dark at this time of night. Remembering thinking this was a dead end. Shortcut easier than walking around the three sides of a square to the Métro station a block away. Hesitating less than an instant at the next turning. Thinking this was the way she remembered, one hand trailing over the worn face of the wall, wall nipping the tips of her fingers. Traffic sliding across the entrance to this side street, too distant to sound like anything more than the swaying of branches on a leafless tree, heels rapping off the darkness on the left, the evening more like night. It was that time of year. Métro shortcut quiet at this time. The sough of a tree: traffic reminding her of that sound, heels beating back from the walls of the next turning. Street beyond narrow. Quiet enough for her heels to beat against the darkness. Quiet enough.

Minnette stopped walking.

Listening.

Waking. No sound other than the spasm of her whole body against the mattress. Blinking at shelves, chest of drawers, wardrobe sketched in grey-blues. Summer. Sun already high and apartment beginning to warm up. Clock reading 5:07. Alarm set for two hours after that. Minnette knowing she would not sleep again. Sitting in front of the iMac, listening to its fan spin, disk drive natter. Staring at a newspaper's homepage. Re-reading the headlines. Scrolling down. Up. Noticing the date. Knowing the date without having to read it. Skimming some piece of celebrity twaddle, as if something so inane and vacuous could somehow anchor her. Looking down at the sunlight pooling under the curtains. Multi-coloured swirls blotting out screen, date, hallway when she looked down it. Waiting. After-images fading. Still waiting, although for what she could not say. Closing the web browser without looking at the date again: her sixtieth birthday a week away. She had no plans to celebrate it, no idea who she might invite. Wanted nothing from it. Except, of course, a good night's sleep.

Waking. No sound other than the spasm of her body against the mattress. Blinking. Waiting.

Waking. No sound. Blinking. Waiting.

Waking. No blinking. Waiting.

To see if the dream was over.

Minnette turned sharply away from the door.

All of which has to leave you wondering: so what? Why all the drama and anguish, Minnette?
　Toledo, of course.
　It all comes back to Toledo.

They got lost driving out of Paris. Somehow. No one wanted to admit they had read the signs wrong and they assured each other the route was easy from now on. They got lost again just before Toulouse. Twice. And it was half a day before anyone realised they were driving deeper into France, not towards Alicante. Minnette stared out of the side window, watching the roadside slip past, telling herself it should feel different to other roads because this road existed as part of a country ruled by a Fascist dictator and seeing only a roadside slipping past. Listening to the cassette player or the radio in the front of the cab. Being drawn into a discussion, feeling less distanced for a time until, without warning, she felt exhausted, no longer cared what she had been saying. Then, Minnette shook her head, shrugging or waving a hand, and sat for an hour, three, in silence but for the music and discussions drifting back from the other seats. The others were sympathetic, even when she told them she didn't want their sympathy. She wished she had never come.

They got lost again.

'It's not far, I'm sure,' the young woman who owned the van insisted. 'Look.'

Her boyfriend swotted away the map she was holding in front of his face, muttered: 'Who gives a fuck', and swung the van on to the impacted dirt along the road's edge.

They set up camp. A crackling fire under the van's awning. Wind drawing smoke on to its breath, breath remaining splinter-sharp, wind's touch leeching heat. Five of them huddling around the fire, light exaggerating the varying amounts of misery in their expressions. From inside the van, the boyfriend banged and thumped about, ostensibly searching for something. The young woman who owned the van rolled her eyes.

'Maybe we're not supposed to be getting there at all.' It was supposed to be a whisper but the scrawny kid with an obsession for British Progressive Rock bands startled at his own voice, looking around the fire almost guiltily.

'Balls,' suggested Yves, concentrating on rolling a joint.

'How about it, Minnette?' The third year reading psychology turned towards her, red hair falling in a swathe across half her face, question coming out of shadow. 'What do the cards say?'

'Balls,' suggested Yves, inhaling deeply around the word.

'Shut up, heathen.' The young woman who owned the van punched his arm, punched him again when he didn't hand over the joint. 'But, yeah,' she hissed, smoking spilling from mouth and nose, 'yeah, Minnette, what do the cards say?'

Pausing a moment or two, then ducking into the van, colliding with the young woman's boyfriend triumphantly brandishing a bottle of cheap brandy, stepping back into the cold to find the scrawny Prog Rock fan clearing off the camping table for her. Minnette began shuffling, concentrating on the question she wanted the cards to answer, a thread of doubt slithering beneath the repeated words, interest and curiosity surely too little a basis to rest any divinatory power on. Perhaps, if Guillaume hadn't gone off—

Minnette sat up straighter. Laid down the first card: The Magician, reversed.

The second crossing it: Judgement, also reversed.

Blinking at them. Coleman lamp hissing as it rocked from the awning overhead.

Third card: The Moon.

'How's it looking?' The psychology student leaned closer. Minnette thinking she could feel the warmth of the woman's body. Thinking she should think only of the question she wanted the cards to answer.

The High Priestess.

Wind humming as it passed over the camp fire. Trees along one side of the campsite gaining weight in a car's headlights. Engine receding. Someone clearing their throat.

She had no faith in this stuff. Not now. If ever. Interest. Curiosity, yes, but faith... since Guillaume... which was silly of her, because he never said, she never said anything either, waiting for Guillaume to... to...

The Lovers.

Knowing the cards couldn't be picking up her thoughts and flinching, wanting to say she had misdealt, reshuffle, start again. Worried what might turn over next.

'Minnette?' The girl who owned the van leaned over the table, passing the joint to the scrawny Prog Rock fan, her boyfriend moaning he was hungry and fucking cold and why the fuck had she chosen this fucking place to stop the night anyway...?

Guillaume. The night he had left. Alone in the attic room. Music filtering up from the floors below. Voices. Footsteps on the stairs. Candles burning. Ignoring it when someone—recognising his voice, knowing it was the founder of the squat outside—ignoring it when someone knocked on the door. Dealing, re-dealing, always the same question. Searching for a better answer. Always hoping the next...

'It's bad.' Scrawny kid holding out his hand for the brandy.

'She hasn't finished.' The red-haired psychology student waving him silent. 'Let her finish.'

Turning over: The Hermit.

Repeating: *This is dumb, this is random, this doesn't mean— It's dumb...*

'Minnette?'

'Oh, it's going to be fine.' Minnette smiled, gathering up the cards and shuffling. 'Yes. We'll hit the right road tomorrow and it'll be easy. We just head south, is all.'

'The look on your face...' The scrawny kid hugged himself deeper into his greatcoat, drawing deeply on the joint when Yves handed it to him.

'Look?' Minnette frowned. 'Sorry. The light's not so clear and—' straightening the edges of the deck— 'I couldn't decide how to interpret the cards.' Putting the cards in a pocket. Not touching them for the remainder of the trip.

In 1588, Florian Rudolphus Dippel published *Numinosity in Darkness*. Long and discursive, illustrated by engravings that are as exquisite as they are bizarre as they are largely impossible to interpret, the core of the book is the assertion that humanity and the entirety of Creation are no more than an epiphenomenon of something greater and more mysterious. He explains:

> *We are not central to the functioning of this Creation (which I term* the Mundanity, *for it encompasses all that we accept and hold as mundane and usual to the bounds of Common Existence). Rather, Accident and*

> *By-product that we are, we are as a Grain of Sand to the motions of a Vast Desert: part of the Whole yet, by any Common Measure, Irrelevant to the life of the Whole. We may term ourselves the Children of Almighty God the Creator indirectly at best, for we have never been his Focus. Further, as Unknowable as we believe the Almighty to be, God, in Truth, is yet more Unknowable, lying beyond the curtilage of the Mundanity in a Realm of Numinosity and Profound Light beyond all of Space and Time and Reason as we appreciate and accept these facets of Creation to be. Indeed, so far beyond us are they, the Almighty and His Creation is, in Effect and Common Practice, denied to us.*

However, he goes on to stress:

> *Do not forget, Accident that we are, we arise from the Stuff of God.*

The Mundanity, Florian Rudolphus reminds us, arose from and lies within the Greater Creation. We do not occupy the centre of the universe, yet, somewhere in every breath, deep within the darkness at the heart of every particle of dust, there is something of the numinous. This, he asserts, is self-evident and true.

The trick, however, is finding it.

A bookbinder by trade, Dippel (his real name was Gerhardt Fricht) published *Numinosity in Darkness* in an ornate and expensive edition of one hundred and seventy-two copies, the number having occult significance to him. Given its radical message, the book was not popular, almost bringing charges of heresy down on its author's head. The vehemence that met his ideas seems to have caught him by surprise and, when a warehouse fire destroyed almost all of the copies of the book and left him heavily in debt, Fricht sold his bookbinding business and left his home town for good. No one knows where he went although, seven years later, in the Baltic town of Lübeck, a Gerhardt Rudolphus Fricht is on record as purchasing a chandlery which remained in business long after his death. If this was Dippel/Fricht, no one knows what he did in the intervening time. At the end of

Numinosity, he promises a second volume in which he will discuss the nature of the Greater Creation and of God, this work to be written once he 'completed certain Investigations upon which I am about to embark'. The consensus is that, aside from this curious footnote to the history of the Occult, Dippel/Fricht achieved nothing except having the good sense to abandon his dabbling with this second volume not even begun and settling for a less controversial, if more lucrative, life as a chandler.

Movements jerky, Minnette scraped the remains of her dinner into the bin.

Poured more wine.

Looked into the almost-empty glass. And decided to fill it again, after all.

Stomach burning as she gulped the next mouthful. Indigestion souring her mood further. Glass striking against the counter-top, first dash of wine flowing too quickly, leaping out of the bowl. Righting the bottle. Resuming pouring more carefully.

It wasn't synchronicity.

Definitely.

Guillaume bothering her on the Quai Voltaire. The youth with the mountain bike on the Métro. M. Jacotey. All random. Meaningless.

Coincidence.

Not signs.

Not omens…

… probably.

Wine pattered against the floor.

Swearing, Minnette grabbed handfuls of kitchen towel, smothered the spillage before chasing after runnels, the puddle around the base of the brimming glass, before slurping excess from its top.

'My cup of runneth over.'

She would be seventy-one next year. That wasn't too old. Not to have something in her life. Something other than memories. Memories and—

'Fuck it.'

Snatching a brandy bottle from an overhead cupboard
—

And leaving it untouched by the sink. Standing on the threshold of kitchenette, living room.

'It's me. It's in my head.'

Talking to herself. The empty room. A room filled with books and notes. A carefully written address and password: things for a summoning.

'I'm giving all this significance because I don't want to be…'

Leaving the sentence hanging, too tired to speak.

Giulio Schifano was reckoned to be the most adept seer and fortune-teller in 17th Century Rome. A former theological student, rumoured to have made a pact with Infernal Forces, Schifano was famous for using a black mirror of ground volcanic glass. It was with this scrying mirror that he claimed to have tracked down an original translation of *The Key of Solomon*, free of later Christian accretions and filled with greater insight than any subsequent version of this famous grimoire. Two years later, Schifano uncovered a book he described as being 'more Fundamental and Rarefied and Greater than the writings of Giodarno Bruno or *The Apocrypha of Hermes and Moses of Aegypt*.' Written in an alien language, he was only able to 'divine some of its innermost meanings' through the use of his mirror and information found in his original copy of *The Key*.

All that is known of what Schifano found in this ancient book comes from a series of letters he wrote to a Swiss physician of his acquaintance. The cosmogony the letters outline is detailed, if incredible.

The Earth and everything we know exists within the fabric of a thirty-two-sided irregular polygon, itself one of many such structures, each nested within another and of almost infinite number; these concentric layers make up the whole of Creation. Because it is irregular, our universe is under constant tension and flux, striving either to increase its number of sides (Schifano called this 'Angelic

Ascendance') or rid itself of excess vertices (a 'Deamonic Relapse') and so achieve a permanent stability. The Earth and humanity were created by refugees from the collapse of an inner sphere of reality known as the Reticule. The refugees may have been trying to perpetuate their memory and spirit (Schifano is vague on this) or they may have been trying to create conduits for intelligences called the Hnivini, whom they believed populated a much higher level of the universe. However, the experiment failed and, ever since, humankind has been left with the sense that it is disconnected from this reality and is intended for higher things. It is this that gave rise to the Biblical myth of the Fall.

The correspondence went on for over three years with the utmost regularity until, abruptly, Schifano's letters became sporadic and cursory; a month later, they stopped completely. Receiving no reply to any of his enquiries, the Swiss physician travelled to Rome. There was no trace of Schifano. Everyone the physician spoke to maintained the fortune-teller had withdrawn from the occult life of the city without any warning, severing ties with patrons and colleagues alike and becoming a complete recluse, all over the course of a handful of weeks. No one knew anything about him after that.

About to give up, the physician nevertheless decided to follow a chance remark, travelling south and east of Rome until, at last, the trail led him to a squalid room in a hamlet on the road to Lucera.

The room's occupant, dishevelled and apparently poverty stricken, certainly resembled the descriptions of Schifano the physician had heard, but the man swore he had never heard of the magician. He was, the man avowed, a simple, devout churchgoer with no interest in Infernal Matters and no knowledge of books in general nor those on the Black Arts in particular. The physician interviewed the room's occupant for several hours, hoping that he would break the man's story and find something of Schifano's whereabouts. Despite the pressure of his questioning, the man's story remained firm and consistent.

The doctor had no choice but to conclude that this was a case of mistaken identity.

Nothing more was heard of Giulio Schifano.

'You saw something?' the German had asked her, pressing despite the reluctance that kept her answers evasive. 'Saw something numinous?'

'I don't think about it much,' she had replied, thinking this was true in a way.

'Was it wonderful?'

'I really can't say,' Minnette told the German in complete honesty.

'But you still think about it. Understandably. It's an extraordinary experience. Of course you carry it with you. But you've never—'

'I had a friend who saw cats.'

'Sorry?'

'Not from the corner of the eye, not like that. They crossed right in front of her. They looked solid.'

'I understand. Yes, there's quite a literature on those kinds of hallucination—'

'It doesn't mean she was mad. Does it?'

'Not at all. Is that what frightens you? That you might have been disassociating? There are all sorts of reasons why you might have an experience of this sort but it's hard to say anything about this particular instance until I know more. Do you think you can tell me all that happened?'

Minnette looked at her therapist without speaking.

'You do not have to talk,' the German had told her, placing a cup of herbal tea on the table beside her before sitting in the armchair opposite. 'It's enough to know you have had such an experience.' They had sat in silence for a while. Minnette listening to the traffic on the road below the German's second-floor flat, cars droning around the supermarket at the end of the street. A snatch of conversation. A dog barking. Sitting room cool although the afternoon had been warm for the time of year. Steam coiling above her teacup. 'You are not drinking?' The German leaning forward, inviting her to sip. 'I think you need warming up. The evenings can be very cold, do you not think?' Taking the cup, shivering, holding it close to her chest so steam rose to brush against her face. 'I never tell anyone what I saw—' faltering over this last word, compelled to add: 'what I think I saw.' The German had sunk back into his armchair, light from the single lamp missing his face as he asked, 'Is not belief the most important thing?' Sipping tea almost too hot to drink, each mouthful as much fragrant air as liquid, leaving lips and roof of mouth tingling once it slipped down, a warmth kindling under breastbone as she had sipped again, sniffing. 'It would be better,' she whispered around the tea's bitter aftertaste, 'if it was true. Wouldn't it?'

She took a taxi, stomach knotting, driver wondering if she was ill, making a joke of it as if she had been drinking too much, Minnette snapping at him, telling him to turn off the fucking radio because the last thing she fucking wanted was to have to sit through more shit about the shitting invasion of Kuwait. They drove in silence, reaching the station long before the train was due. Driver refusing to meet her eye, even when she gave him a generous tip. Trying to hate herself for being so rude and failing. Too expectant. Too anxious. Too scared. Standing on the platform, shade from the awning doing nothing to blunt the building heat, humid air cloying. Counting seconds between each glance at the clock. Worried the train might be late. More than a little unsure she wanted it to arrive at all and, knowing she could back out at any time, standing and waiting and counting off the seconds until her train arrived.
    The train to Toledo.

She left them in Toledo. Said it was a bad trip that had freaked her out. That someone must have spiked the wine they had been given at the party. That she needed to be on her own, get herself together. Yves drove her to the station. Silent until she had her ticket. Offering to go back with her, make sure she was okay. I thought that wine was straight, he said after she thanked him, assured him she could manage by herself. We shared a bottle, remember? Then it was something else, had to have been something else. And Yves, looking into her eyes, agreed that it must have been something, something to upset her so.

In the summer of '76, she had gone to a small rock festival on the French-Belgian border. Originally a friend had asked her along for company and she had agreed because time away from Paris seemed like just what she needed, Paris growing hotter and feeling more tired than she remembered, the city definitely failing to live up to its promise these days. She wasn't interested in the music, had never heard of any of the bands. So, when her friend met an Italian who preferred disco to rock and decided that festivals were for hippies, there was no reason for her to go alone. She watched the opening act, was ready to give up on the whole idea, stayed until the end of the set, entranced despite the unremitting heat and poor sound system. She found them loading up their van, told them their music was dark and beautiful and sinuous and terrifying and still wondrous. The band were flattered, invited her to eat with them. It wasn't more than an hour or so into the meal that they mentioned they shared a house on the outskirts of Nivelles. The attic room was vacant.

Minnette accepted the offer immediately.

A few days later, she met the artist.

'I feel,' she told him, 'like I'm rehashing my life, living in an attic again.'

He made no reply, summer light finding the threads of steel running through his ponytail, neatly-trimmed moustache, sculpting his hands as they rested on the table, inches from her own.

'Perhaps I'll get it right this time.'

The artist stayed silent. Minnette looked away, didn't look up when he asked if he could paint her. Simply gave the smallest of nods.

'What do you think you'll do? Later, I mean.'

November sunshine. Trapped inside the lean-to behind his house. Warm and brilliant under windows streaked by old rains. Minnette wanted to tilt her head to the light. Holding her pose instead, she asked:

'Tonight?'

'No.' The artist let the current sketch fall beside the others lying around the easel. Selecting a fresh charcoal stick, stick rasping across paper. 'I meant later. When you leave Nivelles.'

'I'm not going anywhere.' Used to his insecurities, drawn to his neediness. Feeling she could make his life easier. Not seeing his inability to deal with life head-on as an obstacle.

'Everything passes.'

'No. Not everything.'

He couldn't take her at her word. She accepted the constant testing, the tantrums and depressions. She told him she understood something of his pain, showed him the scars on her arms, told him again she had no plans to go anywhere. Telling the band later that she had been afraid. He had been drunker than she had ever seen him. Tearing up sketches, taking a knife to his canvases. Easel splintering under his pounding feet. All the time sure, sure he would never hurt her. And still running back to hide in the attic room.

The first of two dates in Brussels went badly. The second was better; subsequent gigs in Antwerp, Liège and Aachen better still. Minnette thought she might want to carry on being an assistant tour manager once this string of Christmas/New Year concerts was over. The schedule after Aachen was gruelling, though: a break-neck drive to Metz; then Nancy and the south, before east into Germany, then south again into Switzerland, and further south again after that. Minnette dropped out after Ulm, saying she was going to stay with a friend in Hanover and taking the first train northwards with no plan as to when she would stop.

'I thought you had gone,' was all the artist said when he let her in out of the damp, snow clotting the air.

'I decided to come back.'

He hesitated, hugged her tightly before leading her towards the kitchen, electric light spilling around the half-open door, voice low so she missed what he said, substituting something that she wanted to hear instead.

A numbness had settled over her as the train neared the border with France. Minnette thought distance and something familiar to immerse herself in was all she needed. Perspective and time to think: what she had told Yves and the others couldn't be so far from the truth. But Christmas at her parents' was not what she had convinced herself it might be, the familiar surroundings too familiar, house still a cloistered backwater filled with well-worn obsessions and hobby-horses. And her father, of course. None of it the anchor she needed. She watched TV without seeing what was on the screen. Stared at the flickering burners of the gas fire. Listened to the radio playing in the little room at the back of the house that her father called his 'Study'; the *tack-tack-tack* of her mother's knitting needles. She sat in her old room, trying to read. Her mother suggested she see a doctor. Her father told her to pull herself together. Minnette spent New Year's Eve lying on her bed, listless, half-hoping sleep would wipe out the remainder of the night and aware of the thread of unease over the dreams that would come to wake her up before morning.

Yves called late the following afternoon.

'I met someone at a party,' he told her. 'He'd like to say hi.'

She almost put the phone down when she heard Guillaume's voice. Holding the handset at a distance. Staring at the earpiece.

'Yves said you were ill or something. Are you okay?'

'Where are you?'

'Alicante. I—'

'They made it, then.'

'Uh? Oh. Yes. Yves and the others are here. We met—'

'That's great.'

Silence. Wanting to put the phone down and not able to bring herself to say goodbye or simply put it down without saying anything.

'Sorry.'

'Pardon?' She had heard, although his voice had been buried in the hiss on the line. 'Did you say something?'

'I'm sorry. It was wrong. I was wrong. Going like that.'

Minnette nodded. Belatedly taking a breath, knowing he could not have seen the gesture and readying herself to reply.

'And... I didn't find it. Anything, Minnette. It must be out there. Has to be, has to, doesn't it?' There was more than regret, the line's hiss thankfully smoothing out his voice, hiding most of the inflection and pain. He had hoped to find so much. 'I'm sorry, Minnette, but I didn't find—'

That was when she hung up.

You can't go back.

That was what the artist had said to her.

The old tin box should, could well have been thrown out a move or two ago, if not earlier.

Sure, all the same, it was still here somewhere.

As sure he was right.

The tin box wasn't in the wardrobe. Nor at the bottom of the cardboard box under the bedroom window, that box full of all kinds of things she had been saying she would throw out and still managed to hang on to.

It was only stubbornness that made her hang on to these things. That or habit. Because it wasn't like she hadn't come to believe what the artist had told her.

The tin box was under the bed.

Minnette struggled to stand, knee threatening to lock as her bad hip blazed. Imagining the slowly disintegrating pieces of bone grinding, one against another. The wine she had had with dinner did nothing to dull the pain.

Slumping on to the bed. Eyes squeezed shut.

When the pain eased enough, she began sifting through the photographs in the tin box. Faces she had not seen in decades. A torn picture of her ex-husband, although whether deliberately ripped or not she now had no idea. Her sister and her family. One of Minnette in '79. More pictures than she remembered having. All of them an excuse for nostalgia, which was only another sort of regret.

I have nothing to regret.

Really?

Snaps forming a drift across the bed, box down to its last few layers. Conviction growing.

It's not here.

Just as well?

Almost dropping it on to the discard pile without realising she had found what she was looking for.

Oh, Christ.

Everyone looks so young.

Not that she needed it but there was a note on the back to say this was April, 1974, the six of them standing on the meridian directly beneath the Eiffel Tower. Yves on the right, waving to the camera. Recognising if not recalling the names of the three people on the left. Volunteers or converts: it was too late to make her mind up.

Guillaume always maintained that the meridian through the Tower passed directly through the centre of the Great Pyramid at Giza. She had taken this at face value in those days; never got around to checking since.

He had kissed her just before this photo had been taken. She remembered that. Remembered him saying that this was a place of power, that a kiss here was a seal, a binding that would keep them together and she had said they didn't need that, laughing just before he kissed her anyway. She remembered the laugh, the pressure of his arm around her waist, her hand slipped into the back pocket of his jeans. Turning to the camera. She could see in the picture how she had felt. Remembering that she had been happy even if she could not remember what that had felt like on the day.

Which was strange, because Minnette was sure she could recall everything about the misery that came afterwards.

Albrecht Claes wrote his treatise on Hermetic philosophy in 1619, the book a culmination of over twenty years of study and contemplation. Stating firmly that he had nothing more to say, Claes retired afterwards to the estate of a benefactor, outside Ghent, where he devoted himself to the design and cultivation of knot gardens. Despite, or perhaps because of, his seclusion from the world in general, his book quickly gained a following and a certain notoriety. Although there is nothing within its pages to suggest it was so, rumour inflated into the certainty that Claes had succeeded in the *calculus albis*, creating the elusive Philosopher's Stone, and it was thanks to the resultant wealth that he was able to retire. Claes began receiving fan mail: sometimes enquiries and questions, sometimes blatant requests for money. A regular correspondence sprang up with occultists, alchymists and philosophers across Europe and even beyond. A Swedish mystic and Kabbalist travelled from St Petersburg to spend a single afternoon in Claes' company. Gradually, Claes spent more and more time away from his knot gardens, giving lectures or being feted in one city or another. However, no matter how much he was pressed or cajoled, he never admitted to having made the Philosopher's Stone and, if he also never gave an outright denial, he carefully demurred from taking credit for having achieved what so many had sought.

Yet, in 1628, Claes agreed to manufacture a quantity of the elixir for an extremely wealthy patron.

He failed. Spectacularly.

Whether it was hubris, or simply that so much flattery and attention had convinced him he did possess power,

Claes paid for his failure with a spell in prison. Nothing is known of him after his release...

You see? She closed the book, book sinking into shadows, shadows sinking into darkness. You see? Spreading her hands, hands empty now she had stopped reading, able to read in the dark, able to see clearly and thinking nothing of it. There's no way you can go back, she added, no point to any of it. You can't deny it, can you? Hands on hips as they walked, wall to their right a shimmer in the darkness, her footsteps distant as if they had managed to outpace sound, go further than she or anyone or anything had managed until now, air needles against her face and hands, air an ink that did not stain, hands waving. Can you? she asked again. But there was no reply, the huge shape keeping pace with her a patch of deeper blackness within the darkness, so that it stood out a little, black on blacker, stood out enough for her to see the heft and width of shoulders and neck, the weight of its angular head, sweep of its horns and, deepest and blackest of all, its eyes, slow-blinking, never leaving her. Gentle. Unreadable.

She had come to Toledo to forget.
She returned to Toledo to remember.

Her memory was of a staircase. Two flights, a sharp turn to the left. Stone, treads narrow, the drop between each uneven but always longer than was comfortable. And a handrail, loosely mortared in and cold to the touch. Half a day searching, up one hillside, down steep lanes that curved or emptied into narrow plazas enclosed by buildings or the next rise in the hills, Alcazzar or the Cathedral looking down, cobbles unrelenting under sandal-heel, street map confusing, cars nosing along lanes that should be too narrow for vehicles, ancient doors, brown wood studded, studs dusty or a little rusted, sometimes freshly painted, pausing at a T-junction, a needle-eyed cross-roads, starting uncertainly up the next hillside, street map becoming wadded as it passed from hand to hand, lane to lane, passages and narrow streets twisting, floors plunged into shadow by tall houses with peeling faces, faces in yellow or paler rendering, weeds hanging from the gutters sometimes, sometimes the sound of water rushing underfoot although the only glimpse any drain offered was of dry culverts, an alley appearing, tempting, bringing indecision, the thought that it might lead back twenty years, every meander and snake, each upward slope and blind bend reminiscent of what she had been carrying with her for those twenty years. Reminiscent but not the same, because the coiling streets she had walked that afternoon had been smoke and hazing shadow, not these passageways capped by empty blue, sun straining but without the reach to touch the cobbles, the sunken doorways, the saint watching from a sconce over a closed gateway, until the next coil opened into another little plaza. Sunlight prickling against bare arms, the sweat beginning to dampen her hair as she hesitated. Seeing: semi-darkness, a winter's afternoon so close to the solstice and so overcast it felt like early evening, deepened night. Remembering: air cold enough to draw blood, a silence glacial. Stepping into the shade under a short bridge connecting two tall, pink-faced houses, darkness profound for the first blink, second dissolving the passageway into shifting colours and swirls, swirls parting to show the passage rise and curve sharply. Thinking: *This might be...* And stopping, backtracking after another dozen steps. Seeing and remembering streets of smoke and chill and twilight. And finding instead: shadows thick with humidity, sky blue and sun-struck; voices from an open doorway that revealed itself to be a greengrocers; an old man peering down from a balcony jutting over a cramped street; shop window after shop window filled with Damascene. A gust of cigarette smoke. The smell of garlic and frying pork drifting through the open doorway of a taberna. All interwoven with the ambling footsteps of tourists, a tour guide's commentary, cars and vans squeezing down the roads with a hand's breadth of clearance, the nagging sense of familiarity. An acid sense of disorientation.

What she found was a lane. And a stairhead patched with concrete, passage dropping steeply through a dozen steps to a rectangle of stone flags. Impossible to tell from this angle if it were courtyard to a doorway or half landing leading to a second run of stairs.

Minnette looked uphill. A handful of metres further, the lane began to sweep towards the right, loosing itself behind intervening buildings, houses almost close enough to touch heads.

She remembered a lane bending, up and to the right. Remembered buildings close on either side. Minnette gazed at the lane's rise and curve. And couldn't bring herself to follow it. Not without some sort of confirmation.

She climbed down the first three steps, hesitated on the fourth as a suspicion of metal pipe appeared below.

A second flight of stairs.

Minnette rubbed a hand across her mouth. She would follow the slope. As far as the lane went. However far that was and no further. After that, she'd find the way back to the Hotel Alfonso. Shower. Long shower, then a drink. Several drinks. A bodega and drinks. Maybe tapas but drinks, drunk, a bit drunk, a lot, either. But only as far as the end of this lane.

Slope getting steeper on the curve. Turn completing. Lane dead-ending forty, fifty paces further on.

Just as she remembered.

The second step was narrower than the first, forcing her to grip the handrail as she took the third. And the forth, longer still and sloping towards the fifth, also longer, slope a little steeper, anxiety and anticipation more acute because this wasn't exactly what she remembered, memory thumbed so often she didn't want to admit it had changed and had no choice but to consider that if this was wrong then everything afterwards, all of this was... Remembering, instead, how she had missed the stairs on her climb towards the bend in the lane. But then the afternoon had been so gloomy. And she had been lost in thought, following the lane back downhill after reaching the dead end, noticing these stairs and hoping they offered a way out, perhaps to something wider than the alleyways she had been wandering all afternoon. That winter's afternoon close to the solstice.

It had been incredibly cold. Freezing. She had had no idea Spain could be so bloody cold, snow on the wind the whole time they had driven towards Toledo. And a flurry of snow as they sat in that café, writing slogans and nonsense in the condensation running down the front window, three-bar electric heaters dotted around the room, everyone's nose streaming as a result and all of them laughing about it with the group of kids sprawling across two tables with the air of owning that corner of the room, having annexed it for any wandering freaks and long-hairs, not just for themselves. The house where they held their party had been colder but had warmed up as people came, booze flowed, cigarettes glowing as lava lamps gambolled, vodka bringing a glow to her face, anisette keeping it there through the night as the music shifted, from Country Joe and the Fish to Janice, to the Stones and Led Zep, to the Beatles, who stood aside in the small hours for Crosby, Stills & Nash and Baez and Dylan, until dawn came late and hazy, one of the kids playing Granados on a much-abused guitar, stopping half-way through to say they needed to go back to the café, make everything a circle that joined itself tail to mouth. Like Uroboros, she had said, letting the kid take her hand and lead her out into the chill and half-light. The weight of the hours past were grit in her eyes and joints, sleep an itch, or a guilty craving, something she wanted to stave off either way. Dropping something the kid slipped into her palm, waiting for the rush to come on before retaking his hand, pill making her oblivious to fatigue and cold and the flint sky. Heading back to the house to make another circle of sorts. To wake, hours later, wristwatch wanting her believe it was noon when the shadows and grey air outside testified to a day older, nearer done; body needing her to get up, pee, find something to eat. But hunger gave way to nausea, head tight and fragile. Which might have been the downside of whatever the kid had given her to keep going, or maybe not. Slipping out. Walking. Trying to walk it off. Walking into the new town, wandering through Christmas shoppers and Christmas lights, along wide roads filled with brake lights, headlamps as bright as any seasonal decoration, side streets quieter but still resonating with the bur of traffic. Each breath a phantom, the cold a lover's clinch under jumper and buttoned Afghan. Walking on, nausea a fading memory and headache replaced by the smart of air against forehead, ears, the pain of aching teeth and a jaw clamped to stop it chattering. Fatigue coming in waves that never quite crested, falling back to let her walk, because the need to walk had come on her like the pill's rush and was as hard, harder to shake. Walking until she had to say, later, it had been spiked wine, a bad trip that had left her confused, insisting to Yves that someone had given her LSD and that she had no memory of what happened between leaving the house and the next morning, when he had pulled up in the Renault van as she wandered the swathe of road above the river, old town crouching on the hills above them.

Ever since, there had been a part of her that wanted to believe she had been spiked. And a part that felt guilty about this.

The two flights of steps led to a road.

Just as she remembered.

Vehicles parked the nearest side of the road, hill dropping away sharply beyond the low wall on the far side, view of the countryside beyond the old town bracketed by stone buildings, shutters closed although the sun currently left their frontages in shadow.

Pausing on the edge of the last step. Ignoring the tremor in her hands. Focusing deliberately on the road, trying not to look at the vista beyond the wall.

There were more cars. Newer, of course. And shops, more than she remembered: signs advertising La Casera and Coke, gaudy pictures of ham rolls and boxes of marzipan. Buildings different and almost the same. Wanting them to be more familiar and having to accept she had hardly glanced at them that day.

After an hour or so, she had made herself sit over coffee in a tetería on the edge of the new town, cup and café's warmth making small fires of her face and hands, feet aching at the return of circulation. There was a bus stop outside, route busy: Christmas shoppers, some of them tourists at a guess, an old man who caught sight of her, raised his hat before getting on the bus. Imagining getting on the next bus herself, going to the end of the line, finding another bus, keeping going. Not feeling any conviction in the thought, simply playing with the idea. Which made her think of Guillaume for some reason. Being with the kid who played Granados. Thinking about Guillaume. About how she hadn't felt much about the Spanish boy. About playing with the idea of riding one bus after another. About card readings and Guillaume travelling someplace, looking for—

Coffee cold, Minnette had left the tetería. Walking because there was still something there which felt like nausea. Taking turns instead of buses. Walking anyplace. And finding the streets getting older, narrower, steeper.

Reluctantly, she left the last step and stood beside the nearest parked car. As close to the carriageway as she could without having to dodge the next van or taxi to round the bend. As near as she could go, just yet, to the wall and the view beyond.

In that gap between the buildings on the opposite side of the road: terracotta roofs and square towers making game-board patterns between cypresses, TV aerials adding to the sense of random confusion, river there and gone again behind clusters of low trees, yellowing grassland rising to form mountains, slopes a deep green broken only by old farm houses, villas.

It was... something like she remembered.

Minnette took another step, squinting against sun glare.

That December afternoon had felt endless, the walking and climbing going on for so long it had been hard not to feel something was directing her, that she wasn't wandering so much as searching. A street name; the colour of a door; the relative quiet of a sharp-sloping alley: there was a significance to everything, each detail a waymark on a route hidden until the moment of the next turn when she would at least know the next stage if not the end point.

The clouds had been pressing the last dregs of light out of the day, bringing an early twilight. Lights flickered behind ground floor windows: fairy lights, a candle, the hard, illusory glow of a TV. No memory of the last person she had seen. Taking a turning, climbing a winding road as old or older than anything she had walked along until now. A thread of self-reflection muttering that it made more sense to turn back, find the house they were staying in, get warm, eat, sleep. And going on up the hillside regardless. Deeper into the old town.

Upwards. Always upwards.

Upwards:

Ancient buildings gathering out of the gloom, lanes winding, curling almost back on themselves sometimes so it was difficult not to think of serpents, a dragon in an etching she half-remembered from one of Guillaume's books, dragons like huge slow-worms, slow-worms like serpents under each step upwards, serpents with their mouths locked around the tail of the serpent in front of them, bodies twining one on top of another, vertebrae making the foundations, cobbles and stone setts and concrete patches making the lanes and passages over them, her feet making their own way, or something anyway guiding her, through twilight condensed out of an afternoon compressed by clouds low enough and dense enough to be lost in the twilight of their own making, twilight cold, nose running, teeth aching against the cold, finger-tips aching, ache almost like the need to reach out and touch someone, shivers hunching shoulders under Afghan, fur collar a white shadow in the murk seen from the corner of an eye as she climbed, feet neither of lead nor ice nor like something under her command, a tiny worm of unease and self-reflection twitching, flexing, never strong enough to murmur, faint as the wan streetlight hanging above the next sharp turn, the flickering-black-flickering-white spilling from the television by a ground floor window in an otherwise empty room, never strong enough to murmur faintly that this was not sensible, that this climbing-twisting-climb deeper into the old town was odd, perhaps unwise, perhaps—but the unease and self-reflection faded with the light from the lantern mounted high on the bend in the lane, with the last glimpse of the empty room, and, hands fisted against the frost beginning to shimmer dimly, dimly glinting under each step, she walked, climbing along steep lanes and tight passageways, diverting along alleys that left her breathless, flushed features a spark against the air, sweat drying to needles by the time she reached the next lane, the next cobbled road, taking turns as they appeared, following the ways open to her, feet making their way or something, anyway, guiding her.

Upwards.

Hot and weary, feeling a nausea that came on without warning, Minnette made herself take another step, walk all the way across the road.

Cold and weary, nausea long gone and as good as forgotten—for now; it would return, if only as part of her explanation for this afternoon, for all of this—Minnette walked out of a narrow side passage and on to another lane pushing steeply up the hillside. She wondered, briefly, if, after all, she had been spiked. Her head did feel… spaced, not quite with her body.

A lamp opened its eye, glow a gauze across the mouth of the next turn, prising back the afternoon's dimness just a little, the lane narrow enough that the gauze caught the building on the opposite side, its rendering crumbling, falling away to reveal a glimpse of the flesh beneath; light finding the edges of a gaping doorway, space beyond thick as tar, bottomless, single ground-floor window no less blank, grey enough to become lost, to not be there at all.

Breath gleamed in front of her. Next step taking her beyond the lamp into the guts of the lane, next breath invisible. Right foot finding something hard to grit, to clatter across worn cobbles, fall silent.

Buildings waiting. Lane guiding her. In near silence. Between each breath: a moment when she could pick out a bur of traffic so distant it sounded smothered by kilometres, was almost smothered by the choir of her own nerves, the push of her pulse. Next breath, next step. Nothing else. Nothing but the trailing fingers of the wind against the side of her head; afternoon smoke, a haze of soot fine enough to be invisible, dense enough to turn the upper storeys of the buildings shepherding the lane into a smudge against the grey clouds, the buildings becoming... *Ghosts...* Thinking this was a stupid word to use, thinking she wasn't sure she believed in ghosts, thinking she wasn't sure she didn't believe in magic... and trying not to think of Guillaume or tarot cards spread on a folding table and trying to convince herself to turn back and still giving into the urge to keep walking.

Thinking it was easier to keep walking.

Asking herself why.

And following the curve of the lane through the dense and cold and still of the afternoon. Half-hoping there was no end to the hillside.

A dead-end.

Minnette looked at the wall. The wall acted as if she wasn't there.

It rose, five storeys, maybe only three, but a sheer face, course after course of stones, rendering scarred, chipped, fallen away or smoothed over by the grey cast the clouds were staining everything with, December afternoon about dead because there no going on or up. Only back.

Minnette looked at the wall. One window, high up, unlit. Buildings to the right, left: felt more than seen, their windows catching and losing something pale in the sky, becoming slate, buildings to the right and left feeling hollowed and vacant.

The lane—this lane—had had no branches, no by-ways, had wound itself, successive coils tighter, leading directly... to this.

The end.

Toledo was silent and that tiny worm of unease and self-reflection told her the city shouldn't sound this quiet; another, quieter, slipperier voice hissing that the town was listening; while the balance of Minnette thought only that this was the end when she wanted no end.

She sniffed, cold a buzzing in her sinuses. The air felt prickly, frost beginning to condense out of the twilight on to the walls of the dead-end, the cobbles she was standing on.

The cobbles scintillated. Faintly, at the edge of eye and perception.

Dead-end: she wanted to climb. Not go back. Not have to go back and find another route, she didn't want to go back but go wherever it was her feet took her.

The cobbles shimmered.

Each breath scintillated.

Hillside unmoving beneath her. Anchored.

Cobbles shimmering.

Breath scintillating.

Later, she would forget. Years of replaying this moment—the cobbles' shimmer becoming her shadow, shadow slewing like a lodestone hungry for north, scintillation becoming something stronger, more definite, slipping around a gap between buildings that had had no gap, becoming confusion—smoothed and rationalised the memory into something as simple as deciding the break in the clouds must have opened sooner than she thought, the last of the day's light finding the stairs, limning the stairhead she had missed on her way up-hill. Such a simple explanation and almost not worth its forging, given what happened next, but Minnette held on to it as the years mounted, forgetting that the dead-end lay a distance beyond that last curve in the road and should have remained in shadow as a consequence; forgetting that she had been sure as, drawn towards the shimmering, beckoning light, she had retraced the long, tight curve in the lane, that the exit to the stairs—the stairs themselves—had not been there when she had trudged this way minutes earlier; forgetting how the shifting, dancing glow drawing her back along the curve had made chiffon of the freezing air and how, yes, the light had been touched by hints of rose gold and a russet orange but also by colours no sunset should have: a blue she could not name, a green that bled into a magenta that had been tinged with an electric violet; forgetting how the slipping, swaying glow picking out the stairhead could never have been something so ordinary as winter dusk-light. Minnette forgot all this, all but for one sensation.

As she walked back along the curve in the lane, saw the head of the stairs, the pepper-musk of the frost changed, became sweeter, resinous.

She would never forget that the afternoon had begun to smell of incense.

Eyes closed, last steps to the wall, sun a palm pressing firmly against her head, pushing, pushing hard enough she almost faltered, thoughts running, faster, babbling about the time of day, how it could be, must be the same time, about the same as before, thinking days were longer in September than in December, thinking of turning back, because it was, it might be, better not to know, better to let things alone, better to open her eyes now, mind slewing to Nicolas, to magic, to coming back to Toledo, to—

The parapet wall struck her legs.

Toledo crouched in the valley, hands against the hillsides. Waiting. Only the breeze moved and that lightly, hardly there at all. There were tail lights, headlights, static, dotted between buildings, old walls creaking with the cold,

old stones drawing down the frost, sparkle in the air not moving either. Watching. Or waiting.

The parapet wall struck her legs.

Minnette gripped stone faces rough and cold, holding on to the uneven top of the wall.

Sunlight made her squint, rock a little on legs that shook with cold, fatigue, quavered with a sense of something else beginning to leech out of her gut.

Sunlight touched cheekbones, forehead, brushed the side of her face.

No sound as the lead and granite clouds continued to part. No sound as the sun spilled more light across the city, painting the hillside around her, warming her face even though the air remained frigid. Knees pressed harder against the wall, body straining towards the sun, last of the day's light limpid, more lustrous than gold as it slipped around the edges of the mountains. Thread of self-reflection stammering in her head. Becoming lost in the shafts of burnished light. Surfacing to babble that Toledo was built on rolling hillsides, no mountains this close or this imposing... Vanishing as she stared at the setting sun framed between mountains reduced to silhouettes. A glimmer of light called back from the valley floor, river shrunken but visible among the shadows. Rays, like fingers splayed around the parting clouds. A god's fingers pointing across the hillside, inviting—no, insisting—she look.

Minnette, shivering, had leaned forward a little more to look across the roofs of the old town where the sun directed.

The tower smouldered. Behind it, clouds of indigo and grey denser than soot stood in sharp relief, dark backdrop making the tower look brighter, its face white, stones opaline, terracotta roof becoming scarlet, almost on fire, windows the only thing not lit by the sunlight, each frame black, bottomless tunnels driven deep into the building, deeper than the tower's width, interior bigger and more mysterious than its shining outside.

It was hard not to fall. Hands gripping the wall, tower trying to draw her across the rooftops. Hard not to think that, if she fell, she would be cast across the roofs, pulled directly into the tower. Nothing else seemed as solid. Not now the sunlight had found it, made her see the tower rising above every other building on the hillside, broader and heavier than any other structure she could see. More solid.

Minnette felt herself fading. Wondered if she was on the verge of fainting. Of falling despite her grip on the stones. Heard a voice. A buzzing. Words indistinct. Thought she was talking to herself, denying what she saw, embracing it, babbling in awe, muttering at the top of her voice. No sense of her throat working. Lips and teeth and jaw clenched. Still the murmuring, the words indistinct. Wanting the voice to go away. Ignoring it. Watching the tower. The tower glowing. Becoming brighter. Making her squint. Dimly aware of cold, stone wall, an ache threading each muscle and joint together. Even this becoming lost as she stared, the tower brighter, brightest thing there ever was.

And not able to turn away fast enough as the flare blotted everything out.

Flinching, she saw the hillside run in orange blurs, a second blink unfurling magenta clouds that roiled as she gasped for breath, white light seeming to come back with a third blink.

It was the concussion that struck her, not another flash of light. Too loud to be sound, the wave took her between its hands and squeezed, screaming as she wanted to scream. Yell becoming sound only as it began to reverberate, thunder rolling over itself, over itself, over itself, reluctant to fade as it turned back to shake her a fourth time.

Minnette screamed, scream inaudible even inside her skull. Clawing for a second breath. Wanting to scream again. After-images becoming paler as they hung about her face. Mouth opening wider, hanging. Scream forgotten.

The tower had been split in two.

Memory stuttered. Fragments. Glimpses pieced into a whole: lightning whipping from the clouds, whip striking the tower's face. Face cracking, bursting. Masonry blocks, a haze of rubble tumbling, outwards, down. Frozen in midair, caught in the lightning's flash-bulb afterglow.

Minnette clutched the parapet wall, vision becoming foggy at the edges, a flush of intense cold leaving face clammy, skull tight, nausea a sour taste threatening to swell.

Last reverberation not dying but snuffed out.

Silence. No sirens, screams, no clamour as people stumbled into the streets and roads and wanted to know what had happened, where to run. She knew the stillness was unnatural, could feel it smothering the harsh, uneven sound of her own breathing, heart's pelting. Minnette blinked, a breeze stirring, licking her face. Bringing a whiff of urine, sharp and fresh, damp patch on her jeans-crotch already cooling, too peripheral a discomfort to register before the wind shifted, brought incense again, pungent and sweet against the gunpowder-sharp reek of ozone. Nostrils flaring as the wind slipped away, moved just ahead of the shadows as they bloomed, muting the valley, hillside, made the tower vanish, clouds furling in their turn, sun dwindling. A final ray escaped, glancing across the hillside.

Night hid Toledo, only a few lights in the distance breaking the murk.

Trembling, no rhythm to her breathing and not enough air in any one breath. Eyes wide. Staring. Seeing against the darkness what the last flicker of sunlight had shown her. Broken stones, heavier shards of masonry, a spar, dust between: hanging, never coming to earth, caught in eternal fall like the stones in the picture, lightning splitting rampart walls and tearing them in two. Like—

The Tower. The Tarot card.

Jarring outstretched hands on the blocks capping the walls, eyes squeezing tighter, unwilling yet to see the hillside no matter how much the sun tried to pry her eyelids apart. Waiting. A heartbeat. Two dozen.

Minnette opened her eyes.

Blinked. Looking away to look again. Warm face growing warmer.

The hillside curved away, stone buildings straddling the slope in terraces that looked like they had been laid out centuries ago, TV aerials and a few cables the only concession to the present. It was something like she remembered but the mountains forming the horizon were lower and more distant, less severe, river likewise wider, appearing from a curve in the valley only to disappear in the same way, hillside not as steep as in those memories she had been turning over for years.

Her eyes moved.

No rubble.

Minnette craned.

No shattered foundations or buildings showing signs of recent and extensive repair. No scars left by falling masonry.

No Tower.

And yet she found the alley with no trouble at all.

This was not something anyone could simply walk away from. Minnette didn't, of course. She ran.

Boots slapping against fractured concrete, broken cobbles. Arms milling. Searching for a rhythm and having gravity push her hard in the back. Running to keep from falling. Running to get far away from wall and hillside. Legs never moving fast enough. Hip grazing the first parked car she passed, barking against another, bruises failing to register.

Getting away was all that mattered.

The road curved, unspooling as it wound downhill. Each breath ice and fire and a splinter of glass lodged at the back of her throat. Footfalls pelting off crumbling buildings on either side. And still a silence squeezing the streets together around her, forcing the road to narrow, narrow and twist sharply.

Too sharply.

Minnette's shoulder scraped hard against corner stones, feet tangling, balance capering out of reach, vanishing as gravity let go of her back and tugged just enough on her out-thrown hands. Hands and arms numbing as she hit, rolled, tumbled a second time, sprawling, momentum jolting her across cobbles, hauling her up to dump her on her knees.

Two lamps shone from wall-mounted brackets on one side of the road, their light oddly fragile and casting no more than a faint, reflected glow across the buildings facing them, penumbra suggesting an arch, wooden doors beneath closed tightly.

The need to run gnawed, bubbling into her throat, making it hard not to stagger up, ignore the pain in shoulders and ribs, begin screaming as she started the race again. She had no idea what was making her crawl closer to those overlapping falls of light. One hand raised, palm outwards.

Warm. The air was warmer around the edges of the light.

Rising, teetering closer. The cold remained at her back, to each side, yet the lamplight was warm against her face and hands, warmth beginning to soak through the Afghan, finding tingling skin beneath woollen jumper, cheesecloth shirt, T-shirt: the sun on a crisp winter's day, air chill and burnished by sunlight strong enough to bring a foretaste of spring. Except, hand shading her eyes, she knew the bulbs in those street lamps could never be strong enough to warm like this.

Seeing, in the shade of her hand, the entrance to an alley between the two lamps.

Feeling the terror dwindle. Feeling the buildings and the coiling road and the flesh of the hill itself watching. Expectant. Silence over the old town deeper, poised as a breeze, soft and less than a whisper, seeped from the alley's mouth, warm air threaded with ambergris and sandalwood, tints of attar and sweet-sour shades of patchouli. And something underneath. Elusive if not hidden: pungent, animal-seeming, gone with the next breath.

Later, standing in the heat of a September afternoon, shadow from the building with the arched entrance doing nothing to blunt the heat, Minnette tried to remember exactly how this moment felt and failed to summon anything more than an impression of scented breeze against her face, the memory of there being scents rather than memory of the scents themselves, no longer sure whether she had fallen because she had noticed the light first or saw it afterwards, trepidation and expectation colouring her recollection of stepping forward, thinking perhaps she had heard the whispered litany before she had entered the alley, wondering whether perhaps the voices had begun only as she had taken that first step. Unsure whether, after all, she had walked in silence the whole time.

'Every Breath You Take' was coming from the little tourist shop on the corner. Again. Open windows overlooked the alley, each vacant and quiet. The song ended. Was replaced by 'Every Little Thing She Does is Magic'. Striding back along the alley's length. Again. Thinking how much she loathed The Police.

One of the wooden doors under the arch was open. A car hidden in the shadows. A glimpse of a cane chair beginning to unravel beyond that.

Looking up the road at the sharp turning marking the top of the slope.

Staring at the lights bracketing the alley-mouth.

Again.

Minnette was sure this was the right place, the entrance to the alley she had walked down that night.

Four metres or so in: a sharp bend, just as she remembered. Then a gentle curve swaying away and back towards its original line. Steep-sloping passages branching off, leading deeper into the jumble of buildings standing over the alley. A sharp turn. The latest hit from the tourist shop resolving itself into 'De Do Do Do, De Da Da Da'.

Minnette looked across an open plaza, main road crossing it broader than most, dotted with shops offering Damascene gifts, a bar on one corner with tables lined up in the shadow under its awning, the restaurant on the opposite side offering an outdoor dining area carpeted with artificial grass.

Nothing like she remembered.

What do you remember? the German had asked as he leaned forward in his chair as she hesitated and frowned as if trying to sort impressions and memories before telling him about the working they had attempted in her last year at University and mixing that up with months later on the Aegean island with the cup of land between the hillsides and the farmhouse that had creaked when the wind was still was still was still nodding the German nodding his eyes on her and not blinking not blinking as he suggested when she paused that she needed tea that she should drink tea drink tea drink

'One drink. What could that hurt?'

Looking at him. Knowing she could turn away, pretend she had a tutorial, her tutor that semester sympathetic and sure to let her hide in his office for an hour or two, long enough for this to be over. Knowing that and knowing that Guillaume already knew what she was going to do.

Hard to say exactly where she had imagined their first meeting taking place, so many imagined meetings to choose between, expectation growing over the last six or seven weeks, rising more once his post card found her in Copenhagen. A betting shop on the edge of a crumbling housing estate in Leeds, however, was not one of the places she had pictured.

They sat for half an hour without speaking, the magician absorbed in the images on the dusty TVs screwed to the nicotine-stained walls, tilting his head sometimes to listen to the breathless race commentary over the tannoy.

Old men in dowdy jackets and overcoats, cigarettes clutched in the corner of the mouth or between yellowed fingers, fading tattoos a blue-green smudge on a hand's back or an exposed wrist; younger men covered in brick dust or in paint-spattered overalls, or wearing jackets made out of denim or plaid, fur collars as stained as the room's walls; women now and then, placing a bet for someone else or risking their own money: too earthly, too grim and mundane to be the place where there could be a chance of enlightenment, transcendence.

Hard not to wonder if this was a mistake, if the German had been right all along.

'They believe there's always a chance the universe is going to change for them.'

The magician's voice was soft. Minnette almost startled, face growing hotter, wondering whether, and dismissing the notion in the same moment, he might have overheard her thoughts.

'Some believe more strongly than others, but they believe the same thing.' He lifted a finger, indicating the race coming to a climax on the screens. 'Even if they think it's nothing more than a flush of excitement, a couple of minutes when they have more in their days than early shifts or bills or a gaffer who's a cunt.'

The race finished. A young woman trundled a pushchair up to the window and collected winnings.

'Tell me something you believe in, that you believe you witnessed.'

Minnette hesitated, shrugged, the image of a winter's afternoon and the night afterwards overlaid with memories of the German, of Guillaume, of a séance Guillaume had held.

'The table rose,' she finished.

'What do you think it was?' He turned back to the TVs on the wall, punters studying the form of the next race.

'I…' Nothing seemed adequate.

The magician glanced at her, seeing her uncertainty.

'Good. That's a good place to start.'

The barman gave a sceptical look.

'It's the heat. It's very hot this evening. Isn't it?'

He shook his head and she was ready to argue, more than happy to argue that she was right, when Minnette realised she had spoken in French. '*Es muy...*' scowling over the word for 'hot' and wiping at the hair sticking to her forehead instead, pantomiming wagging the collar of her blouse to encourage a breeze, about to demand another beer, knowing the Spanish for that, and remembering she had only just walked into the bodega, saying instead: '*Una cerveza fría por favor*', fingers drumming on the edge of the bar, hoping the barman was going to refuse.

Instead he nodded and placed a sweating bottle and chilled glass in front of her. Disappointed, Minnette was tempted to complain about the slow service. Remembered the last bar. And mumbled a thank you.

Climbing on to the high stool was harder than expected, almost tipping off a second time before managing to perch uncertainly on its edge. Elbows planted firmly on the bar, she began pouring beer. It slopped out in a rush, climbing over the side of the glass to hit the marble counter. Snatching serviettes from the dispenser, corralling the spreading froth, Minnette took a gulp from the glass and spilled the beer down her chin.

The barman was polishing glasses when she looked up, challenging. Staring until there was no doubting he wasn't laughing about her with the customers sitting further down the bar.

Minnette took another gulp, managing not to spill any this time. Thinking: *This is a fucking useless town, utterly fucking awful, fucking useless place filled with useless people who don't know their own town even when you fucking explain and explain to them what you're fucking looking*—and barely glancing towards the old man when he said good evening and sat at the next stool, lifting her glass and finding that, somehow, it was already empty.

'Another beer—huh, I mean: *ot'o... otro cerveza...*'

'Can I help, madame?'

'Miss—' quite happy to have found an excuse to cause another argument and, seeing this man's expression, changing her mind— 'thank you.'

His French better than her Spanish, it was a surprise when a tall glass of ice water appeared in front of her along with olives, flat bread, slices of lightly-salted Manchego the old man insisted she share with him. Minnette was going to refuse, before nodding, taking an olive to seem friendly and quickly following it with bread and cheese, conscious she had eaten nothing all day.

The old man told her about his dog. About his neighbours. A nephew in Madrid. Minnette nodded, deciding to say nothing about her day or why she had come to Toledo, deciding she had had enough of the town, of—

'And you, mademoiselle, are you on a short holiday?'

'I'm—' *not going to say anything—* 'I'm—' *just shrug and stay silent—* 'I'm...'

She didn't tell him anything. Not everything, anyway. Not exactly.

'All day. All af'ernoon, I searched all af'ernoon. And I couldn' find it. Foun' the alley, or what the alley is now. I think it was the alley. You can see th' problem right there, can' you? Bu' I kep' searchin' and— What d'you think?'

'I'm not sure, mademoiselle—'

'Well, 'xactly, and how d'you think tha' feels?'

'It must be quite—'

''Xactly. Awful. Fuckin' awful way to have to live. Years. I mean, years, almos' twen'y years.'

'You're upset, mademoiselle, and I'm sure whatever it is that's upsetting you is very bad, but I don't understand—'

'No, me neither. I'm always hopin' someone'll explain it. Tha' would be grea', really grea', 'cause otherwise I'm jus' mad, I wen' mad and saw things and they was real, seemed real, looked very fuckin' real and if they seem, seemed real, if they was really real lookin'... you see?'

'I, um... I'm not—'

'No, no, no, me neither, me neither, 'cause tha's the point: if they are, if they was really real and they seemed and fel' and look, looked, real and you—me—if I couldn't, can't tell what is and what isn', then how do I ever know was is or isn'? You see?' Pausing, frowning, head heavy as she looked around the bar, fan spinning overhead, faces reflected in the big mirrors on the walls, toreros staring blankly from the frame holding their yellowing photographs, framed postcards of happy couples smiling for the camera looking back no less vacantly, room suddenly narrow and long. 'Is it hot? Feels very hot. Is it?'

'Yes. Rather. But, sorry, I'm trying to understand: did you see some—'

'You know a buildin'? Long wall, big wood door at th' end? Stone? Walls o' stone, door's wood, big, heavy, somewhere, somewhere here, nearby?'

'Sorry, I don't think—'

'Di'n' 'xpect you to. 'S alrigh', no one does, no one. 'Nother beer? Been a lon' day, hot, walkin' all day, and hot, very ho' after all tha' searchin'.'

'Would you like some more water? Would you like to talk to, um, the police, if you saw something so distressing?'

'Wou'n't help. Forge' it. Really. For the bes', jus' move on and forge' it, don' you think? I do. Yeah. Should've. Years...'

'Please, mademoiselle, let me get another ice water, perhaps something else to eat, you're very upset and very —you're in no state to—'

No listening, weaving carefully between the tables, bodega very dingy despite wall lamps and ceiling lights, lights much less bright than they should be, thinking of the air conditioned room in the Alfonso and how to get there, thinking of the first train back towards France in the morning, sick of it all, digging in her bag, not able to make sense of the unfamiliar currency and feeling sick, sick of the whole thing. Leaving without looking back.

It was the book slipping forwards and dropping into her lap that woke her.

Which made no sense because she had been reading the book, words slipping past, turning pages as they went, forming new words and new pages before they turned and turned—

Minnette blinked, glow from the bedside lamp prickly.

The photo of Guillaume and her at the Eiffel Tower beside her left hand, the box of photos threatening to slip from the bed.

Retrieving the book. Arthur Hailey's *Airport*, much read, almost as much as *Hotel*, both old favourites because they were so trashy, so ordinary. So believable. Skimming: Patroni working desperately to clear Runway 30; Ada Quonsett getting caught on board Flight Two; Bakersfield's struggle to get to the dinner party Cindy wants him to— Not what she had been reading while she slept. All of it what she remembered and nothing like what she was remembering: the long road, narrow like a passageway, dark but with a suggestion of dawn about to break, each turning darker when she took them but becoming the long road, narrow like a passageway, dark with a suggestion of dawn about to break, each turning as empty as the last when she took it but suggesting—

Looking up. Bedroom door half-open. Unsure whether she had left it like that. Blinking, light from the bedside lamp bright and prickly. Making her squint at the sliver of hallway visible through the gap between door and frame. Heart beating. Beating faster. Squeezing eyes tight shut. And opening them to stare, frown deeper. Waiting.

It wasn't the biggest party Minnette had been to. It looked like it was going to be the most colourful, the oddest. Guillaume's flat was packed. There were hippies, of course, and a scattering of Maoists and Trotskyite radicals looking at everyone else with the contempt that only fair-minded, caring people who know—because they keep telling themselves they are fair-minded and working in the interests of the greater good—that they are vastly more superior than everyone else. Both were in the minority. Of the majority she encountered, as she wandered through the crush, glass of wine almost forgotten as she watched, sometimes talked, more often eavesdropped: a couple of would-be alchemists eagerly discussing quantum theory and its impact on the search for the Philosopher's Stone; a witch, her cat draped across her shoulders, the animal trying to lap gateau from the laden fork the witch gestured with as she talked animatedly with a palmist and a Surrealist film maker Minnette had heard made most of his money from 8 mm porn films; a group of Rosicrucians looking faintly glum, together with a middle-aged man in a mauve Rayon suit who, apparently, was a senior member in the French lodge of the O.T.O., but looked suspiciously like a minor civil servant, out for a bit of louche living; a Sufi who drew underground comics for a living and was about to start work on a new magazine called *Métal hurlant*; several people who claimed to be followers of Ouspensky; and rather more followers of Gurdjieff; a geomancer talking earnestly to a man who claimed to be reincarnated; a young rock musician who had just come back from Germany, where he had lived at an 'acid ashram' deep in the Bavarian forests for six months during which, he claimed loudly, spilling wine over himself, he had communed with entities in orbit around Saturn, these entities hip enough they had given him all the major licks for his next album. All this and an 8 mm print of Kenneth Anger's *Invocation of My Demon Brother* on permanent loop in the bathroom, a tiny audience of druids, astrologers, tarotmancers, and so forth watching its images dance over the tiles while people excused themselves, ducked under the flickering beam and made more customary use of the facilities.

Minnette spotted Yves, apparently entranced by a Persian-looking woman talking to a small group of guests about Sumerian astrology. Hard, however, not to suspect he was much more entranced by the astrologer's plunging neckline. He waved, grinned, returned to his contemplation of the profound.

She raised her glass in a toast to him and went to take a swig. The wine was gone. Minnette got a refill, hunted fruitlessly for Guillaume, launched herself back into the throng, catching a snatch of song from the hi-fi, something about a yellow brick road. And becoming lost in the overlapping conversations, the groups coalescing, fragmenting, forming again: UFOs, astral travelling, the power of the pyramids, the Great Ancestors who survived the destruction of Atlantis, Egyptian magic, the Bermuda Triangle, the forthcoming harmonic convergence, runes, visualisation, sigil magic, UFOs. Listening, joining in sometimes. Trying not to smile, act like this was a sideshow.

'Enjoying yourself?' Yves seemed to have lost his Persian astrologer during the hours since they had last crossed paths.

'It's interesting.' Whisky, she had decided, was definitely the right drink for this gathering. Minnette took another mouthful. 'Definitely interesting.'

'What's that mean?' Yves was very drunk indeed.

'Exactly.'

Not drunk enough.

'You seen Guillaume?' She drained her glass, whisky burning on the way down to a largely empty stomach. Like Yves, she wasn't drunk enough. 'He asked me to this menagerie and then pissed off somewhere hours ago.'

'Over there—' wine glass waved under her nose, directing her attention to the far side of the room and a knot of people in deep conversation— 'been there for ages.'

'Probably bloody avoiding me.'

But he seemed just the opposite, apologising for getting caught up in conversation, for having failed to find her in the crush. Saying he'd asked Yves to look out for her, offering brandy, a joint. A seat beside him.

'This is pretty wild, wilder than I thought. Enjoying yourself?'

Minnette took more brandy, telling him it was a great party as she fiddled with the stopper on the bottle.

Although the other guests were beginning to wind down, the group here in the corner around Guillaume was too settled to begin to break up yet. She listened to them, tried not to stare at Guillaume, and admitted she was down because she had kind of hoped he was going to pay more attention after he had tried so hard to get their friendship going again… unless it really was only going to be friendship… and that that thought alone was enough to make her think all this talk and all these people were ridiculous.

Crazy.

'But people see things all the time—' Guillaume gestured, meaning more than the freaks and weirdos beginning to drift away from the party, his own brandy forgotten as his passion increased— 'it's just down to being in the right place, being worthy—I guess worthy… receptive, say—yeah, I mean, an old mind, being prepared to believe—'

'But can you believe everything you see?'

They turned to her, waiting for her to say more as she tried not to blush and squirm and think of The Tower, of the impossibility of that and what had come afterwards.

'You'll know when something is true,' Guillaume said after another moment.

The pain from her bad hip finally made her move, turning awkwardly, no position seeming to offer any relief until she was sitting upright.

Airport slipped to the bedroom floor.

Grunting, she caught hold of the box of photographs, dropping the picture of her and Guillaume and the others at the Eiffel Tower inside before lowering the lot to the floor, wincing as she tried and failed to get the paperback without having to actually get out of bed.

With a grunt, Minnette gave up.

In the darkness after turning the bedside lamp off: Wriggling to find a position that her bad hip would tolerate. Staring at the ceiling as it grew more defined the longer she lay there. Knowing it was not so many hours until the alarm would go off, start another day.

Closing her eyes. Telling herself to sleep.

Watching the partly-open doorway through lids themselves held partly open. Waiting. Wondering.

Wondering when the dream might start. Might end.

Perhaps it was only the novelty of it all, of being here— his flat, his bed—that kept her from saying anything straight away, burrowing a little deeper under the duvet as he talked, letting him talk while revelling in being warm, in a warm bed in a dry apartment, one that didn't smell of damp and mould and incense sticks used to hide the smell of damp and the stale smell clinging to the squat's hallway and kitchen, a smell that came back to her at odd times, when she was at university or a café. But not here, where there was only the ghost of fresh linen from the recently-laundered bed clothes, the scent of Gitanes and Marlboros in the ashtray, and the smell of him, warm and real and beside her at last.

Minnette stretched out her legs, feet and toes straining before she relaxed, listened to Guillaume talk.

'I knew I was hurting... well, hurting you when I went. I know I've said sorry...'

He had. Several times. Particularly in the early hours of this morning.

A smile came without warning. She placed a hand across her face, worried he might see. Not wanting to loose the joy that was making her giddy even if there was still a thread of reluctance to admit how much she had wanted this and how much she had tried to pretend otherwise.

Minnette traced the line of Guillaume's shoulder blade as he leaned across to the low bookcase beside the bed, lighting up a fresh Marlboro. Muscles under her finger responding. Him looking back towards her, smiling around the cigarette as the lighter flame glimmered in his dark eyes.

Guillaume shook his head.

'But, I mean it when I say the only thing that made sense to me then was going. "Then": makes it sound like it was years ago, instead of—'

She was going to enjoy this moment. Revel in it. That was what she was going to do. Smile still there, inside. Revel in this, in being—finally... finally!—with Guillaume. For however long. A long time would be good, but even if it was this, only this, then this was... was...

'I was sure. I believed, you know?' Leaning forward, hugging his knees, smoke coiling around his head. 'Completely.'

His sitting like that let cold air creep under the covers. The morning sun had lost the bedroom window, drifted out of sight before a cloud dimmed its face. It was spring, weather schizophrenic enough to flip from sunny and temperate to dank and rainy in the space of an hour. Back again. Sometimes.

The window in her room at the squat leaked when the rain hit it.

Guillaume took a long drag on the Marlboro, held it out for her, one leg sliding flat, his foot brushing her thigh. Lingering. Heat of contact distracting as she drew on the cigarette, loathing the taste, wishing for one of her own, and taking another mouthful of smoke.

'Classic mistake. And I'm obsessing, I know.' He grinned as he took back the cigarette, free hand caressing her upper arm, the side of her breast. Minnette smiled, sliding a hand under the duvet towards him.

Guillaume frowned, drawing deep and sharp so the tip of the cigarette glowed harder.

'But it did seem like all I had to do was hit the hippy trail, hang out in all the right places, stay open until something told me to strike out on my own. Like something would lead me in the right direction.'

Getting angry was an option. Affront would come easily, she felt the acid in her throat, a flush of adrenaline laying copper over her tongue and making her nostrils tingle. Tired. Tired of hearing him say this, wanting his attention. And thinking she must, obviously, not deserve it because otherwise Guillaume would be—

'Are you rich?' Leaning across him for her Gitanes, curling around to lie half across his lap as she lit up, waving the lighter to indicate the bookshelves, the expensive hi-fi, the portable TV, concert posters and mystical symbols and framed prints, the size of the room itself, the flat.

'Hm? I guess.'

'You guess?'

'How about you?' Hard to tell what his expression meant: playful challenge or something more defensive. Minnette shrugged.

'Nothing like rich. My family are very provincial, very square. Papa is—' a flash: not a memory, but several, running together, different years and places making a composite: the lectures and homilies on how she had to live, what she should do with her life, on the state of the country, the need for firmer government, and on and on; the look he gave her whenever she did anything he didn't approve of; the feeling that nothing she did was ever likely to please him; arguments that had started over things so trivial she had no idea what they might have been; her father saying— 'Papa is a senior foreman in a factory and Maman volunteers at the church when she's not working at the beauty parlour—she's co-manager—and my sister married this guy who owns a couple of electronics companies. Their first child is on its way.' Drawing on her Gitanes, casually turning her head away to let out the smoke. 'Ordinary. Not worth the breath.' Not looking back as she made her voice sound light, playful. 'Your turn. Are you rich?'

'My parents are.'

There was no telling from the tone of his voice, but she thought there was a change in the tension of his body.

'They're divorced.' Guillaume tugged at the pillow behind him until it was a little more firmly behind his back. Leaning against the headboard, one hand resting on her thigh. Turning away himself as he drew on the last of the Marlboro. Smoke tumbling over the rucked duvet as he continued: 'She still lives here, in Paris. And he lives… New York, Vienna, Maui some of the time.' A shrug. 'Mostly I hear from their lawyers.'

A trust fund paid for the flat, his tuition. The hi-fi, the TV, other things were gifts he felt guilty about taking from his parents and took anyway. 'The trust fund stops when I graduate. When that happens, I'll… get a job, feel less like I'm letting them use me to spite each other.'

A bitter undercurrent no longer being hidden, she wanted to say something to him about his parents, his life, and couldn't think of anything that didn't sound idiotic. Silence stretching. Moment near gone to say anything at all.

Minnette hugged Guillaume, face pressed against his chest so she could feel his heartbeat.

'It's okay.' Stubbing out his cigarette, he put an arm around her shoulders, cradling her as she tried to cradle him. 'It's just how it is. Been liked it since I was eight. I'm used to it.'

Silence. Only not silent: clocks ticking, traffic outside, water running through pipes somewhere in the building. She wanted a true and perfect silence.

Guillaume took a breath, about to speak. Let it out, unused. Spoke after all.

'It's why I left like I did. Partly. I was hoping to find… something. Anything would have done, so long as it showed there was some *thing* beyond all this, some sign there is a deeper, more valid and truer reality than trust funds and parents and… I don't know.'

Wanting to ask: *Doesn't love count?* Hurt he wasn't feeling like she was feeling. And still on the verge of telling him. Of saying: *It might have been hallucination. I might still be crazy. I'm scared it'll happen again. More scared it won't, I suppose, more scared I'll never know why, never have a reason, some sort of explanation for what I—I think I saw. And what I saw was, was*

—

Staying silent. Feeling the moment lengthen. Grow colder. Grow—

'We keep looking.'

Not sure where the words came from. Repeating anyway:

'We keep looking.'

Not meeting his gaze when he replied: 'Together?'

Feeling hurt he had to ask and wanting to make it sound like a joke when she told him: 'Yes, if you like. If you think I can help.'

'That would be terrific. Amazing.' Smiling as he hugged her. 'I wasn't sure how much you wanted, I mean whether you really believed—'

Thinking of Christmas and Toledo and telling him: 'I'm not sure what to believe but I'm willing, I want to search and study and find out more, find out about magic and everything we've talked about, everything.'

'That's terrific,' Guillaume said again, holding her tighter, kissing her as Minnette kissed him back, assuring herself that there was truth in what she had said and that there was no reason to feel guilty, no reason to say anything about what might or might not have happened last year. Not yet. Not until she knew more.

'Belief makes everything.' Bending to pick a young child's plastic hammer from the floor. Toy hissing, sand flowing around its interior. Placing it neatly inside a cardboard box from the cupboard under the television in the corner of the room. 'Belief is the tool that makes the world we exist in.'

Continuing to talk about belief as he put away other toys scattered across the carpet. Irregular Lego shapes. Darth Vader missing cloak and lightsaber. Bond's white sports car from his last but one movie. Face passive as he spoke. Even, grey light coming through the net curtain softening but not removing the gaunt planes of his face.

'Belief is power.'

Sitting on the edge of a settee half-hidden under a length of curtain being used as a throw, aware of something sticking into her thigh, a toy car perhaps, aware of voices coming from a radio somewhere in a back room, of a faint smell of beeswax and sprouts, of the heat coming from the gas fire opposite the settee. Still unwilling to speak as he paused over a football programme.

Leeds United vs.—

Missing the name of the other team as he placed the booklet on top of the other toys.

'Did you know I had a son?' His back to her as he spoke.

Minnette shook her head. Hurriedly adding: 'No.'

Sliding the box under the television, gently closing the cupboard doors: 'Our lives are shaped by belief. His mother believes our son is better off living away from me. I see him once a month.' Pausing, still not looking at her. 'Sometimes less.'

Swallowing. Managing: 'I'm sorry.' Embarrassed it was such a glib thing to say.

The magician rested one hand against the cupboard doors. And straightened abruptly, taking a breath. Standing to look through the front window, glass rain-streaked, drizzle showing no sign of letting up, no sign of becoming proper rain. 'And—' tone as soft as before— 'what if—' turning to face Minnette at last— 'I told you I got these toys simply to fool you?'

Staring at him. Confused. Thinking she had mis-heard, must have mis-understood. Looking at the magician's bland expression, rainy daylight casting his face into shadow.

'You turd.' Flush making her hot, heart pounding. 'What would I say? I'd say you were a lying bastard.' One fist raised, trembling as she lurched to her feet. 'All those letters, postcards, the fucking time I spent trying to get your phone number, all that crap you said when we met, I can't believe—'

Flush deepening, eyes wider, words running out and leaving her mouth hanging before it shut, lips growing tight. 'Bastard...'

'Belief is a tool.' Walking from the room. Not even gesturing so she was left dithering, deciding she should follow after all.

'You manipulative shit.'

If only to keep swearing at him.

The magician climbed to the first floor, stairs complaining as Minnette stomped after him.

'I should never have— You're a liar, playing head games. That's not power, that's not magic. I've—' a fraction's pause, long enough, despite anger and self-consciousness, to wonder whether this admission should be made now, if at all— 'I've seen things, performed rituals, I know what it's like to be close to—'

'I made you feel sympathy for me—' turning sharply as he spoke, forcing Minnette back on to the landing just as she had one foot on the upstairs hall— 'then hate me—' his torso bending towards her so it felt like an attack, arms moving on their own to ward off a blow that never came — 'in the space of seconds.'

The magician's voice was calm, hands hanging loosely.

'I made your world change.'

Opening a door, going in without waiting for an answer.

Deep breaths. Shaking her head, one expression half-forming and being pushed aside by another. Angry, scared, humiliated. Cheated.

'No. No. This isn't magic.' She barged into the room. 'It's psychology, cheap mind games—'

A cupboard against one wall, door ajar and offering a suggestion it was filled with magical paraphernalia. Objects of all kinds—some occult, some obviously not—filled the shelves around the rest of the room. There were books. Not as many as she had dreamed might be here, but a lot of books, ring binders, notebooks.

Minnette closed her mouth, searching for the dropped beat of her anger.

'It's bull—'

'Why—' reaching into the cupboard— 'does this sword have power?'

Balancing the ritual sword on flat of his palms.

'Because... because it's been blessed, because the Guardians of the Four—'

Propping the sword against the cupboard doors and plucking a paperback from a shelf. 'And this? Does this have power?'

The magician tossed the book at her. Minnette fumbled, book thudding to her feet. Stooping after it, she saw the cover. A swordsman, skin white, baroque pillars framing him, mist coiled around black armour, black sword.

Straightening sharply. 'Of course it doesn't—'

'No.' Striding towards her, snatching up the book. 'Of course it does.' The magician brandished the paperback in front of her face. 'If I believe it does. Believe hard enough, completely enough.'

Opening her mouth. Thinking better of what she might have said. And shaking her head. 'No.'

The magician nodded. 'Yes.'

Do you feel that you have been chosen? the German asked as she tried to swallow away a mouth dry from the tea that had left little bits of leaf stuck between her teeth and had left her feeling dry and warm and drained of words and now just now just as he spoke and she fell silent just at that dry and warm and hazy moment noticing that the room was dark and that it was night outside and that outside was as quiet as inside and that she felt hazy and light and the German was asking her again if she felt that she had been chosen and shaking her head as the shadows began to waver and slip around her as the German whispered close to her ear from where he was sitting in the armchair opposite her and she lifted her hand to see the shadows fall away away away darkness falling away as the armchair glowed as the chair glowed as she blinked and swallowed the bitter taste in her mouth and watched as the luminescence clinging to the German's face fell away and spread and made shadows that made her look look look across the room at the half-open door to the kitchen

They met up on one of the galleries, floor creaking underfoot, Guillaume placing a finger over his lips, gesturing towards the wide hall beneath them, hall silent but for the rustle of pages and the scratch of pens, shrugging, pantomiming a question, Minnette holding up a couple of index cards, aisle and catalogue numbers scrawled on them. Pointing back along the way she had come.

Guillaume followed.

Through a book-lined arch. Past a series of heavy bookcases set closely together.

To a junction.

Where she hesitated, both of them finally deciding left. Up a complaining spiral staircase. Behind, below and all around, pages whispered, spines creaking gently, pens moving, stopping, flowing again, and voices, sometimes voices, voices murmured and low and almost indistinguishable from the pages, the soft breathing, soft breathing of all these people reading, wandering, writing, padding shelf to shelf, researching, noting, making notes, all these books waiting.

Less than an hour later, they weren't lost. They padded shelf to shelf. Hoping to find what they were looking for.

'Maybe its all in some special collection, after all.'

'That's not what the assistant told you. Is it what that assistant told you?'

Minnette had to shake her head. The assistant had said that they would find most of the books they wanted on these shelves. Somewhere.

The Bibliothèque nationale restive, silent feet moving. Between book presses, shelves. Pages whispering.

They found Lévi's almost forgotten *Dialogues Infernal et Angélique* and a reprint of Hohman's *Discussions Towards a Path*. Guillaume wanted to linger over both. Paging forwards to pause. Switch to the other book. Compare passages in each. Pen moving, stopping, set aside before finding a flow again. Reading stooped over his shoulder, standing after a few minutes, he oblivious, standing with a hand resting on his shoulder as he read and made notes, weight shifting from leg to leg, needing to keep looking. 'I won't be long.' Lips brushing his head, feeling Guillaume nod before leaving him at the table.

Climbing, staircase maundering.

Books peering towards her as her head cleared the level of the next floor.

Pausing at one shelf, turning to run a hand over another.

A straggling zig-zag across the floor, padding shelf to shelf. Taking the next set of stairs. Downwards. Pausing.

Striking off at random. Library huge.

The huge library smelling of old paper, fragile words.

Minnette walked the length of one aisle. Turned left. Along the narrow passage between a pair of ornate presses. Back-trailing, following another pathway to another dead end, and turning back, to find the way blocked by a heavy trolley, books spine-inward so a voice whispered, *Blind*, hesitating, voice inside whispering 'blind' again as she turned, leaving the trolley, sightless volumes, chose another track between the shelves.

High windows at the end of an aisle gave a pallid light, softening blue with a copper so it felt like dusk, a little later, possibly, like it was winter not spring. Ironwork groaned. Lights flickered, dimmed. A cough, muffled, distant, following around another turning, scaling a ladder to a high shelf. List of book titles very bright. Taking another turning. Paper bright in her hand, white sharp, almost glowing, corridor gloomier than the last.

A fluorescent light above the tops of the bookcases hummed, clicked, hummed, twitched again. Next light six, ten paces further down the corridor. Too little light to read. What was written on the list. Minnette stopped. A fluorescent light overhead hummed, twitched, shrinking in on itself to glow only from its ends. Spasming. No one around. She should. Ask directions. She should ask, speak to someone. Next light ten, fourteen paces further on.

Hummed, twitched. Too little light to read by. Shelves flexing. Spasming. Next corridor twenty, forty presses further, further on, gloomier than the last.

Minnette stopped. Taking a breath. Frowning. Smelling old paper, old ironwork, scents of oak and metal, copper, a hint of dust and a hint of a scent behind the dust that was too faint to be more than a suspicion and licking her lips, feeling palms damp, book list crumpling as her fingers tightened, licking her lips, smelling dust along the corridor. Light softening, blue a shade of copper so it felt. Possibly later than dusk. Winter shelves muttering, voices almost as frail. As the pages, dry-lipped, voices almost as cracked as the spines, dry-mouthed words becoming. Yellowed, a hand almost touching. Between her shoulder blades. Neck hairs rising over muscle twitching.

Not turning.

Paint- and chalk- and marker pen-scrawls covered every piece of equipment; crushed beer and cola cans littered the concrete; concrete daubed with paint, a spray pattern framing a dog turd; empty tubes of glue among weeds at the edge of the play area. The magician paused, stopping her from coming through the rusting gate. Minnette glanced at him. All he had said as they got on the bus to cross Leeds was that he was going to take her to a place of power. This was not what she had thought he meant.

A group of youths watched from perches on the tubular climbing frame. One with a lopsided mohawk, shaven sides of his skull pallid, eyes like a reptile. Another: a shock of black hair limp across a bloodless face. Their only movement the wind tugging at their clothing.

The magician ignored the youths, leading her towards the centre of the playground. He touched a crushed lager can with the slender toe of one boot, nudging the can to one side, back again.

'What do you see?'

Confused, still not sure whether she was doing the right thing in being here at all, Minnette made an effort, turning slowly, itemising all, including the grubby corner-newsagent's across the road and the smears of fresh dog shit on the pavement just outside the peeling railings.

The magician said nothing. Rummaging inside a plastic carrier bag emblazoned with the key-like logo of a supermarket chain, he took out a postcard, holding it to his chest. 'It's of this place when it opened. Council were so proud.' He told her the history of the playground, how the city council had invested in its construction but not in its upkeep, how the councillors' pride had turned to despair with the local residents, whom they blamed for the state of the play area when, in fact, it was the councillors' unwillingness to see that maintenance was as important as new construction, new projects, new headlines, that their lack of involvement helped breed indifference and a sense of abandonment that had made this place what it was now.

'But,' the magician finished, 'they were dead proud of it when it opened, made postcards and everything. So, tell me what this place was like. Describe what you see on here.' He held out the card.

It was blank. Not even a postcard, simply rectangle of white cardboard.

'Tell me what you see on the postcard.' Tapping a finger on its unmarked face. 'Tell me what's in that photo. Tell me everything you can see there, everything you know is there, in that picture.'

Holding the card in front of her, mouth opening, closing, turning her head: the litter, the graffiti, the almost catatonic youths draped on the climbing frame; thoughts stuttering, backtracking; asking, *How much of this is true?* thinking how convincing the magician had sounded: matter-of-fact, disgusted by the councillors' complacency, talking as though he had witnessed it all. Speaking with utter belief.

'Well...' Looking at the rectangle of card. 'There's the climbing frame.' Wanting to see a photograph instead of a blank. Resisting the urge to glance around. Visualising the place as it might have been. 'And it's clean, of course—'

no, no, seeing the playground as it had been— 'almost shining in the sunlight.'
'Colour?'
'Grey. Metal grey.'

When she finished, Minnette looked at the postcard. Looked. And saw—

'Yeah, but you have to understand that alchemy wasn't something they found for themselves... No, that's just the point. A group of pale-skinned people, with reddish-blonde beards, brought it to them, taught them that and agriculture. Now, why would South and Central American people choose such skin colourings if they weren't recording something that had happened, that was true, eh? Those teachers from across the sea weren't simply some lost tribe from elsewhere on the continent. They were foreigners, from a very sophisticated civilisation that seems to have suffered a terrible disaster. Destroyed, practically.'
'So... What? These people were the survivors of Atlantis, is that what you're saying?'
'No. I don't think it was Atlantis. I don't think there was an Atlantis. I think that name is simply a shorthand for something else.'
'What? Don't sit there like that, tell me, I've got classes soon.'
'Is that the time? Got to go: lecture. Sorry.'
'Minnette! You can't go now. Come back!'
'Tonight? Guillaume's?'
Minnette waved, running from the café, lugging a shoulder bag, a copy of Blavatsky's *The Key to Theosophy* clutched in her hand.
Early summer, 1972: she had been living with Guillaume for almost seven weeks.

For almost seven days, she had to go through similar exercises, telling him details of memories of events that had never taken place, seeing faces absent in a crowd. On the eighth day, the magician refused to see her at all. On the ninth, he phoned to say he was too busy that day, she should get the paper, start looking for a job and a place to live, because she was going to be staying in Leeds a long time. But, as she sat on the edge of the bed in the hostel, looking at the walls, too excited to think, and thinking even so that this was both what she wanted, had wanted for some time, for years, and yet completely unlike what she had been searching for, someone stuck their head around the door, telling her to go down the lobby. The magician waiting by the entrance, placid, not saying anything other than she was going to go out and walk around the city and see only red plastic macs: 'People are wearing nothing else today. You should make a list of styles, numbers, that kind of thing. Find me. Later,' he told her, Minnette squinting into the low sun as she watched until he turned a corner, shivering because the air was unseasonably bitter; blinking away tears from the cold wind as she saw passers-by in heavy coats, jackets, a Goth from the Poly with a huge portfolio case under her arm, wind tugging at the skirts of her air force great coat. The Goth's red plastic great coat.

The headache lingering into the following day had only a little to do with the depth of that cold snap.

'I understand. I do,' she began the following evening as they walked along a terraced road stranded in a sea of rubble, every street around it in the process of being systematically demolished ahead of large-scale redevelopment. 'Visualisation is important, of course, but...'

Closing her mouth. Regret as gritty as the wind coming off the rubble heaps.

'You tell me.' The magician concentrated on the pavement, face pale in the half-light, becoming shadow under the widely-spaced street lamps, speaking as if she had asked: *Why?*

'Visualisation...' Wiping a thumb across her streaming nose, fumbling for a tissue, damp tarmac glimmering, cold biting through her knitted cap, pinching skin left exposed by tight loops of scarf, head and eyes smarting, wondering if she was getting a cold, saying: 'It allows the magician to direct Power. The Powers can only be manipulated and evoked if the magician can focus on them completely. There can't be any space for error or for confusion. An adept has to be able to conceptualise one of The Powers before calling it down—'

'This is what you believe?'

His stride lengthening. Leaving her trailing behind him. Wanting to shout, let out some frustration. And not sure what to say.

New Year passed before there was chance to notice Christmas had been and gone.

The second week of January: sitting on an unheated train trundling towards London.

'I don't—' Words blurted, bitten off.

The magician sat in the opposite seat. Legs stretched out, crossed at the ankles, hands clasped loosely in his lap. Minnette sat with fists buried under each armpit, jaw clenched to stop it chattering. Wearing every jumper she owned, leather bike jacket almost too tight to zip up. He in clothes light enough for a spring day, oblivious to the cold.

Shoulders hunching, trying to stop her knees drawing up.

'I mean, the training—' Mouth closing firmly. Hearing petulance and knowing it wasn't only from the cold or the fact she had no clear idea what this journey was for. Telling herself: *Patience. He knows, he must know—* and letting out a breath. 'It's not that I don't understand the importance of visualisation. Obviously. Without thought forms having weight and texture— You can't influence the aetheric unless you can picture, not just picture but create a total object, a, a *map*—'

'Map?'

It was the first thing he had said in miles, in tens of minutes.

'Yes. More so, obviously—' Trying not to squirm against the hard seat-back, not sure if this explained enough. About to add more. But the magician settled deeper into his seat, eyes loosing focus.

'Don't confuse the map with the territory.'

'I'm not.' Bridling. His voice off-hand and dismissive. Suspicious he was leading towards another trap, another demonstration that what was there to be seen was not truly there—

Minnette tightened her arms around herself, cutting off the thought. Concentrating instead on smoke-stained walls, weeds aged with frost, cars on a distant road. Before sitting straighter.

'Look: the visualisation training I accept.' Pausing an instant, expecting him to mumble, 'Really?' under his breath, the magician seemingly lost in his thoughts. Not fooled, Minnette pressed on. 'And, of course, I accept that different ritual approaches offer different strengths and emphases, nuances—Cagliostro's Egyptian master ritual has different affects to a similar kabbalistic ritual, which is more closely tied to—'

'Is reading the map the same as walking the ground?'

His voice a murmur, gaze focused on nothing. Train bucking. Train freezing. Anger a welcome distraction from feeling she was saying the wrong thing. 'I'm not claiming to be an expert. I've studied but I know there's more to learn.' Feeling no matter what she said he would find fault, anything to appear superior. 'But I understand some things. That power comes from linking with the *anima mundi* through intermediaries—elemental powers, angels, Group Forms if you're adept enough to attract their attention—and that power only flows through ritual—' an image in mind, quickly ignored, of a hillside, a warm light, voices— 'and that ritual relies on the correct Correspondences, the correct Intentions, because within Humanity is all of the Universe in microcosm and within the Universe is all of Humanity in macrocosm and if the ritual is judged and performed right, that which is inside us causes change in that which is in the Universe...'

Words drying in her mouth. Thinking: *I'm cold. I'm tired.* Thinking: *He's not listening*, magician staring at nothing, legs stretched out and hands clasped. Thinking he had heard everything and considered all she'd said beneath him and that thought making her angrier, uncertainty and insecurity easier to dismiss that way, better to think him arrogant than to think everything she had learned was wrong, which, in turn, summoned hillside and light and voices and she attributed all three to memories of the Aegean, to days and weeks in the sun in the cup of the hillside, Aegean leading to thoughts of maps having nothing to do with anything and that he was trying to distract her with doubts and suggestions that she was missing the point, failing to understand—

The train lurched. Wheels squealing. Carriages juddering. Slowing to a graceless stop.

Glancing out the window. Once up and down the carriage. They were the only passengers she could see. Dismissing the train. Wanting him to reply.

'There's an order to everything, there must be, has to be and through that—'

The train lurched into motion again, trundling forward at a slow walking pace.

The magician sat up straight. 'We're stopping here.'

The station was barely a halt, countryside beyond hidden inside a cowl of freezing fog. After five minutes, the conductor came along, apologised for the unscheduled stop, the fact the carriage was so chuffing cold, but if they wouldn't mind changing to the train just down the end of the platform, they'd find that was good and warm.

'This happen often?' Minnette asked the conductor. The man—a Sikh, Yorkshire accent so broad she founded it almost incomprehensible—shrugged.

''Ardly ever. Good luck, in'it, though? 'Ad enough of freezing on this train, me.'

'Luck has nothing to do with it,' the magician muttered as they strode along the platform.

Halting. Staring at him. Stumbling into a trot. Catching up. Whispered questions bringing no reply, only a glance it was impossible to interpret in any way other than the suggestion he had brought about the train's breakdown.

The magician said nothing else for the remainder of the journey.

The new train was much warmer.

That night, lying in a narrow bed in an overheated flat in Clapham, there were dreams of the Christmas road trip and Toledo, confused gasps of wakefulness briefly interrupting their flow but unable to hold back the foaming impressions long, dreams merging, parting to offer a glimpse of her reflection trapped in a window, herself as she was now—hair short, the planes of her face clear and spare and eyes outlined in black, biker jacket over skimpy white T-shirt— not as she had been nearly ten years before, window becoming the warm glow of the two lamps framing the alley's mouth, alleyway whispering, sometimes in French, sometimes in accented English, sometimes in a language that seemed familiar although the words slithered out of reach to leave nothing but the feeling they had meant something.

No sense of time but, after a century or an instant, the need to run gripped her, leeching into heart and bone but not thighs and knees and feet, legs rusted tight and reluctant to move.

Minnette staggered.

Minnette—

—ran. Made herself move. No amount of speed and effort enough. Alley mouth closing over her. Alley branching. More branches suggesting themselves beyond that. Knowing each branch harboured yet further branches and seeing them through walls at once solid and hazy. Running, taking a turning and that turning unfolding into a street that remained firm and hard-edged only for the time it took her to make the next stride. Buildings sagging as they fell back, re-forming into another branch, another lane, another turning.

Light cold with nothing of the deep, almost technicolor sheen she recalled when waking. A near-monochrome that struck her as richer than common experience, more real.

The dogs appearing, their voices metal grinding against flesh and nothing like she remembered.

Sky empty, not filled with white ravens.

And the woman with the veil so fine, so white it had been iridescent, billowing in a breeze that touched nothing else, standing on the shadow cast by a bridge that had neither start nor end nor means of support, the woman did not unstopper a bottle and pour but took a cracked bell and a ram's horn and a handful of mandrake that squealed with pain. Cobbles becoming slabs of black and white marble becoming a river of mercury becoming a door of copper braces and limestone becoming the shadow of a face encased in iron becoming holes in the light becoming the hillside, the hillside straining, wanting to flatten and converge on the horizon of an infinite plane on which The Tower—

The Tower had stood over her earlier. In the same dream. Another dream. A dream. And it had been much as her waking memories formed it: grown from the hillside, its eye on her as she ran down the alley between the two lamps. This Tower stood uncertainly, its perspective reversed, too broad at the top and too narrow at the bottom; body grey, not gleaming sandstone; sheathed in a mesh of falling masonry but these blocks and ever-falling shards had no weight, not defying gravity but simply floating, as insubstantial as any cloud, almost as pale.

Turning, watched on all sides by empty windows, alleyway sagging, beginning to fold in about itself, Minnette ran away from the grey Tower.

The grey Tower stood in front of her. Teetering. Provisional.

Turning, watched on all sides from empty windows, alleyway surging, clouds of ash rising with each slow, swift-moving footfall, Minnette ran away from the grey Tower.

The grey Tower stood in front of her. Willowy. Reticent.

A door at its base appearing. Spilling light across the ash.

Minnette tried to run.

The Tower's blocks were words, letters at least. Between them there was air, nothing but air. Though even that was untrue because the words were the air and it was the air that was nothing at all. Nothing, not even the space between one footfall and the next.

Minnette woke up screaming.

Breakfast: radio tuned to Radio 2, owner of the flat singing along to Barry Manilow as bacon spat in a frying pan, cereal crackling as milk hit the bowl, fresh tea spilled across the table in a narrow spray of drops, dark gunge caking the mouth of a bottle of brown sauce. The magician watching her as she ate. Not mentioning the screaming. Minnette not volunteering anything.

That night, another dream of The Tower. Only there was no Tower. Full moon casting shadows from walls and falling masonry but The Tower itself absent. Instead, there was a feeling of dread squeezing, forcing her out of the doorway where she was hiding and into the open. Acutely aware of being exposed. Of being in view of The Tower. Not wanting to see The Tower, knowing it was not there to be seen and being terrified of glimpsing it.

The parapet wall gave as she hit it, flexing and pushing back. Minnette sank to her knees, cowering. The Tower watching. Its presence boring through the stones, wall thin enough to let her, to make her see The Tower. Its presence. Its reeling absence.

She looked away. Eyes squeezed shut.

Seeing The Tower. Rising on its narrow base. Long shadow teetering as the sun shrank.

Running. Over cobbles. Over flagstones. Over earth baked harder than concrete by the pressure of The Tower driving her to run. Knotted streets passing by without her moving. Turn approaching. Past. Already become another doorway, deep and hard and solid. And The Tower's shadow leaking through the roof of the building opposite. Staining her hands. Clogging her throat.

Running. Over cobbles. Over flagstones. Over earth groaning under the weight of The Tower, moaning at each footfall, looking down and seeing nothing, not earth nor stone, nor even her feet. Knotted streets passing. The Tower's shadow leaking through.

Again.

Running. Street hemmed in. By a wall. By turnings. By doorways, doors half-open. Again.

Running. Footfalls almost silent. Hemmed in. Breath silent. By a wall, by a door half-open. Moaning each time she caught sight of The Tower. Something insubstantial becoming solid. Again. Running. A solid mass becoming tenuous. Running. Again.

It came to the wall in the end, dream overlapping with memory, this wall longer and longer the longer she ran, knowing that The Tower was not there, knowing that it was almost there, that it was behind her.

A hand outstretched.

The wall would last forever. Minnette knew that as she reached the doorway, recess a sliver of shadow that unfolded into the blue half-light, the magician standing back to indicate the sun was rising and that night was growing deeper.

The moon, horns raised, nodded.

Hiding was no use. Minnette hid in the doorway. Feeling The Tower through the heavy sandstone lintel, the step to the door. Feeling: the weight of masonry tumbling, of a presence that was no presence, The Tower looming overhead on the point of crashing down. The Tower thinner than a promise never made.

The magician reached deep into his mouth, struggling to take hold of something, eyes passive and empty, simply a space where something might have gone, arm bending as he reached for something that wanted to remain always out of reach. The magician reaching deep into her mouth.

Minnette beat against the door. Fists bouncing off the ancient wood. Soundless as she struck the panels again until the door began to give, opening to cast a stream of light across the pavement and the edge of the road as Minnette trudged closer, frost glittering on her arms, breath becoming a cloud of motes that gleamed in the light from the doorway ahead, door feeling hard and unforgiving under her hands. The Tower walking beside her. Standing over her. The Tower standing back to indicate that the sun was rising and night was growing deeper.

The Tower a tremendous weight on the point of collapse, door opening to cast a stream of light across the pavement, The Tower an inconceivable void teetering on the point of swallowing, a shadow breaking into the light, unable to scream, shadow of The Tower becoming vague, harder to recall, scream a pressure and a hand pressing tightly over mouth and nose, a hand outstretched—

Not so much a scream as a choking sound.

Jolting awake.

Second yell harsher, louder until she cut it off.

Sweat binding a corner of the sheet to one thigh, the opposite calf, remainder thrown off the bed, sweat prickling down back, between breasts, not sure which room this was. Remembering Clapham. Slumping against the pillow.

A grudging light filtered through garish rayon curtains: dawn, later: no way of being sure. But sounds insinuated through the walls: a radio DJ, voice muffled; the rattle of the grill pan being taken out of the stove; unidentifiable thumping. Light oozed under the bedroom door from the bulb in the hallway. Staring at it, unsure. A disco hit on the radio. Light not changing. Watching the strip of light, unable to convince herself she hadn't seen a shadow cross it, conviction that someone was in the hallway, listening, fading reluctantly.

Pulse slowing. Adrenalin's fire dwindling. Leaving shivers. Hauling against the sheet, wrapping it tightly, pulling it under her chin, hugging herself. Sure it was time to get up. Lying still.

In the hall outside, the floorboards shifted. Gently.

'You have three days.'
It was the first she knew of a ritual.

The whispering had stopped.
Standing very still, head to one side. Interrogating every creak, every movement of the wind.
The whispering had stopped.
Sky beginning to shallow, not so deeply blue. Frost glimmering faintly in the light from a small laundrette. Rows of dormant washing machines staring blankly out of the window with their single eyes.
Breath shallow. Heart beating. Shivering. Exhaustion an after-image to every breath, an undertone to every blink.
Toledo slept. Dark, solid. Waiting. But solid.
Shivering, Minnette stood very still. Listening. Waiting.
The litany had stopped and the street would not change again.
Resting a hand against the glass, glad it was cold, glad it was hard and unresisting. Watching the washing machines watching her, bulb behind the counter at the back of the laundrette dull, bright only because the night hadn't ended —

Glancing back at this thought. Hand on the window, steadying. Hoping for reassurance. Or the first sign the road was about to change.
Car engine. Attenuated by the brittle air, indeterminate distance. Starter motor whinging, grunting. Sleepy. Reluctant to wake. No, that couldn't be it. It was the cold, the damp and the frost. The starter wasn't alive. Wasn't about to suddenly...
Engine catching, revving, changing tone, receding.
Shivering. Hand pressed harder against the window pane. Forehead on the glass. Both solid: bones of her skull, laundrette window. Washing machines looking back. Washing machines standing inside the empty laundrette with their doors hanging open. No life. No sign of life.

Toledo asleep. Dormant, Toledo dormant. Sunrise close, another day about to—

Minnette turned around sharply.

'I thought it was you.'

After the therapy sessions came to an end, there was an ill-tempered week spent with her sister in Rouen. Then came four months working on the outskirts of Paris, catching up with emails at a cybercafé that throbbed to techno and worldbeat and smelled of mildew and stale pizza. Then came a period where there was no job and nowhere permanent to stay.

All of the books and notes went into storage again.

In 2004, there was the job at an antiquarian bookshop in the third arrondissement that paid okay, better than okay as she was happy to work weekends, late evening opening.

Looking at larger flats, spacious enough for books, papers, notes, magazines. Spacious enough to bring everything out of storage.

Opting for somewhere small.

'I don't have a lot of things,' Minnette told the housing agent. 'This place will do fine.'

No dreams. None that she remembered.

'I thought it was you.'

The manager of the antiquarian bookshop was very happy that she was happy. 'You're so diligent, Minnette,' he told her, 'and so careful with the books, so good with the customers.' Smiling, nodding, thanking him for being so kind as to say so. Going back to the small apartment, with its three rooms, its bare walls, bookcase filled with trashy novels. Listening to the drone of TV through the wall. A voice in the hallway. An argument quickly stifled.

'I thought it was you.'

He stood back, smiling.

No memory of the dream. Only that there had been a dream.
Nothing to worry about.
Probably.

She left the antiquarian bookshop with one week's notice, telling the manager there was another job, repeating that there was nothing he could change that would make her stay.

A small bookshop and stationer's a short train-ride from Paris: that was where she ended up after six weeks of being unemployed. Getting a reputation amongst regular customers for being surly and crabby took much less time.

A junk shop with delusions of grandeur and a reputation for books followed. 'I hate books,' Minnette told one of the customers, aware the owner was in earshot. 'I'd stay but you look like an idiot,' Minnette told the new owner when the business was sold a short time later. The previous owner thought this was funny and wrote her a glowing reference, 'even though you were a terrible employee.'

An auction house. A second-hand bookshop specialising in paperbacks. A repository holding expensive books bought as an investment. A short spell in the branch of W.H. Smith's near the Place de la Concorde. Getting fired from that coming as a relief. Settling for a summer contract at Shakespeare & Co., where she could sit behind the till, pretend to be reading and claiming the grimace on her face was rheumatism in her leg; or camp in the antiquarian shop next door, usually giving the impression that the profound silence of the tiny, book-lined, room was inviolable; and sometimes finding herself drawn into conversation with collectors from Tokyo, Sao Paolo or Oslo.

None of it mattered. None of it seemed concrete enough to matter.

Which was the insomnia. She was sure. It was the insomnia.

'I thought it was you.'

Not more than a metre away. Smiling.

Jostled by a tourist, another pedestrian. Taking a second step back and tempted to dodge across the road.

'I saw you and... They say it's a small world.'

'Not large enough, obviously, Guillaume.' Glancing pointedly at her watch.

'How long has it been, Minnette?'

The years had marked him, turned his hair from dark brown to granite. Beard gone. Eyes—

'Do you need that? Wouldn't contacts be more practical?'

Guillaume took the monocle from his eye. 'I think it gives me an... air.' He handed it to her.

Hesitating before holding it to her eye. 'Plain glass?' Her mouth twisted with disgust. Taking in suit, cravat, silk pocket handkerchief. 'What's next? Spats?'

He took back the eyepiece, slipping it into a waistcoat pocket. 'I happen to like dressing this way.'

Minnette raised an eyebrow.

'So...' Guillaume drew out the word. Fleetingly, he seemed uncertain, searching for something to say, something other than this sparring. The moment passed and, in retrospect, she decided it had never happened, forgetting his expression, the tension in her shoulders.

'So, I hear you're working in second-hand bookshops now?'

'And I saw you on TV.' His face blank this time, so she added: 'You're toupee looked like it was about to fly off,' and only in the moment of speaking knew there was a chance of stemming this flush of anger.

'I'd hoped we might be friends.' His manner stiff. 'I've recently moved back into the city and—'

'And I don't make friends with media frauds.'

He fitted the monocle over his eye. 'I've admitted my mistakes more than once, Minnette. Said sorry, for whatever that's worth, done my best to make amends—'

'Not with me.'

'Well, we haven't seen—'

'You never said sorry to me.'

Pushing past him although the pavement was empty enough to avoid contact entirely. Ignoring the flower of pain down her leg, telling herself, amongst everything else, that she wasn't suffering from arthritis and desperately trying not to limp, walking as quickly as she could, breath growing short, berating herself for not doing more to keep fit, for being so weak the ache in her leg was making her cry. Turning the corner, assuring herself she would soon forget this. Telling herself she was wrong: Guillaume had not said anything as she walked away; that she had misheard the one word he had spoken.

In their second or third session together, her analyst nodded as Minnette admitted she couldn't find any truths inside her head any more. 'What's there's so jumbled... Is that common?'

'What did you think?' Analyst's voice gentle, expression interested without being pressuring. Minnette liked that, found it reassuring.

'I think...' Her analyst was easy to talk to, obviously interested in helping her. It made her want to open up. Minnette liked that, found it reassuring.

'I'm not sure,' she finally mumbled.

An envelope was waiting when she got back to her room. The magician had already left the flat. No choice, then, but to open the envelope.

A typewritten sheet of instructions. Times, places she had to visit, things she had to do or collect: a card from a telephone box on a street near Elephant and Castle; a broken compass from a flea market in Muswell Hill; both items to be carried anti-clockwise around the Circle Line for seven stops, before being deposited in the last station's lost property office; a narrow street in Rotherhithe, which had to be walked five times over a period of forty-seven minutes; a junk shop in Hackney which had a phrenology bust she needed to buy, the bust to be left in front of a former haberdasher's in Snow Hill... and so on.

Notes followed each instruction. Snippets of history, background information, comments that offered explanations without exactly enlightening. For instance, the magician explained that the haberdasher's, now boarded up and awaiting redevelopment, had once been a language school where a German immigrant had attended English lessons for two weeks in 1924; the immigrant, who it was claimed was both linked with The Order of the Stella Matutina and obsessed with the writings of Jahn, had hollowed out a niche in one of the school's walls, installing an effigy made of lead and bronze in the niche, the effigy a device of sorts, a talisman. After installing the device, the German disappeared completely. The talisman, likewise, had vanished, yet...

And so on.

Confused, resentful and trying to push that aside, Minnette found a single word, handwritten, at the end of the instructions:

Believe.

Insomnia made a desert of most nights. Sleep might come while reading, consuming and unexpected, disorganising words and pages, making it harder to keep track of lurid plots, interchangeable characters, but vanish by the time she went to bed, wakefulness lasting deep into the empty, harsh hours of early morning. When she eventually woke, stiff, gritty-eyed and mouth tainted, there was little sense of having slept a handful of hours but rather of having simply ceased to exist for that time.

And her sleep did seem empty.

The street remained solid. No matter how quickly, how suddenly she turned, trying to catch it in the act of reshaping itself.

Window pane cold and grimy under outspread fingers.

Reluctant to leave the pool of light outside the laundrette. Taking an uncertain diagonal path across the road.

Not sure what to feel. Uncertain where she should go next.

Shivering growing worse.

Conscious of frost gnawing forehead, cheeks, ears. Hands numb. Legs no less so, aching. Tremor forcing her jaw to tighten, teeth painful.

Breath short. Palms clammy. And weak: weight of every muscle and bone and blink and nerve-twitch draining.

Road wider than expected. Path weaving.

Quivering. Air tasting metallic.

Pausing. Staring down the empty road: a street light, darkened shop windows, two cars. Staring. In case what she had experienced earlier was going to start again. Was not freak accident, momentary insanity.

Vision blurring, clearing as she took a step, managed another.

Minnette tripped over a cobble, stumbling the last few steps to the opposite side of the road. Dizziness making her footing uncertain. One last moment of wondering whether this was because the road was changing. And her flailing hand grazed the wall of the nearest building, cold making skin sensitive. Blood oozing as she looked. Lips dry as she brought knuckle to mouth. Saliva just visible around wound.

A gentle blush tinted one half of the sky, casting the rooftops into silhouettes.

Night almost over.

Numb with more than the cold, she continued walking.

Late in 2005, a friend of a friend of a friend suggested interviewing for the job. 'You know a little about that sort of thing, don't you?' the friend of a friend of a friend had asked.

Minnette said she might think about it.

The friend asked two weeks later whether she had followed up that job. Saying she had tried and failed to get through to the shop seemed like a good excuse until an instant before it left her mouth. Minnette offered instead that Shakespeare & Co. had been very busy, that there was too little time to look for another job.

'That's why you really should go after this one. And it's management, don't forget. You're wasting yourself on being an assistant. More money, more chance to stretch out—'

Minnette said she might think about it.

'I don't think they've found anyone yet, but you don't know how long that might—'

Minnette said she would think about it.

'I don't believe in any of this crap,' the assistant told her on her first day.

It wasn't only a bookshop. There were tables with displays of crystals, scrying stones, dream-catchers. Panpipes and soporific synthesiser drones played constantly, a bland backdrop against which the tabletop waterfall, sitting under the Yin Yang banner in the opposite corner, gurgled tinnily.

The assistant gave Minnette a short tour of the back of the shop. Puddles lay across a stockroom frequented by mice and laid siege by mould. Only two of four lights worked, tubes fizzing loudly when the switches were thrown. A kettle stood forlornly on a small table in one corner: the staff rest area.

'Did she show you back here?' the assistant asked after warning Minnette not to use the kettle as it fucked up the electrics. She didn't need to see Minnette's head shake to add: 'No, thought not.'

'I mean, I suppose you have to let people decide for themselves and that,' the assistant continued as they sat behind the counter sipping styrofoam coffee from the café on the corner, 'but I don't understand how anyone can make themselves believe all this crap. Do you?'

Minnette stared at the titles on the shelves and gondolas, the carousel of Karmic Offers by the door—

past life healing; crystal meditation; finding your spirit guide; chakras and dieting: claptrap, all of it, nothing but New Age claptrap—and gave the assistant a sympathetic look.

'Haven't a clue.'

Gradually, a dream began to shape itself in the short, barren hours of unconsciousness that were all the sleep she got. Days at the New Age bookshop long and draining and familiar by then, the dream found her intermittently at first, leaving dim impressions and a vague unease that were almost unnoticeable in the grogginess of each morning, forgotten by the time she plodded out of the flat. But, over weeks, a month or so, those dim impressions grew stronger, dream coming more frequently, lingering enough to give a sense of what was happening in her sleep. A sense she carefully chose to ignore. Consciously, at least. Over-the-counter sleep remedies and soporific herbal teas began piling up along the kitchenette's narrow window ledge.

She had trouble sleeping. What else should she do?

The nostrums had no effect. The insomnia worsened, lying cold and unspeaking in bed beside her each night and the thought that, at least, she did not dream was no consolation. But, after nine or more weeks of this, the insomnia relented and she slept through the small hours again, those hours a blank. Minnette threw away the remedies and herbal teas. Contemplated going to a doctor. Hoping sleeping pills might bring the blankness on sooner and lift the fatigue that still freighted each day. Whisky, somehow, seemed less dangerous than barbiturates.

A glass each evening became two, nights still dreamless. Which, she was sure, was just how she wanted them, even if they were no more restful. Better, Minnette told herself, to sleep badly than to dream. As weeks past, it began to seem the dream would never return. A bout of insomnia—that was all it had ever been.

The dream returned.

During its absence, it had evolved something of the quality of a memory relived, a texture as disturbing as it was difficult to pick out from events experienced while awake. It's texture and taste coloured each day: mornings abrasive, afternoons caustic, evenings repellent.

The dream started with her laying out a circle, setting up an altar, lighting candles, beginning a ceremony. Always, darkness lay beyond the circle, hardly touched by the candlelight, a growing sense there was nothing there to touch. As the ritual progressed so the emptiness pressed closer, outer edges of the circle diminishing, vanishing, candles waning until Minnette was left standing in darkness, granted sight by the dream, watching nothingness creep closer, close enough, in the last, to touch.

Sodium light staining main roads. Side roads dimmer but for feeble lamps running worms of silver across pavement, tarmac, each surface damp. Surprise it had rained mixed into a dizziness, the pressing feeling of time slipped, melted, reformed into night without any intervening day.

She had lost a day. Spent it without noticing.

A residential street. Silent although a few windows were lit, curtains glowing. No other sign there was anything in those houses, that they were anything other than façades. Hunching deeper into her leather jacket, pushing such ideas away and picking up pace. Heading towards a hint of sodium. Needing a main road. Something well-travelled. Solid.

Road deserted. A chip shop, lights diffused by a haze of condensation. Familiar enough to make Minnette think of her bedsit in Leeds, two storeys above a corner chip shop, to feel nostalgic, sense memories of the smell of fat and vinegar, the feel of a hot packet of chips cupped in cold palms, newsprint rough against fingertips.

Shop deserted: no one waiting to be served, no one behind the counter.

Imagining: fryers standing, open mouthed, fluorescent strips overhead dull, steam running down window-glass cold and hard and unresisting.

A bus rattling past. A glimpse of empty bottom deck, courtesy lights making the space look flat, more like a sequence of photographs pasted to the windows, each motion-blurred so the real speed of the bus was disguised as it slipped by, paused at a stop for less than a minute, a few seconds, for a long period that had no name because it had no duration.

Handbrake grizzling. Bus drawing away, turning a corner, Minnette thinking, too late, that she should have run, taken the bus wherever it was going, sat under one of those lights in the downstairs salon, ignored what the windows were trying to make her see, ridden the bus as far as it went, wherever it went, should have run and taken that bus.

Road deserted. No idea when the next bus might appear. No concrete, certain idea, of where she was, of how this part of London lay in relation to those she was familiar with. Refusing to dwell on the possibility she might be genuinely lost or stranded, because this was a major city and such things had to be impossible. Pushing fists deeper into pockets, walking faster, one Doctor Marten boot striking the dank pavement ahead of the next boot, aware of shop fronts and doorways, doors nestling in the depths of each, one Doctor Marten boot hitting a tight-rope-narrow line along the edge of the curb, so there was a better chance of spotting the next bus, or a taxi, or working out where she was, watching the line of the curb, worrying at memories of the ritual, not feeling they were enough to account for time gone, for the lateness of the hour, Minnette admitting the ritual had affected her, disturbed her, impressed her, had unnerved her, and walking along the curb always careful to keep as much space between her and shop-fronts and doorways as possible.

The ritual ended in the early evening, around 6, as close as she could to tell.

Minnette knew exactly when it started: 4:56 in the morning.

She and the magician had left the overheated flat in Clapham in the middle of the afternoon—*Yesterday afternoon*, she reminded herself—entering the nearest Tube station as the sun was setting, carriages cramped, passengers blank-faced, closed within themselves. Emerging above ground to find night advancing. Taking a bus, its windows turned into mirrors, giving little hint there was anything beyond them other than a few near-formless shapes condensing out of the dusk. Another journey on the Underground followed, Minnette staring at the maps at the head of the long stairs dropping down and down to the hidden platform. Wanting to convince herself she was reading them wrong. Positive they could not be following a long spiral across London. And watching the magician as, silently, he led her through thinning rush hour crowds, one platform to another to a train, to a station whose name she missed, to another train, another platform. Feeling they were going in circles. Trying to push that aside because it made no sense. It made no sense.

They walked the last stretch. Suburban streets. Houses set back behind overgrown or barren gardens, or masked by paling fences: demure, distrusting, watchful, calculating, anxious, exhausted, uncaring. Streetlights widely spaced and mounted on old, concrete columns, the taste of lost gentility, frowsy and self-conscious, adding to the January dankness.

Lost in thought. Not noticing the magician turning up one overgrown path. Having to run back. Pause. A torch beam's glimmer leading her to the right house in time for him to finish unlocking the door, go inside.

The house felt deserted. Bare bulb hanging from the ceiling, bulb low in wattage so the hall seemed darker with it on. Breath condensing. Passageway bare, unheated. Cracks in the faded paint on the walls looking as though they might be painted themselves. Corners grimy, with dirt or shadow it was hard to tell. Parquet floor gritty, dust merging into the tiles to keep secret any marks made by other recent visitors.

The house felt deserted.

Yet, as the magician locked the front door, there was a faint creak of weight shifting on the floor above, the suspicion of air being displaced inside the closed ground-floor rooms.

The air in the hall smelt housebound. Another, deeper breath brought traces of another scent. Warmer, spicier, more recent.

Incense.

Scalp crawling. Neck growing tight. Minnette took another deep breath, struggling to relax as she told herself it was okay to be nervous, trepidation before a ritual was natural, thrusting hands into jeans pockets to stop herself worrying at her bottom lip. Wanting to be angry. Or at least confused. Something else than this, unable to keep still and having nothing to do but stand, wait, searching for distraction, doubt, say, because this was not what she knew, wasn't how rituals should be constructed, that would be something to think... Fingers clammy, almost trembling. Neck tight. Scalp crawling. Trepidation before a ritual natural.

Another breath. The house smelled damp, shut up. Like an empty house. 'Who owns this? Whose house is this?' No way of keeping silent, although the question came out as a strained whisper.

Shaking his head, expression indicating silence, the magician opened the cupboard under the stairs, bringing out two simple black robes.

No instructions. Pulling robe over street clothes as he did. Sitting on the hard parquet when he did. Taking off shoes and socks, exposed flesh smarting as the air touched it.

The house was cold. *And empty*, Minnette reassured herself, trying not to startle at every creak. Telling herself: *It's the house settling, it's the cold, the wind, the house settling*, and glancing towards the magician, knowing she should be concentrating on the ritual. Chill deepening as night seeped through the house, knowing she should be preparing as the magician was, turning thoughts and feelings to the ritual. Noting every creak, every shifting air current. Minnette sitting on the hard parquet, chill deepening, Minnette sitting as the house flexed, as the street outside grew stiller, lights extinguishing, electric fires cooling, ticking as rooms cooled, as bedsheets were tucked in, electric blankets turned down, turned off, rooms mostly silent, hot milk drying on the sides of mug or glass, breathing becoming gentler, deeper, street mostly dark, houses mostly somnolent, growing a little restive in dream, dreams growing sparse, becoming a breath neither drawn in nor quite on the verge of release...

The magician stood. A single motion breaking the silence and turning about itself to become him checking his watch, unstrapping the watch and laying it on the floor, to become the magician standing and walking silently, almost silently, to stand by one of the two closed doors at the hall's far end.

Disorientation. An instant of surprise. Recollection and understanding tugging her to her feet. Aware of the cold, gritty floor against bare feet, the sense of no time having passed jarring with knowing that hours had vanished. Stomach tight and body trembling. A waft of incense as she stood beside the magician. Magician with a hand on the door handle, head bowed, eyes closed in concentration, lips moving. Not praying: realising he was counting down when he mouthed, *Now*, turning the handle, leading her into the room, lighting the first candle. Door closing behind them.

The ritual beginning.

The ritual was exhausting. The ritual was exhilarating. The ritual was interminable. The ritual was over before she quite accepted it had begun.

'We should know.'

Sitting cross-legged in the hallway, leaning forward to prop forehead on an arm resting across knees. Exhaustion and hunger indistinguishable. Happening across a memory of an Aegean sunrise, a farmhouse, muscles aching, his hand on her thigh, a memory of sleep finding him before it turned towards her, sun looking for chinks in the shutters, ways inside as he breathed, hand hot against her skin, a memory of—

'We should know soon, shouldn't we?'

Door to the ritual room wide open, room mostly in darkness. Outside: evening: no sign or memory of sunlight since the day before; little sense of intervening time. A deep ache through shoulders and back, thighs stiff, stiffness unyielding no matter how deeply she pressed chest into crossed legs, tried to relax. Sweat cooling. House as cold as the night before. A humming tremor gripping jaw, neck muscles. Shiver running into her fingers, fumbling socks, Doc Marten's. Dry throat making speaking difficult.

'We'll know soon. I know it. We will. Won't we?'

Standing, beginning to pace the width of the hallway. Memories and emotions jumbled. Wanting to speak. Keeping silent because the magician was silent. Pacing the width of the hallway. Touching a crack in one wall. Turning. Reaching for a mark on the opposite side.

'We'll know.' Words spilling. 'I know we'll know.' Touching the crack, hand flattening across the rough paint. 'Soon. I think soon.' Fingertips lingering as they found the mark on the other wall. 'Yes. Has to be. The sense of, of—' testing the solidity of the opposite wall again— 'power, I've never felt anything like—' palm flattening, wall hard and unresisting— 'I mean, it was incredible, wasn't it?' Hand on the wall, steadying. 'What do you think?'

Stepping into the middle of the hall. Turning.

The magician was gone. The second door off the hallway ajar, fluorescent light filling the gap, sounds of movement beyond hard to distinguish.

Sitting, wrapping her arms tight around her ribs. Beginning to rock almost at once, jaw aching from the cold and the effort of not babbling.

Images of the ritual playing out, fresh and bright and indistinct and hazed and jumbling and fading as they came and vivid and disturbing and exhilarating and transient and absent and unnerving as each became the next and the next turned and returned and returned.

Rocked harder.

Seeing—

A hand brushed her shoulder.

Jerking, cry high and shrill. And embarrassing. Magician already walking back down the hallway, stance betraying neither comment nor judgement. Robes gone, replaced by long coat, black in this light when she knew it was blue in the light of day. A shadow walking away down the hallway, sitting, back against the door to the cupboard under the stairs, facing the open ritual room.

'Eat,' was all he said.

A plate of bread spread thickly with jam and a mug filled with fizzing cola on the floor in front of her.

Minnette did not feel hungry.

'Is this... Is it...' Voice croaking, unwilling and uncooperative. Swallowing. 'The rituals, your rituals: always like this? This, this—' Feeling a bubble of gas worm from thorax to throat. Seeing the plate empty but for crumbs, dregs in the mug. No recollection of having eaten, trying not to wonder how much time had passed as she tried again: 'Are they?'

'Depends. We'll discuss it later. Tomorrow. Afterwards.'

Torpor settling over her, draining through joints into muscle. Much colder in the hall than she had thought. Looking at the wall ahead, unable to spot crack or mark, unsure where to look and unable to settle for the idea she was looking in the wrong spot. Torpor becoming a need to stand, knees and thighs protesting.

'It worked.'

Walking down the hallway, sole of each foot a bed of nails, pins and needles prickling, path weaving, footing uncertain, a fire pit to be crossed, doorway to the ritual room on the far side.

'Didn't it?'

Fingers of one hand curling, nails digging into a clammy palm. Other hand gripping doorframe, wood uneven under layers of yellowing paint.

'Did it?'

Minnette stared into the ritual room.

Single candle, wavering, only one still burning on the dinning table that served as their altar. Flame steadying. Incense overlaying the damp of a house kept closed and empty for a long time, parting to reveal the faint trace of sweat on the room's breath from the two of them closed in there for so long, door tight shut.

At least two: Minnette squirming away from the memory and unable to stop it welling again: a moment towards the end of the ritual when she had been sure there was some… one standing behind her. Hard not to flinch, spin round, sure there had been a presence visible at the corner of her eye.

A draft of air toyed with the last candle on the altar, light bending into a sinuous coil around the edges of the room. Glancing down at her shadow sketched across the bare floor by the hall's unshaded bulb. Aware of the magician seemingly lost in thought.

Movement played across the wall opposite the altar.

Glancing towards it, stomach clenching as she assured herself there was nothing to see and seeing a wedge of light spreading across cracked plaster, colour and size wrong for it to be the candle, a shadow swelling from one side, wedge swinging open wider, letting the shadow come closer. Knowing shadow and light behind it had nothing to do with the altar candle, light too steady and white, knowing where and when she had seen this happen. Watching it happen again. Running before it had chance to end. Leaving the front door gaping. Magician giving a single shout, shout lost in the sound of her own breathing, own boots thudding against pavement.

No pretence of browsing, simply walking up to the counter and polishing his monocle.

'I was passing, noticed you looking enthralled.'

'Browsing or buying?'

'Neither.' Guillaume tucked the monocle amongst the folds of his pocket handkerchief. 'I saw you and thought —'

'If you're not interested in the stock can you piss off? I've got paying customers to see to.'

They were the only people in the New Age bookshop.

Drumming her fingers on the counter-top, avoiding Guillaume's eye. Hearing him draw in a breath to say something and getting in first.

'I'm just doing this as a favour, the owner's a friend of a friend...'

'Oh.'

No inflection in his voice, although she looked for something in the syllable to rise to. Resenting that absence. Realigning the displays on the counter with stiff, prissy movements.

'It's just temporary, is it?'

Wanting to say yes. A spark of pride making her blurt: 'Actually, I'm the assistant manger—' Regretting the tone of her voice, sure the admission sounded too much like pleading. 'I'm expecting a delivery any minute. I need to check it, put it away out back. I think you better go.'

'Have you become interested in this sort of thing now?' Guillaume glanced at the titles on the nearest shelves, at the displays of crystals and woodland spirit figurines. 'How are you?'

Ready to bite back at the first question and feeling trapped by the second, Minnette walked stiffly around the counter and opened the door. 'Leave. Now.'

Sure he was not going to say anything as he stepped out onto the pavement. Ready to slam the door on him anyway.

'Always running away, aren't you, Minnette?'

Door striking frame. Pavement empty. Guillaume already out of sight by the time she stirred.

An illuminated road sign stood impassively beside the crossroads. Splayed fingers pointing the many ways open from here. None meant anything. Gaze running over names, letters, willing them to make sense. If she had an *A to Z*. If she was less tired. If...

A pedestrian crossing's lights showed red, lamps fulminating bull's eyes.

Turning back, staring at the road sign.

A mini-cab swept past before Minnette could react: the first traffic for some time. No real idea of how long she had run, how long she had walked afterwards, how far she was from the house. Perhaps one of the names on the sign was familiar. Vaguely. It did nothing to help her work out where she was, decide where she should go next.

Hesitating. Walking away from the crossing.

Pavement ahead sparkling faintly, air casting needles against her face. Despite the thickness of the boot's soles, her toes were starting to numb. Noticing the cold for the first time. Shivering. Heel slipping, balance thrown but not lost.

Next row of shops unlit, grills covering each window. Doorways sunken into shadow. Minnette veering closer to the kerb, pace increasing.

Until she saw the light.

Next morning, a warm front unexpectedly enveloped the city. The hard frost of the night melted, drying in bright sunshine that held steady throughout the afternoon, a south-westerly bringing an unseasonal spike in temperatures. Sunset over Clapham that evening was stained a deep, violent red that faded slowly into a night that was cloudless and mild.

Unable to find the borrowed latch key there was no choice but to ring the bell.

Lights dimmed by the sunset through the corridor windows.

Ringing the bell again.

No sounds from inside. Hard to tell if the hall light was on. A stillness about the front door, the flat beyond, making her think it was wasn't, that there was no one in.

Shoulders slumping, Minnette sniffed, knuckling her eyes and sniffing again, shifting weight unsteadily, sniffing and tight-closing her eyes, tempted to sit beside the door, standing too much effort, joints smarting, eyes tearing because she hadn't slept in almost three days, sniffing, trying the bell again.

She had turned away from the last door.

As morning rush hour coalesced and children began to go to school, Minnette had found a railway station, standing on the platform amongst countless people absorbed in the morning paper, the prospect of a day at the office or on a building site or behind a till in a shop. Took a train. Got off after a couple of stops. Wandered. Found a Tube station. Recognised a few names, destinations and routes feeling a little firmer. And getting off after three stops, crossing to a different line. Leaving the Tube two stops after that. Walking. Not exactly aimlessly though not with any conscious purpose at first. Later, when chance brought a familiar landmark and she had to admit she knew the way back to the flat, more or less, Minnette pretended she needed more time to think, that anyway she could not trust the direct route in her head, taking a more circular, longer route, doubling-back several times, pushing on until dusk turned the sky red, until she could no longer stand walking and knew there was no choice but to go back to the flat.

She had turned sharply away from the last door in the row.

Sitting on the floor of the corridor, looking at the sunset. Turning over the day. Remembering bright sunlight making silhouettes out of tower blocks, warm breeze on her face, on her arms once she had shed jacket and jumper. Remembering train platforms and carriages, although these were mostly interchangeable. Thinking of the night before. The ritual. Needing to leave the house. Needing time to think over the Working she had helped the magician perform. The sudden warmth of the day that had followed, the cold of the night before. The walking. Light growing stronger. Walking through cold, darkness, deserted streets. A crossroads, next row of shops unlit. All of them dark behind metal grills. Doorways hidden. Walking along the road, the row. Road bending gently, unlit windows and doorways spilling shadows across the pavement, pressing her out towards the edge of the curb, bringing the end of the row into view a few steps sooner, bringing the light dusting the pavement into view beyond a gentle bend in the road, a few steps, a few steps closer, and seeing light coming from the door, the half-open door of the very last shop in the row, seeing the light—

Minnette frowned, unable to remember what happened next, assuming she must have walked past the shop, that the door couldn't have been open at that time of night, sure she must have simply kept walking, positive that that was how it had—

Security chain rattling, latch turning. Looking up to see the magician. Clambering stiffly to her feet. Looking at the magician. Face flushed by the sunset, corridor warm and almost as mild as the evening framed in the windows.

'So—' ruddy light doing nothing to make his expression any less ambiguous '—what do you believe now?'

Their first ritual working together was a failure. No particular surprise, perhaps, as the working had been ambitious—something they both felt during the days leading up to the attempt but which neither admitted until a week or two later. Even so, it left them both waspish and cynical immediately afterwards. All Guillaume was willing to say about it during those days was: we have to try again. The repetition fuelled her anger, searching harder for something to blame. I wanted it to work, she admitted to

Yves, whose sympathy made her even angrier. A friend of Guillaume's, an alchemist who had come to Paris as a refugee from the collapse of the Prague Spring and who was normally pessimistic about almost everything, suggested the ritual might have worked but not in the way she and Guillaume had expected. Minnette's reply was scornful and harsh and protracted enough that the Czech alchemist left Guillaume's flat in a hurry and avoided her from that point on.

'What the fuck are you doing?'

Staring at Guillaume. Grabbing the brandy bottle from the floor. Filling her wine glass almost to the brim.

'I mean it, Minnette. That was, that was— He was only trying to make you feel better.' Guillaume putting the bottle in a cupboard, leaning against the door to stop her topping the glass up again. 'Why? What's fucking wrong with you? I'm disappointed, too, you know, but I don't—'

'I'm not disappointed.' Yelling the sentence a second time. Taking a large mouthful of brandy and choking, almost dropping the glass. 'I'm not disappointed,' she managed, gulping air, deciding not to bother with the rest of the brandy, and admitting she had hoped for something, for something—

'I am disappointed,' Minnette told him.

so that is it and she tried to hold on to those words and she tried to focus on the German's face as it drew back together and made itself again and mouthed the words So that is it and that was how it was and those words found their way into her head without touching the air in between mouth and mind and she nodded or she thought she tried to nod because her head was loose and her neck was soft and slipping and it was more pleasant to sit and melt and the German smiled a smile that was fading light and a face that was not connected to a body but floating over her as she floated and melted and knew there was no need to nod or speak as the German's smile faded into the darkness and the only thing in the darkness with her was his voice whispering that this was their secret now and whispered this is our secret now

He talked for most of the train ride back. Describing without making clear. Making statements that were questions that seemed to refer to two things at once. Questions that did not feel like they were asking for an answer but which were not statements. Asking for descriptions of her experiences, her impressions, what she had felt before the ritual, during. No mention of the weather.

Either she struggled to find an answer at all or feared she would never stop talking, words pushing one over another to pour out, words evaporating to leave a residue that had no name, could not be described.

'What we see is what we believe strongly enough,' he told her, gesturing vaguely at the view slipping past the window. 'What we see is what we believe.'

Warm weather persisted, unseasonal, distrusted, embraced. Half-demolished streets loosing their dankness, puddles between heaps of rubble glimmering as they dwindled. An item on local TV about an ice cream factory thinking of putting on extra staff. Winter coats vanishing from the streets for three days straight.

Warm weather persisting into another day. Sun shining from a cloudless sky.

Warm weather turned into two inches of snow in the space of an hour.

Sunshine and a flush of warmth. Bigger than usual crowds to the banks of the Seine. Middle-aged couples leaning on the bridges to watch the long-hairs and freaks sprawled in any available shade; younger people of less hippyish tendencies strolling arm-in-arm or necking. Street artists and Sunday painters, traffic filing and lurching along the road as tourists snapped views of the Palais du Louvre or the Île de la Cité, wandered from stall to stall along the Quai de la Tournelle or the Quai des Grands Augustins. Fly-blown copies of *Paris Match* vying for space with dusty box sets of Satre, Camus, *Tour Eifel* key rings. Drifting slowly through it all, sometimes pausing to look over the parapet at the random carnival down on the riverside, walking on to the next bookstall, the one after that.

Guillaume shook his head and laughed. Waved a broken-spined copy of Pauwels & Bergier's *The Morning of the Magicians*.

'Magical texts used to have this habit of turning up just when you needed them.' Paging through the sensational potboiler. 'It happened to MacGregor Mathers. Lots of people. Crowley, too, wasn't it?' He gave her a mock scowl. 'You have to work harder at it these days.'

'Isn't it more valuable, if it comes with effort? If it's not—' hesitating for a fraction of a second and pushing on— 'not handed to you.'

'S'pose.' Thanking the stall holder with mock gravity, carefully putting the book back. 'I suppose that is true.' Putting an arm around Minnette's waist, Guillaume guided her towards the next stall. 'I mean, the effort adds to the whole process of—I don't know—mystical development —does that sound too pompous?' She shook her head. 'But I wonder how long that takes. Mystical development.'

'It'll happen.' Sounding sure and surprising them both by how much.

'It's not the power. Not the power, exactly.' Guillaume studied an American reprint of *The Cosmic Doctrine*. 'But what the power brings. The insight. The understanding. Isn't it?'

She made no comment, let him lead her along the Quai des Grands Augustins.

Casually, Guillaume asked: 'Do you think that can happen? The right book appearing, a teacher coming along? Do you think there's some hidden cabal of occult masters guiding you, or that Chance or Fate might just decide to, I don't know, say grant you the knowledge you need, the power?'

'I don't know.'

They both stopped at the next stall, Minnette wandering to the far end as Guillaume browsed, pausing over every book. Or so it seemed. She looked at the spines, covers facing her. None of the titles registering.

'I understand it's better to gain the knowledge than to have it handed to you.' Guillaume held up one of the books. 'There's so much to learn, though. Feels like there isn't the time to get it all in.' Shrugging, paying for the book and handing it to Minnette. A volume of Castenada. 'I just wish, sometimes...'

Surprised by the gift, smiling as she read a passage at random, kissing him, feeling she should say something more than simply *thank you*.

'You never know when you're going to turn a corner, or look across a hillside, and see something unexpected, transcendent, otherworldly.'

Meaning it to be no more than comforting, some words to lift his mood. Realising there had been something in her tone, her expression, to make Guillaume tilt his head to one side, expression puzzled, intent.

'What do you mean?'

Picking a book from the stall at random. 'Nothing. Just being silly.'

Holding up the blue-marbled notebook. 'What's this?'

It had been lying against the bedsit's door that morning. No note. Nothing to indicate it hadn't been left by accident except suspicions bordering on certainty.

'Yours.' The magician pushed his shopping trolley between trays of fresh potatoes and winter cabbages.

Elderly men leaning on the handles of their trolleys as if leaning on the bar in the tap room, having animated conversations with other elderly men, their wives dropping sliced-whites and toilet rolls into the cart before plodding off in search of instant jelly. A young mother struggling with two children and an over-full hand basket. A middle-aged man in carpet slippers despite the rain, shuffling past with a shopping list held out in front of him, blinking, a stranger unused to foraging alone.

Self-conscious, Minnette bit off one reply and chose another.

'I have notebooks. Lots of them.' Riffling the blank pages in front of the magician's face. 'What's this one for?'

The magician dropped a bag of carrots into his trolley, hesitating over the swedes before angling off to a display of half-priced sausages.

'Fill it,' he told her, tone sounding as if the answer should be obvious. 'Fill it with the truth.'

She slipped out of bed just before dawn.

Pausing to watch Guillaume sleep, listening to his gentle breathing. Going into the other room to sit beside the window and watch the city wake up. She liked doing this: the slow build up of traffic, early morning shoppers, people on the way to work, light changing as things got busier. A small pleasure. But not the reason she had been lying awake for so long.

The Christmas vacation was not fading. Not in only a few months. The memories felt whole, not one moment lost. Not that she needed them all. The Tower would be enough. She could describe the lightning, the explosion, The Tower crumbling and not coming to earth. And she could tell him about the alley between the two lamps, the warm light, the voices, the path twisting and changing. She could tell him about trying to be sure it had stopped and wouldn't start again. He'd understand how that had been. Guillaume should be able to understand that. Understand how none of what happened made sense, how it couldn't have happened, how she wanted it not to have happened. The terror that all of it had happened only inside her head. The terror that it hadn't, her hand trailing along the sandstone wall, stones rough and cold and rooted deep into the ground. Wall endless. Until the light. She could tell him about the light falling across the icy pavement and the door opening and the shadow—

Minnette made no sound as she cried. Fists clenched tightly over her jaw. Hating her silence. Hating herself.

hearing as he sat back as he faded as the room grew brighter and darker and fainter as she felt her head grow heavy and soft as she saw through closed eyes seeing the door to the kitchen ajar when it had been closed when he had made a point of saying he would close the door because there was a draft and seeing a shadow somewhere a shadow somewhere behind the door but not being able to look because the room was his face and that had become almost nothing but light and she watched him through closed lids watching him sitting back in his chair sitting and smiling and not moving as he spoke as his voice whispered in her ear and she felt his breath against the side of her face words less than a whisper as the German said I know what it is you saw

The press works had been closed for eighteen months. A layer of snow had done nothing to hide weeds and cracked concrete, the stains of rust and oil outside. No wind, only the sound of traffic in the distance and a feeling that the site had been abandoned a long time.

'The security guard is a mate of a mate of a mate. We won't be disturbed.'

The magician set down a cardboard box, emblazoned with Tony the Tiger's face, in the middle of an area that must once have been filled with heavy machinery. Straight lines and grooves in the concrete were all that remained. He turned slowly to look around the gutted factory.

'You agree?'

Blowing on her hands, words fading on the icy air as she spoke. 'We've been through this.'

He had let her help formulate this ritual, determining time and place as well as the focus of the ceremony: several pieces in the local press about a young girl who lived on the estate near the playground; hope of a new treatment in America; her family fund raising. Minnette had suggested they hold the ritual in a place familiar to members of the family, the magician finding this derelict factory after a handful of phone calls.

'I'll prepare the altar if you set the bounds.'

Weak sunlight filtered through grimy skylights. Light turning blue, becoming no different from the darkness roosting beneath the roof struts by the time the circle was finished, seven torches shining across its diameter, beams criss-crossing, tugging at their shadows as they made the final preparations.

Adjusting the items on the altar, feeling a vibration as she touched each one, a vibration that might have been nothing more than excitement, hands steady when Minnette held them in front of her, no sign of shake. Closing her eyes, breathing deeply, smelling the cheap perfume they were using as incense overlaying lingering machine smells, air cold. Searching beyond the hum of adrenaline for a deeper feeling. Genuine, she was sure. Not imagined and made real through imagination alone. Had to be, Minnette assured herself. Taking another deep, slow, breath. Had to be.

'How?'

Turning towards the magician before her eyes opened, look of surprise on his face quickly smothered.

'You know that.' His voice was calm, betraying nothing. 'We've been through each step. You formulated how we're going to help—'

'No.' Making a sharp, frustrated gesture, as her voice rose above the low murmur the derelict's open spaces had imposed on them both. 'No, I mean *how*? How is it we can do this if there's nothing here—' another gesture: everywhere, the world, the whole of creation, not simply this place that had no purpose now— 'but what we think and create and imagine, *how* is *this* possible?'

Stared at her for a fraction of a second, long enough for her to see he understood what she had meant by 'this': not just ritual and exercise of power over a plastic world waiting to be re-formed, but something wider. Going back to the preparations. No answer: only a glimpse of his expression as he turned away. The suspicion the magician did not know how to answer.

The news that the little girl's family had won a jackpot on the football pools was covered on local TV, radio and on the front page of the evening paper.

She was only there a little over five months before the New Age bookshop closed following an electrical short caused a small fire, although the closure owed more to a faulty sprinkler system whose pipes had burst. Most of the stock water damaged, not burned.
  A terrible accident.
  That's how she described it.

A new job. A new place to live: a district where Erik Satie had lived towards the end of his life.
  A happy coincidence was what she told everyone.

The dreams of nothingness and darkness encroaching faded. Stopped.
  Not something she told anyone, telling herself it was one of those things, not something she could have controlled or predicted.

The previous tenant had installed shelves from floor to ceiling, her landlord telling her she could take them down if she wanted. If she wanted to fill-in the holes and repaint the wall, that was okay, too.
  She wasn't doing work for free, not with the rent the way it was she wasn't: that's what she told friends, anyone willing to listen, that's how she explained the shelves staying up when she had so little in the apartment.

The shelves began to fill. So did the apartment as boxes came out of storage, as she spent a little more time, a little more time, a little more each week or month, a little more time reading, studying old books out of storage, buying, little by little, new books to add to the shelves.
  This she explained to no one. Not even herself.

And so the dreams, of nothingness and darkness encroaching, faded, quite co-incidentally, to be replaced by —

Minnette slept deeply enough, remembering dreams only vaguely if at all and never talking about them or how she spent more and more of her time as months became another year, days another week, weeks became blurred. Never talking to anyone about either.

'Anyone'...
There really was no one left. Only the reading and studying. And memories, of course.

Sitting as the other students spilled from the lecture theatre, writing faster to get down that last point, knowing there was an hour to the tutorial and still feeling pressure of time, pressure to not miss something important, underlining a phrase the lecturer had used, thinking it particularly important, adding another underline, pausing.

Room better than half empty. Suddenly self-conscious, feeling rushed.

Minnette looked at her notebook, sure she had missed something. Cramming books and notes into her shoulder bag. Hurrying out to slow in the corridor, suddenly caught by the feeling of newness, university strange even after being here almost a month, knowing a handful of weeks shouldn't be enough for it to all—course, university, Paris —seem familiar and ordinary.

Glancing up. A loose group of students across half of the corridor. Not all first years, although her Yves was among them. She had met him a week or so after the start of term, on the edges of a small crowd sitting in a café, neither really taking part in the conversation, Yves suddenly turning to her and saying he thought they should be friends because he had no ambitions. 'You look like you wouldn't mind that in a friend, unlike some of these people,' he had told her.

Yves saw her, beckoning her closer, Minnette slowing, glancing at the other faces in the group. And deciding she felt more like being alone, shrugging apology, pointing to her wristwatch as she hurried by, focusing on the exit, avoiding eye contact with the people nearest Yves.

Outside, groups of students loitered around the steps or on the fringes of the lawn beyond, rest spreading out: for the library, other lectures, the nearest café. Burying her chin under loops of scarf. Setting off at random, thinking she needed exercise, that there was no reason not to wander for a while before going to her tutorial. Cheeks flushed. But that was the cold, Minnette decided, walking faster, side street broad and almost empty but for cars parked nose-to-tail along both gutters, walling-in the narrow footpath—

'Excuse me?'

A touch on her shoulder, light, not enough to slow her. She could pretend to be lost in thought, to have not noticed. It might be someone playing a joke, someone about to molest her. It might be something terrible, she thought, taking two more strides before the hand brushed against her arm again.

'Excuse me?'

She had noticed him a couple of times. A year or two older, good-looking, hair falling past his shoulders in swathes of tawny brown. He had been among the group standing in the corridor, standing beside Yves. Good-looking. If you liked that sort of thing.

'You're Yves' friend, aren't you? Minnette, isn't it?'

It didn't sound like a pick-up. But then, it couldn't be a pick-up, Minnette reminded herself. Noting his hair was washed, beard neatly trimmed, that his clothes were cleaner and newer than the counter-cultural make-do of most people she knew.

'Yes.' A small shrug to make it seem like she had nothing to hide.

'Bit overwhelming, first year, isn't it?' He smiled. Minnette managed to stop herself smiling in return, tried not to stare into the young man's eyes, glad the breeze was blowing along this street, that it would explain ruddy cheeks, a flushed face. 'Yves was saying how hard you've been working. I think he's a bit jealous.' Laughing, smile warmer. 'It gets easier but it's easy to get buried in all the work they pile on you in the first few weeks.' Not knowing where to look as he told her: 'My name's Guillaume.' Looking only at him as he added: 'I thought you looked a little lost. Can I help?'

Not that she was sure she wanted her memories.
　Or that she trusted them.

Sitting with him at the restaurant, pretending it was only lunch, that having lunch with him was ordinary, something everyone did, mind turning over the past, the past since Nivelles, setting off with nowhere in mind and simply following whatever route came along, until Hamburg led to Bruges and Bruges led to Lübeck, although from Lübeck she almost kept going northwards, wandering ever northwards, but without a destination because a destination meant an end, because an end required a decision and it was too early to decide... 'He has a reputation, but don't we all—' the old woman in Lübeck smiling, patting the pink frills and strings of pearls around her neck, obviously familiar with the stories about herself, voice filled with the gravel of chain-smoking, ashtray already half full when Minnette sat down, glass of cherry brandy within easy reach, old woman sipping without pausing in what she was saying, waiters topping up as they passed— 'but he knows, you see, he does know, that I have to admit and you, yes, I think you'll find that out, that much, my dear—' taking a sip of brandy, lighting another cigarette, a waiter pausing to fill the old lady's glass before disappearing through the bead curtain behind the bar, old lady drawing deeply, cigarette coal a sharp eye crackling— 'yes, I think you'll see that much, because he —' squinting through a wimple of smoke, Minnette's heart beating faster as she tried not to fidget, as the old lady drew again on the cigarette— 'yes, you he will see, but don't get me wrong, he is polite, not like some, my dear, he'll listen for five or ten minutes before he tells you he has somewhere else he must be but that it was a pleasure to meet you, he—' a sip of cherry brandy— 'has a touch of that old world charm when he sends them away but you, you I think he might tolerate for an hour, no more, so—' stubbing out the cigarette, voice changing, loosing something of its huskiness— 'be ready with your questions and listen to the little he says—' old lady draining her glass, standing, waiter appearing, holding out her fur coat for her to slip arms into, shrug on as she walked towards the exit— 'although it might not be what you've been hoping for: you might well be better with the Englishman, he has...' turning to look at Minnette before tugging open the door, door swinging shut and leaving the sentence unfinished, Minnette sure everyone was looking at her even though the other customers seemed absorbed by the football game on the TV beside the bar, not sure what she should do next and going to the nearest railway station, buying tickets to Düsseldorf for the next day, which was not really a decision as much as a way of deferring decision, perhaps until the man in Leeds wrote again, perhaps until... but he had not dismissed her after ten minutes, inviting her to eat with him that evening, then this lunch, which, although she tried not to show it, was exciting and Minnette tried to stop knotting her fingers together in her lap, to show that she was ready and receptive and could be trusted with whatever truths and insights and secrets he wanted... and the German talked as he munched potato salad and sipped beer, politely and gently, like an elderly uncle or a grandfather, taking an interest in her, Minnette mentioning she had once visited the Aegean and the German delighted because that was a place that had always struck him as being beautiful, that he had always wanted to visit and—would she believe? but then the world is fuelled by coincidence—had spent the morning searching for picture books on, even calling in at a travel agent's, although their literature, he thought, lacked authenticity, did she not find that to be so? he asked as he took another mouthful of beer, prompting Minnette to drain a third of her own glass, feeling hot although the restaurant had not seemed particularly warm when they had come in, wanting to turn the conversation in a different direction, nodding as the German went on about the Aegean and how enchanting it must have been, quite a magical experience, he was so— 'I got stomach 'flu,' she blurted, 'I was vomiting for almost five days straight then didn't have the energy to think for three weeks after that, and then I went home again... sorry...' she added, concentrating on the plate in front of her, peripherally watching as the German sat without moving for several seconds, at last giving a tiny nod and bending over his salad again...

Every day was full.

Gripping the handrail, rocking with the motion of the bus, staring absently through the windows, a list of all the things that needed doing after the morning's lecture becoming a memory of the squat, Sebastian/Patrice watching as she left that Christmas before going—before going on—

Life was busier these days, last year of the course the hardest. Minnette ran from the bus stop to the lecture hall

There was a lot to do.

An hour and a half later, still scribbling notes as she hurried from the lecture. Thinking there would not be enough time to get to tutorial and arriving early, which was good, a point about the coursework nagging, needing to be gone over. Tutorial overrunning. Five minutes. Twenty. Tutor, apologising, cutting off Minnette, apologising but insisting, already late for another appointment. Not content they had covered it enough and standing outside the tutor's office as he hurried up the corridor. Remembering she had promised to phone a friend, seeing the queue for the pay phone, long, slow moving, fretting over not phoning, at having promised then forgotten, forgotten about eating too, standing in the queue for a few minutes, fretting about the slowness. Ducking out. Heading towards the cafeteria. Changing her mind and joining the back of the queue again. And thinking it probably didn't matter, that eating made more sense, being hungry the reason why she was having trouble making up her mind—

Minnette spotted a young woman from the course sitting at a table near the door to the first café she tried. They were supposed to be collaborating on a joint project. Minnette had agreed. But it hadn't been her idea, wasn't what she wanted. Not that the other woman was unpleasant, no, only that Minnette thought she could do a better job on her own, preferred working on her own, at least this time, so it would be better, more polite, yes, more polite not to talk to this student until that was sorted out.

Which was something else that needed getting 'round to, needed adding to the list of things to do, the next café too full, spotting one of Yves' friends, one of the others on the road trip, sitting at a half-empty table, the café too full, too noisy, not wanting to sit somewhere so cramped, not wanting to sit next to someone, not wanting to sit in a place that was so noisy, even if half the tables were empty…

Fourth café almost empty but for a knot of Guillaume's friends crammed around a couple of pushed-together tables, talking animatedly. Trying to slip away and one of his friends spotting her at the window, practically dragging her inside. Ordering the cheapest thing on the menu, hunching over the plate, looking up only when spoken to directly, saying little, whether she knew the answer or not. Leaving them, saying there was a lot to do that day. Which was true. There was coursework, the final dissertation. So many things filling up the days. Walking very quickly. No destination. Walking faster. Longing for the next corner, to be swallowed by the next turning, the alley— Really having to get on, so much work, enjoyable work, the course work, final dissertation, all thoroughly enjoyable, that was true, of course, but a lot of it, a—

Seeing one of her lecturers coming out of a shop. Stopping at the curb-side, about to cross, pretending not to hear. Having to turn and smile, lecturer calling her name, happy they had bumped into each other because there were a few points about Minnette's dissertation. Which she definitely wanted to go over with the lecturer, she would, she would call by and talk about those few points, points that had definitely been bothering her, talk about them tomorrow, the day after, when there was a time that was good for them both, not now, even if it was only going to take a few minutes, because she had to get to the bookshop, had to go— The lecturer nodding, fishing inside her satchel to hand Minnette a reading list, which Minnette took after a moment. Glanced over. Promised to come by the lecturer's office, to talk over those points, to talk over her detailed outline, which was very nearly finished, very nearly, she told the lecturer, face in a smile, face straight and honest and not the face of someone who had yet to start an outline, had done nothing more than pile up a few books in a corner of the flat and leave a notepad on top, a promise written on the pad, a promise to start.

She would start tonight.

Minnette nodded as she walked away. Wondering which was the best route to the bookshop from here.

She would start tonight, she promised as she walked into the bookshop.

Early. She was early for her shift. So little time in the day. So much course work and then doing a shift at this underground bookshop. Working here almost a year. A distraction. Welcome but a distraction. She did tell people that, sometimes; did think it, sometimes: putting stock away, organising shelves, tidying the magazine racks, helping hippies find books by Leary or Hesse or Reich or Velikovsky or— It was easy to get wrapped up in the work, easy to fill the periods when there were no customers by leafing through another book or rearranging the window display. Easy to feel a little guilty about it, afterwards, although, after her shift, she decided to go to the library rather than back to the flat. Finding a quite table. Stacking piles of books around the edge. Like a wall. Ducking behind. Starting notes for the dissertation.

Waking with a jerk, heart thumping. Tables occupied by people who hadn't been there when she had sat down. Confused. Taking some of the books from the table, placing them on the trolley for the librarians to put away. Thrusting notepads into shoulder bag, conscious of time passing, time pressing, remaining books tucked under-arm to be put into the bag on the way to the exit. Mouth of the bag closing in on itself, books slipping—*You should have done this at the table, idiot*—muttering, undertone growing flustered, books slipping, almost falling, slipping away, struggling with bag and books and missing the voice, hearing 'Excuse me' finally and realising it might have been the fourth time.

He had very long hair, a denim jacket that reeked of patchouli, acne. A first-year, she guessed, staring at him blankly as he held out a book, mumbling that she had dropped it. Shaking herself, making her hand rise, seeing the title, backing away, 'Keep it, it's not mine,' first-year insisting she had dropped it as she hurried away, life too busy for her to waste time on mistakes like this, too busy these days—

Leaving the first-year holding the copy of de Gébelin's *The Primitive World*, a stylised Tarot deck on its cover, The Tower visible if partially hidden by The Hanged Man, rushing from the library into the early dark of another late winter's day.

Their current apartment was minuscule compared with the one they had first lived in. A ribbon of kitchenette off a living room that would seem cramped with no more than a few bits of furniture but which held a sofa, bean bags, three mismatched chairs, a stereo on a small table, records. Books lined the short corridor to the bathroom and bedroom, macabre antiques filling any left over spaces, posters drooping from those walls too warped to hang shelves from. The building's foyer smelled of drains. The stairwell of the vinegar the concierge used instead of floor cleaner. It was the best they could afford after Guillaume's trust fund had ended with his graduation.

There had been a chance of more money but the last thing he wanted to do was continue studying. At university, at least.

Pushing the front door closed with her backside, Minnette hefted three string bags of groceries into the kitchenette: just about all her food budget for the month, an extravagance she would have to scrimp to make up, but Guillaume wanted this evening's dinner party to be special. A new group of friends he was cultivating, plus a sprinkling of people he had known for much longer.

She fished out the present from one of the bags, unwrapping it carefully and turning it over, checking it hadn't been damaged in transit. The display stand was actually meant for a plate, the stand having been left at the back of a cupboard by a previous tenant. No sign of the plate.

Wrapping a tissue around the stand's prongs and setting it beside the stereo on the narrow table in one corner of the living room, she balanced the present so the boards wouldn't be marked: a book by the English occultist, Israel Regardie, quite rare, anything but cheap.

Textbooks propped open in any available space. Making intermittent progress on the dissertation as she prepared dinner. Wiping her hands on her apron and making some rough notes, checking the alarm clock that served as a kitchen timer, the meal hopefully ready just in time for the guests to have settled in. A moue of discontent at the thought of another evening with Guillaume's friends and knowing it would help him in his work, sure it was disloyal and unfair to think otherwise, dismissing her feelings, turning a page, picking up a pen to make another note, pausing to stir a pot.

Staring into rising steam.

The present nagged.

Turning down the heat, Minnette went to look at the book again. Guillaume would be delighted. It was worth the cost, worth using the money set aside for this month's rent. Putting it gently back on the stand, moving it so he was sure to see it when he came in.

Yes. Minnette nodded. Guillaume would be delighted.

Nine o'clock came and went. No sign of Guillaume. Makeshift serving dishes, empty plates, a few bottles, a half-dozen ashtrays overflowed across the cramped living room. Smoke filled the air. As did music from the stereo, although that was almost masked by the conversations that overlapped, flowed together from time to time, split again. Trying to concentrate, playing the hostess as best she could when all she was interested in was the clock, not whether everyone had had enough to eat, drink, their opinions about anthropology, politics, pop music or esotericism. Stabbing out a cigarette, Minnette almost refilled her wine glass, changing the record instead, swapping Bach for James Taylor. No one seemed to mind and she didn't care if they did.

The conversation guttered, stalling completely. One or two of the guests moved restlessly. Hoping no one would notice as she checked the clock again, lighting another cigarette to cover the action, feeling the evening had been more strained than it should have been. Even given Guillaume's absence. She could have made more effort, first impulse to turn them away, no matter that the meal, the month's food budget, would have gone to waste, not feeling like entertaining. Admission making her feel guiltier for how the evening was turning out.

Pouring more wine. Minnette swallowing half the glass before brightly asking if anyone wanted more to eat, was the music too loud, or not loud enough, what did everyone think of... No idea what they might have an opinion on, head hollow.

One of Guillaume's friends stubbed out his cigarette, made some remark about a sociologist on television who had caused a minor scandal with some off-hand remarks in an interview. The details had passed Minnette by, aware only that it was being built up in the newspapers and talked about a great deal. Soon, the others were deep in discussion about the story.

She drained the rest of the wine in a single mouthful.

When Guillaume finally returned, some twenty minutes later, he was full of smiles and apologies, expansive and charming, smiling and joking, smiling and apologising again as he poured himself wine, sitting cross-legged in a narrow gap in the midst of his guests, waving a hand theatrically and launching into a clearly exaggerated but very funny tale about his day, why he was late.

Minnette was the only one not laughing.

In a lull, she opened her mouth to ask him what he had really been doing all day, all evening. One of his new acquaintances—a journalist, or a production assistant in TV, she couldn't remember which it was—pressed Guillaume for his views on the latest rash of UFO sightings, enthusiastically expounding a theory that flying saucers navigated along ley lines, their engines running on 'geomantic energies'.

Minnette drained her glass.

As the journalist or production assistant rattled on, Guillaume gave Minnette a wink.

They eventually left.

Not as drunk as she should be. Upending the remains of the last bottle over her glass as Guillaume showed the final guest out. Wanting to be drunker, a hazy numbness and the first signs of hangover the best she had managed so far, neither doing anything to blunt her anger.

'That went well, don't you think?' Rubbing his hands together and pouring a brandy. 'Very well.'

Watching him, knowing he was never going to offer her a nightcap.

'Yeah.' He nodded as he sipped. 'Great.' He turned towards her, lifting his glass. 'Thanks. For everything.'

'Bastard.'

No reaction. Minnette screamed the word a second time, scooping a dirty plate from the floor and hurling it at him. Guillaume dodged easily, one hand across the top of his brandy to stop it spilling.

A couple more plates, some screaming, and the anger burned out, becoming something tar-like and smothering.

Slumping into a bean bag. Tears refusing to come. She buried her face in her hands.

'Go to bed, I'll tidy up.'

When he didn't move, she said it again, more loudly and clearly.

'Look, I'm sorry.' He knelt, proffering his brandy. Shaking her head, pushing the glass away. Guillaume leaned closer, trying to get her to look at him. 'I am sorry. Time got away from me. I was thinking things over and then I had to do something about it, about what I had decided. Had to. It was too exciting.'

'You could have phoned.' They weren't really words, more breaths where the words could have been, closing her eyes, trying again. 'Do you know how stupid I felt, all your friends here—'

'Some of them are your friends, too.'

'—and me, me without a clue where you were, making excuses, more or less pleading with them to stay because you couldn't be any more than another five minutes, another ten, and you so wanted to see them, have you any idea how that made me feel?'

'I—' He reached out to touch her, thought better of it, sitting back on his heels, apologising again, saying of course he appreciated all she had done that evening, all she did to help him all the time, which was why he had been late.

'A surprise. I was going to save it as a surprise, Minnette.'

There was a tone, a subtle twist in his voice that began worming, setting off doubts as it worked deeper, promising that, tomorrow, the day after perhaps, she would begin to suspect it had been she who had spoiled the evening and not him at all.

'What surprise?' Feeling very tired and wanting this over almost as much as she wanted another drink.

'We're going to travel. Egypt, Greece, Iran, the old places where magic is still alive. We'll search it out, find it at its source. Do you see, Minnette? Not in books but where it's alive, and, and in the air.'

Wondering if she was more drunk than she felt because, no matter how clear the words were, she failed to understand anything he was saying. Guillaume told her his plan again, enthusiasm forcing him to his feet so he could move between the serving dishes and empty wine bottles, repeating how wonderful it was going to be, an adventure, an exploration. And soon, too. They should go soon.

'But... I have finals, a dissertation—'

'Doesn't matter.'

'What?'

'No. Listen. Defer it. Pick it up when we come back.' He knelt in front of her, gripping her arms. 'None of it matters. It's not real anyway, it's a distraction. You said yourself how exhausted you are.'

'Well... yes.'

'You let it pull you in, distract you, make you forget what's important.'

'Graduating is important.'

'Of course. On one level.' He made eye contact, smiling, his face alive. 'But think of the things we talked about, all the things we've hoped to learn and experience. We can't do those here, buried in the day-to-day.'

'But...' Struggling to think and finding only deeper confusion.

'It's out there. All the wonderful and the... numinous. You know?'

Looking into Guillaume's eyes, unsure what her own expression must be, tar-like weight souring, acid flash something she didn't want to name.

'It has to be out there, I can't believe it's not, Minnette, and I want us to go and find it. Together.' Unmoving as he wrapped his arms around her, hug awkward. 'Don't you think it's out there, waiting for us?'

They didn't speak for much longer, letting him help her up as he apologised again, guided, half-carried her to bed, turning off the lights in the flat as he went, the book Israel Regardie on its stand, quite forgotten.

Asking if she had heard of him, this Englishman, as he unlocked the door, standing back to let her go into the flat, Minnette standing uncertainly in the hallway as he closed the door, excited to be here, sure this was going to be the start of something, hoping that might be so at any rate, and shaking her head, shrugging, saying she had heard something, rumours, things in passing, which was true, not thinking she should mention the letters because there had been no reply, at least not to the first or second, and the third, the fourth, the fifth, they were, they were too… not sure how to think of them, what the right description might be, but sure the letters weren't, couldn't possibly be worth— 'He seems interesting, his ideas, you see, yes?' the German led her into a small kitchen, offered to take her coat, hanging it on a hook behind the door as he asked if she would like cake, a cup of tea, the day being rather cold he thought, did she think it was cold? which she had to agree it was, happy to have tea, cake, hand resting on the back of a kitchen chair, taking its weight, ready to sit at the small table, the German shaking his head, indicating she should go through to the lounge, offering two different sorts of cake, wondering if she would be so kind as to remind him whether she preferred milk in her tea, pipes knocking as he filled the kettle, telling her about the little shop where he bought teas of various sorts, the neighbour who had baked the cake, a charming person, a Polish refugee who had come to the West at the end of the '60s, the election of this actor, Reagan, to become American President a disturbing turn of events—relaxing a little, words washing over as she agreed and stepped through the connecting door into the lounge, wondering if this meant the German might have accepted her, lunch, dinner, their meeting this afternoon resulting in him inviting her here, to his flat, all that, she thought, all this must mean he had—

'Not to say I have doubts, or distrust, you must understand, my dear, but this Englishman…'

The German looked at her, Minnette pausing on the threshold between the two rooms.

'Make contact. Discuss. Consider. Enquire. These are things we must do. Yes?'

Frowning, because this was too much like he knew she was in contact with the magician in the north of England. Frowning because that couldn't be the case.

'With caution. Of course.'

Trying to erase the frown in case it was misinterpreted. In case it was too much like an admission.

'And then we must choose. Yes?'

Finding an answer of some sort, struggling to keep the conversation moving, mumbling about hoping all that might be so, or that she wasn't sure, was too inexperienced yet, was only just beginning her studies, talking, talking, talking. Taking a breath. Thanking him for the slice of cake he handed her. Not moving, plate resting in her hand, the German going back into the kitchen with the words: 'And then we must choose. Unless a path chooses us.'

Giving the scoop a shake, shovelling chips into a bag. Steam condensed on the chip shop's window, runnels forming. Giving the scoop a shake, shovelling chips into a bag. Rain hitting the outside of the chip shop's window, runnels forming. Giving the scoop a shake, shovelling chips into a bag. Fat crackling. Customers waiting. Fat spitting. A queue. The radio repeating the same song. A dog, shape indistinct beyond the steam. A queue forming. Bark repeating. Headlights dull. Headlights stronger, flashing in the rain, brake lights flaring, dying, flaring, dying. Giving the scoop a shake, Minnette shovelled chips into a bag. Tears brimming at the corner of each eye, runnels forming.

'The world,' the magician told her again, told her again, told her again, told her again, told her again, told her again, 'the world is only what we see and we see only what we believe.'

The manager looked, doubt shading into scepticism, discomfort, as he pulled a large handkerchief from the pocket of this trousers, watching her closely as he finished wiping the inside of each nostril and shook his head.

'I don't think any of my customers are going to be thinking about that. They just believe in you giving them chips when they ask for them, alright?'

Nowhere to go that morning. Lying in bed. Listening: dim noises filtering through the floorboards from the flat below, the chip shop below that; traffic noise; ebbing; surging; pigeons outside the window, picking at the window ledge, cooing, maundering obsessively; no rain. No rain. Seeing: faintly yellow light through the curtains, sun presumably half-uncovered somewhere over the city, no clear idea of where east was in relation to bedsit, window, bed. Staring at the ceiling. Thinking: *get on with some reading.* Telling herself she would get on with some reading, would get up and make coffee, sit and drink, stand again, tidy the bedsit, read, make notes, start. Start the day, she told herself, thinking she might sleep an hour or so more, being tired, being for the best as she would not be able to concentrate on reading, making notes, starting the day. Turning over. Feeling mattress against shoulders, sheets and blankets and one foot peeking out at the end of the bed. Cold. Lying on her back and conscious of sounds and, assuming without thinking that the sounds meant the city was moving around the building, around the bedsit, around her lying on her back, a door closing, footsteps clumping closer, receding, no one on the staircase, a voice, perhaps a voice above or below and a cat, mew soft, risers creaking, footsteps pausing in the hallway outside, her door a shape at the edge of her eye, silence drawing out, enough to make her wonder if she had drifted off, slept, missed her unknown neighbour climbing down to the street door, silence on the landing. Almost silence. There was always some noise in a city. Everywhere. Minnette stared at the ceiling without moving.

The pay-phone in the hallway finally stopped ringing.

Unconsciously relaxing. She would get up after another moment or two, go out, start the day, look for work that was better than the chip shop, a second-hand bookshop, say, read in a café for a while, walk, get up, start the day she promised herself.

The pay-phone in the hallway began ringing again.

There was nowhere to go, muscles growing stiff, staring at the ceiling, listening to the noises through the floorboards, the window, a bus, a lorry, lying in bed without making any further movement, Minnette told herself.

The magician followed her on to the bus. 'You're frightened.'

'No, I'm not.' Sitting, getting up and changing seats, pushing past him as he tried to sit beside her again. Ending up at the back.

The magician sat in the last but one row, legs in the gangway. Facing out the side window. Windowlight glinting from the corner of the eye nearest her. Glinting as his eye moved.

'You're not? Then why hide?'

'I'm not hiding.' She stared out the opposite window.

'You don't answer the phone, don't come to study any more, leave places when I walk in, cross the road if you see me—'

'I'm not frightened.'

'Then why hide?'

Not listening. Not answering. Only the view out of the window sliding, shifting, lurching as it changed. And a vague anxiety about where the bus was going.

Pausing at the foot of the staircase. Hand resting on the Yale lock. Taking a breath. Before opening the door to the street. Snow last night. Falling into the road, road silent, cars vanishing, white line showing the snow where to go, white line white snow white breath against the window glass, cold radiating, draft slipping through the tight-closed window, cold fingers, breath misting window window misting snow snow making everything fade malleable slip impermanent snow falling over— Snow over and already slushy, gutters running with grimy melt-water that looked like lead under the morning overcast. Minnette stepped out, tugging the front door closed, a sharp yank, wood swollen, a bad fit. Pulling up the bike jacket's collar. Hunching. Looking at slush mixed with smears of dog shit. At litter fighting its way to the top of a waning snow drift around the base of the bus stop. Glimpsing the empty litter-bin strapped to the bus stop's pole as she walked past. Boots uncertain on the melt, balance equivocal. Eyes on toecaps, on the pavement. Seeing winter boots stained by slush and dirty snow, the white training shoes of a boy in school uniform. Watching the boy searching for a stretch of compacted snow long enough to slide on properly. Glancing: slate-blue numbers on her digital watch; Doc Marten's navigating the pavement; a gobbet of slush riding on the toecap. Checked her watch again, time not registering previously; hour early enough there was no rush, no urgency. Go to the supermarket, or a Wimpy bar. Go to the indoor market. Although that required a bus journey, a wait at either end beside a post with litter around it and an empty bin girdled to its waist. But no urgency to get back here, to the bedsit, to the chip shop, to do the lunchtime shift. Picking up pace anyway. Watching each step because the pavements were treacherous, because it made sense to, considering how quickly she needed to get to the shops and back, keeping her eyes down as she walked, walking faster, eyes always carefully down, not trying to see anything on the periphery, blanking the corner of each eye, not wanting distraction, avoiding registering anything because anything might cause a reflexive twitch, head and eyes moving before the movement could be stopped, eyes registering something, anything that might be around, anything that might be out there, eyes and brain acting together to interpret, form shapes and patterns and so she concentrated on putting one boot in front of the next and avoiding ice and slush and skids of dog shit and litter and feet and ankles or trouser cuffs, seeing only what was immediately in front of her, only that. Because anything else might be dangerous.

Standing in the middle of the playground again. Youths missing from the climbing frame, a biting wind flicking a crushed beer can against the tubular steel uprights. The magician asking: 'What do you see?' and turning in response, slowly, once around, taking in rubbish, spray paint and marker pen, ice clinging to the path-way, crisp packets stuck to the railings.

'Nothing.'

A narrow corridor led from the side door to a small lounge bar at the rear of the pub. Slipping through the door ahead of him, picking up pace on hearing the magician follow the corridor in the opposite direction, towards the toilets. Only one light ever worked along here: navigation by the feel of dog-ends underfoot, the smell of cigarette smoke and stale beer from the bar hidden beyond an abrupt angle in the wall, bend masking the low-wattage bulb hanging over the entrance to the lounge. It wasn't so dark it was difficult to walk. Minnette's pace quickened.

A door opened, shaft of light cutting through the gloom as the rattle of bottles in a plastic crate underscored a gruff voice mangling Madness's 'It Must Be Love'. The publican's shadow fell across the width of the corridor, silhouette filling the doorway.

'Oh, sorry, love, didn't see you there.' He hefted the crate of mixers, closing the stockroom door and standing to one side. 'On you go.'

When, ten seconds later, she hadn't moved, he rolled his eyes, stepping around her without another word.

Minnette, attention fixed on the now-closed door, didn't notice.

'It comes down, mind, to will: to see—' the magician waved his half-empty pint glass, indicating the far side of the small lounge bar, the rest of the city on the other side of the etched glass window— 'is to believe strongly enough to see, something most people just take on trust. Or don't know what they're doing. See?'

Nodding. Even though she wasn't listening any too closely. Even though she was actually not looking at the magician, his waving glass, the interior of the nearly-full lounge at all. Looking between wandering patrons, across intervening tables. To the door to the corridor.

Pale fingers turning, turning, turning the empty pint glass by quarter turns. The magician sitting back. 'Now do you understand?'

The fruit machine trilled, paid out. Coins vomiting from its mouth to the cheers of the group of men swaying around it.

'Yeah, I understand.' Watching handfuls of coins stuffed into jeans pockets, jacket pockets. 'I understand but...' Coins dropped and retrieved by hands already full of coins. 'I understand what you're saying but there's more. Isn't there?'

The magician sighed, giving a pitying look. 'You only *believe* I'm wrong. It's... everything, a state of mind: will and belief, there's only will and belief and nothing beyond that than what we shape and believe. Only that. Nothing else, nothing concrete, nothing *true*— You see? No 'true', only belief in 'truth'. Right?'

Shaking her head, watching coins being dropped into the fruit machine, tumblers spinning, the group swaying as brightly lit symbols clicked into place, cheering, heckling, tumblers spinning again, coins still held in their hands or tipped into drained pint glasses until they were needed to go back into the fruit machine, always the next go, the next after that.

'No.' Shaking her head firmly, appearing certain, argument more stubborn posturing than reasoned thread. Unspooling that thread, thinking: *This is true because because*

because because I say—and not sure whether that was what she meant or if that was what was so, *This is true because I believe*—and being firm about that as the argument roved, turned, turned back on itself, became a silent dead end, the magician getting another round of drinks, launching into an analysis of her personality, Minnette having failed to understand anything, to truly see what was happening and what had happened and what could happen, Minnette acting on nothing more than prejudice and fear and closed-mindedness, Minnette stupid in a way he hadn't thought she could be when he had agreed to teach her, Minnette staring at him as he talked and provoked, and maintaining her belief that all he was saying was wrong, maintaining her belief in her belief even if that belief, if that belief, if…

Shovelling chips into a bag. Never answered the pay phone in the hall. Listening to him telling her again, telling her again, telling her… Keeping belief. Keeping silent. Keeping the blue, marbled notebook on the window ledge where it was impossible to miss. Listening to him. Keeping silent. Not stubborn. Belief. Having belief. Keeping that belief. Keeping—
    'What is it you've seen?'
    Keeping silent.

The pay phone kept ringing.
    Lying on the bed. Listening: dim noises filtering through the floorboards, from above, from below; traffic noise: surging, ebbing, surging; rain. Seeing: sodium light through the curtains, sun presumably somewhere else in the world, light streaking and running; seeing rain at second-hand; seeing the ceiling first-hand. Thinking. Telling herself. Closing her eyes. Listening: dim noises filtering, traffic noise ebbing, surging; rain. Pay phone ringing. Frown of concentration deepening. Seeing: shapes probing the darkness under her eyes. Hearing dim noises, muffled, mute traffic ebbing, rain… No rain, dim noises dimmer, ebbing. No rain. Frown of concentration

deepening. Smelling: hot chip fat, faintly; the old rug beside the bed, musty: faintly; disinfectant block, seeping, scent seeping through the lath and plaster and old paint and older wallpaper of the wall between the bedsit—fading—and the communal toilet next door—fading—frown of concentration deepening, feel of the much-washed purple nylon sheets and rucked blankets above and around, purple sheets beneath lower back and shoulders and buttocks... fading, against her body, her body against pillow and mattress... frown of concentration deep.

The phone no longer—

The curry house was already half-full, more people coming up the narrow staircase from the street, people heading the other way, conversation hauling itself over the sitars pumped through speakers drooping from balding flock wallpaper, plastic table cloths sticky under sheets of white butcher's paper dropped protectively over each table, elbows rucking the paper, lager glasses staining the paper, room hot, room narrowed by conversation, voices pumped against flock paper going bald, carpet black in the light from lamps on each table, table lamps staring fixedly at steaming plates: prawn pathia tandoori chicken lamb vindaloo with extra rice, rice on the carpet looking white, wriggling in under the lamps mounted on the walls the lamps mounted on either side of the entrance to the kitchen, curtain swinging, stirring air and conversation voices whispering, rising-falling laughter tasting of fizzy lager and cumin fizzy lager and fenugreek, sitar and shennai hauling themselves into the room falling-rising elbows wriggling in the light from tables, shadows clotting a floor looking black, lamps shining dim, rice on the carpet looking white in the half-light lamps on either side of cutlery hotplates sizzling litany gone to pieces, voices overlapping lapping at plates at lager going flat at wine by the glass at tables lining each wall narrowing, to become shadows scented and shifting under the warm light mounted beside the sounds of litany or sitar or cutlery slicing rice scented with cardamom spilling across a carpet that looked hard as stone, rice looking like frost coating the narrow aisle winding through the half-full curry house.

The middle-aged woman from across the corridor, with the lacquered hair and mole on her lip hidden by layers of powder, came out when she heard the door opening and asked do you know, lovey, if the 'phone is working, pointing to the pay-phone screwed to the wall beside the stairhead, because I tried it this morning, you know, the middle-aged woman with the lacquered hair gesturing towards the silent pay-phone screwed to the cracked plaster beside the top of the next flight of stairs, and it was silent, you know, no dial tone or anything and I suddenly thought it might be, you know, one of those new ones, the middle-aged woman from the flat opposite gripped the high neck of her sweater, fingers white against the black, no, call it Davy's grey or anthracite or black olive or onyx, fingers pale against the wool, knuckles pinker, hallway cold, no snow outside, not yet, no snow but cold, fingers smarting, hands hanging as the middle-aged woman continued one of the sort you put money in first, you know, do you have pay-phones in Paris, it is Paris isn't it, I always wanted to, you know, go there but, well, anyway I tried putting in money and still the 'phone didn't do anything, hallway taking both hands, a draft working up the twist of the stairs, one flight, the next, working its way up from the front door to take both hands, hands cold, smarting, don't worry, though, squeezing the high neck of her woollen sweater, fingers white against the dark, don't worry, I got my money back, lovey, the woman from the flat opposite laughing high and short, the kind of laugh someone nervous should make, cold air beginning to seep through skin and flesh, bones aching, knuckles turning red, laughing again, looking away, glancing back and, yes, looking away again, blinking so, so I was wondering if you knew if it's out of order or what, because I was expecting, the woman with the lacquered hair licking lips red with lipstick and her lips will be thin, not bloodless exactly, but pale like her face under powder, flawless under lipstick and opening to take a breath, to ask, having heard the door open, did you hear it the other day, on and off for days it was, ringing, wrong number I suppose, seeing the woman with the pale, thin face hug herself, hallway draughty, the woman with the pale, thin face hugging herself, hallway draughty, draft brushing hands, cold working in, bones beginning to ache, concentrating too hard to spare a thought to make them stop although stopping them aching should be easier, easier than a face pale, lips thin, a mole, than a—a flawless mouth forming the words on and off I was told, lips thin as the woman nodded lacquered hair, head beneath, not that I was in all the time, of course, ligaments and tendons shifting, seeing that a fraction before, aware of the draft gripping her hands, ligaments and tendons shifting under skin thin enough to let veins show purple, but I heard it and I thought it was quite frightening, you know, because honestly, you hear things, don't you, hear about things happening these days, don't you, watching as this woman paused, making the pause into which she tilted her head and, no, she won't try to make eye contact, that wouldn't be right, her gaze strays off a little to one side, lacquered hair and thin, pale skin under overhead light under powder, continuing, as she should, when the pause was long enough, and I thought, hands white and lips pale under lipstick, I thought it was disturbing, you know, laughing again, sound brittle in the hallway, a confirmation that the next thing should be a shrug, seeing the middle-aged woman shrug, draft gripping both hands tightly, squeezing, hard to keep all the threads going, the corridor, the single light overhead, the 'phone, now silent, now mounted inside a small hood on top of a narrow shelf at the head of the next flight of stairs, the middle-aged woman from the other flat giving a laugh, rueful, unsurprised, when she should have shrugged, expecting a shrug, the image real in mind, under hair dark and cut short, under scalp growing tighter, under bone, and now it didn't seem to be working at all, hands aching, have you any idea, have you tried to use it, head tight, have you heard, relief coming as both hands buried into jeans pockets, shoulders hunching into a shrug, zips on the bike jacket giving a tiny rattle, a tiny rattle as shrug ended.

'I don't know anything about the 'phone,' Minnette told the woman from the flat opposite, stepping towards the stairs leading down to the street, 'I've never used it. Sorry.'

The curry house was becoming full, people coming up the narrow staircase, laughing, waving, filling vacant seats, chairs' feet stumbling, dragging menus, taking menus and making jokes, stereo speakers offering sitar music, offering popadoms and lime pickle, crumbs finding space on the white sheet of butcher's paper protecting the plastic table cloth protecting the table that creaked a little as elbows and crumbs fell on it, chairs creaking, raita white on lips, speckling, making no other sound on the carpet that looked black, cutlery and a glass and a woman's voice talking about Les Dawson, a man's voice masked by someone across the table, reaching across the table for pickle, his wife turning to the waiter, shadows clotting the flock peeling from the walls, pen over pad, another tray of pickles, table full, an arm reaching, apology turning into a question, question stirring, stirring to be interrupted, waiter looking, waiting with pen poised, crumbs dotting the paper across the table nothing like rice, like frost, nothing left in her glass and agreeing that, yes, another lager would be good, room hot, room narrow, black, elbows rucking paper and, yes, another—waiter telling everyone he would be right back, enjoy, fizzy lager and the smell of mango chutney, missing a joke and laughing because everyone else at this end of the table laughed, air hot humid hotplates steam fragrant enough to be incense, table leg, that woman's knee, table full, pressing round her, curtain litany whispering tamarind, laughing louder, room full and hard to concentrate, white paper faces, faces leaning across the table, laughing because everyone laughed, sweat clammy and mouth filled, lime, chilli, sour and metal-threaded, woman's knee on one side, husband leaning across the table to talk, words smothered in cutlery and glass and other tables' conversations under sitar music as he nodded, reply making everyone laugh, not laughing but watching.

The magician did not look up from his starter.

sitting back and watching him through closed lids and seeing shadow and seeing a wall and seeing a shadow move as light moved as she saw I know what it is you saw whispered I know seeing him through closed lids become almost nothing but shadow and no light not moving as she whispered to him as the German fell silent as the German whispered whisper whisp

The pay-phone would remain silent.

The present had used up all her money: that was how it should be remembered.

Pigeons no longer spoke, no longer sat on the bedsit's window ledge.

He had betrayed her: that was how it had been.

The notebook with the blue marbled covers lay on the table, the table stood beside the window, the window let in light, the light grey or sodium or streaked with rain, the rain fell, turned to snow, turned to nothing.

The artist in Nivelles had been an acquaintance, friend of a member of the band: that was all it had been.

Rug beside the bed, toilet, room across the hall... the room across the hall was silent, probably vacant.

The German had been a nice man who bought her a sandwich and waved when she got on the bus and had said goodbye: that was all he had said.

Books lay open beside the bed, bed lying beside the books and the books and the bed lying beside the pen, pens, blue and black and red, ends clotted with dried ink because they leaked because they were never used.

Stomach 'flu, coming back from the Aegean before their trip had really begun, plane landing in Naxos and getting sick: that was exactly what she remembered.

Notebook forgotten, pigeons silent, pay phone always silent, toilet, room across the hall, fat sputtering in the chip shop on the ground floor, notebook—

She had filled the notebook with these truths. Just as she was asked. Just as was necessary to make them truths: the city, the light, the pigeons that had whispered to her as she had dreamt, the rug, the landlord and the bedsit, the bedsit and the pay phone, the pay phone and the silence, the silence and the chip shop, the chip shop and—

The chips were always the same.

Foot of the staircase, Yale lock submitting with a twist, breath exhaling to reveal the door opening to reveal the street as it had been in the image held in mind during the slow descent, one step at a time, feeling each step, a creak underfoot, each creak heard a fraction of a moment before sound was conjured from stair.

Minnette re-called a dream of wan light, air cold.

Saw: rime of frost along the curb, a Highland Toffee wrapper clinging to the gutter, chip papers made waterproof by grease, a litter-bin beside the chip shop's entrance, an orange Cresta can, sides squeezed together, lying at an angle, an angle of... at an angle to the litter-bin. All seen in a single glance.

Felt: door handle, brass smoothed by use, cold against skin, skin and bone and ligament and muscle and tendon. Door swollen. A bad fit. Sharp yank, tugging the front door closed. All experienced in a series of instants.

No sound. Except traffic—a yellow van, exhaust coughing, the 07:51 bus running three minutes late next in line, a dented brown Austin Princess lurching to a halt behind that—and the shout of two school kids running down the opposite pavement, arms and legs with that elastic, dis-coordinated motion of young teens, purple blazers under arctic parkers and Adidas bags flapping against their backs. Seen and heard in the time taken to take a single breath tasting of exhaust fumes and frost and the lingering scent of the chip shop.

This was all as she had visualised.

Walking. Hunching, pulling— No.

Walking. Pulling up the leather jacket's collar. Hunching: a clear image of hunching against the cold. But not looking down. She would not keep her eyes down today. She would look up, the image—of herself, hands buried in jacket pockets, hunched against the cold, yes, but walking with her head up—this image very clear in mind, in memory, in mind and memory: Minnette would walk down the road, looking up to see the litter-bin strapped to the bus stop, pavement underneath bare, no litter, no dog shit today...

Minnette looked up as she walked down the road. Seeing the litter-bin strapped to the bus stop. Pavement underneath—

Frowning. Seeing the image, the memory. Remembering: staircase, Yale lock, door swollen, but silent —she had overlooked the sound of it closing—traffic, slate-blue numbers on her digital watch showing the time, and the white of training shoes, a boy playing truant; no: seeing two boys running running to school this time because it was going to be morning, glancing at the slate-blue numbers on her digital watch and thinking: *The bus is four minutes late this morning*, visualisation clear and sharp, seeing the bus stop, the queue at the bus stop, the pavement clear of litter and shit, litter *in* the litter-bin this morning.

This was all as visualised.

Minnette looked up as she walked down the road: bus stop, bus queue, litter-bin strapped to the pole, at its base —

The bus pulled up to the stop.

Doors would hiss, first person in the queue making a joke as she climbed up the steps, bus driver's voice hidden inside traffic noise, the shouts from those two thirteen year-olds, but there would be the suspicion of a laugh.

The bus pulled up to the stop, the woman at the head of the queue making a joke with the driver as she climbed on board, the driver laughing.

Minnette glanced at her watch. *The bus is four minutes late this morning*, she thought. Glancing at her watch. The time was among the slate-blue numbers.

Frowning.

Re-calling a pavement hard underfoot, a wall. Dismissing both.

Only what had been visualised. Only that. Minnette looking up and around as she walked away from the bus stop, air cold against her face, shoulders hunching under leather, remembering how the hunch and tension of the muscles should feel, feeling the bunch and tension of the muscles. The pavement would be hard underfoot, unyielding. The pavement was hard underfoot. The light this morning would be grey, but a paler grey because the sky would have cleared overnight, been very clear overnight night, enough to cause frost, but a front would have moved in at around 06:21, bringing light cloud and light breeze, and the city would be there, around her as she walked down the road, the chip shop out of sight but, surely, definitely, still there, still existing because she remembered and saw it in her mind and remembering and seeing it in her mind made it exist, the city existing even though she could never see it all, remember it in any detail, but it too had to remain if she kept it in mind.

A dream of wan light, air cold. A pavement hard underfoot, a wall.

Minnette would walk down the road. She had visualised that.

Wan light, air cold. A pavement hard underfoot, a wall. She had seen...

Nothing could cease to exist. Not if there was remembrance, the weight of it in mind.

Wan. Cold. Hard underfoot. Wall.

Minnette looked at the city. Feeling its expanse, its weight, its detail. Feeling its solidity.

It was true because—

It was in existence because—

It was wan, cold, hard underfoot, wall long and air cold.

No snow but frost.
It was frosty this morning.
As she had thought it would be.

The curry house was becoming empty, people going down the narrow staircase, laughing, hands trailing over balding flock wallpaper, leftovers and takeaway in silver boxes, in grease-stained bags, making jokes, footfalls hollow, covered by sitar music, crumbs on the carpet, carpet dark, air humid, stretching, lingering too long. Paper beside her plate empty, perfect in its way, untouched by tikka sauce, by pickle smears, by the crumbs that lay dark against the paper's face elsewhere. Hand resting in the patch of almost white, table taking on the cast of the room, wan light tinged, humid and warm, air of the long, narrow room straining a little more, spinning on, conversations spinning on, another beer? another glass of brandy? any more ice cream? Nearly-empty plates, stained, streaked, picked over, debating the possibility of another bottle of wine or going home or all going to someone's home because the evening had been a classic. Finger tracing a path across the white. Wasn't the evening a classic? Finger tip finding itself in mid-air.

'Yes—' looking up from the paper beside her plate—'it's been great.'

'You seem like—'

'Oh, just tired. Working at the shop. All that.'

Head moving involuntarily towards the magician. Seated at the opposite end of the table, he was leaning forward towards the young woman perched awkwardly at the table's head, making a comment, young woman giving a titter, titter drowned in a gulp of lager.

Minnette felt herself watching: lager glass resting a moment against the young woman's bottom lip; lager glass descending through air that was stained with lamplight and humid and close, warm in fact; young woman swallowing, neck muscles moving in concert; lager glass meeting the table, resting there, cupped by one of the young woman's hands, the other resting over its mouth. Sealing it shut.

And, while watching, aware of a pressure in her gut. And thinking she shouldn't have had prawn pasanda after all. And remembering; something. And turning to the couple sitting beside her and smiling and feeling that the smile was a mask or a sketch or an accident or a deliberate thing she was creating just in this moment, an instant where what she was about to say—that she felt fine but tired and yes, she had enjoyed the evening, it was good to get out, to have an evening off, she had enjoyed it, really —was real, a truth that couldn't be contradicted, a thing that was certain.

'Sorry. I'm very tired.'

Minnette's face arranged itself into an expression she could not predict. The wife reached out, patted her hand. Hand leading her into a debate, squeezing wrist before letting go and hanging in the air as a ragged alliance formed around vanilla ice cream, coffee and brandy. Minnette looked at her wrist. At the wife's hand. Nodded yes, yes to more coffee or ice cream or brandy. Yes was as good as no: words not forming inside her mind, only a mood that might have been summarised by those words.

She caught herself looking down the table, towards the magician.

Looked at the white, perfect paper beside her plate.

Hand dropping. Feeling around the back of the chair. Searching until it found the shoulder bag she had brought with her that evening. Finding a way inside, inside of the bag misdirecting her, confusing hand and whatever else might be connected to it.

The barrel of the ball point pen felt chill against the fingers of the hand.

Minnette looked at the pen a moment. Did not look towards the magician. Thanked the waiter when he brought whatever she had ordered. Minnette saw that it was tea. The steam rising from the cup told her it was mint tea. And she discovered that she did remember ordering a mint tea after all.

The ball point pen stopped moving.

A series of lines lay across the no longer perfect white paper. Minnette added some more. Thinking nothing. Watching someone else make a grid-work of clotted blue ink. A maze unwound from the grid lines. Pen digging deep into the paper. Deciding what should be on the paper where there had been nothing before the pen came along. Corridors with unsteady walls, but walls that turned about themselves, winding, tighter, inescapable. At the heart of the labyrinth, letters small and overlapping, she saw the pen had left a message:

je ne l'ai jamais cru à toledo

She covered the writing, first with her hand, quickly dropping a napkin over plate and maze before glancing as casually as possible down the table.

The magician seemed interested in something else.
and yet he stopped her

a voice sounded

can i help
    can i help yo—

a touch on her shoulder light spilling across the pavement could pretend to be lost are you lost voice someone playing a joke shadow larger two more strides before the hand brushed broader wider looking as he added

Minnette turned

'Piss off, will you?'

Slipping from under his hand, Doc Marten's thumping on the stairs.

'We need to—'

'I'm tired, I've got a bad stomach, I've got an interview for a job tomorrow, I want to go home.'

'You never mentioned a job interview.' Voice neither indignant nor exactly neutral.

An over-long stride, awkwardly on to the tiny vestibule's floor. Balance retained by grasping the handle of the front door. 'I don't tell you everything.'

'No. That's right.' Feet hitting the stairs, following, becoming louder, heavier, faster.

She spun, sure he about to crash into her, back pressing against the front door's handle as he stopped, one foot on the last step, other on the scuffed tiles of the curry house's postage-stamp-sized vestibule.

'You saw something.' Leaning towards her, voice low, insistent, face dipped into deep shadow by the short length of fluorescent light above them. 'In London. At the end of the ritual. You saw something. I put it down to tiredness, emotion.' The magician rested a hand against the front door, close enough to smell vindaloo and lager on his breath, cigarette smoke on his clothes. 'I was wrong.'

'No. Piss off.' Reaching behind her, shoulder straining as her hand searched for the door handle, searched for leverage, having to lean closer to him for the door to begin to open, aware of the smell of him, warmth of being so close. 'I didn't see anything.'

'Oh.' The magician standing back. Face falling, realising he had made a mistake, shoulders dropping as he stepped back on to the stairs, let her open the door, feet almost tangling, almost falling into the street, dank night air gripping her face, making her eyes smart but stopping her from looking anywhere but up the road, not back, she was not going to look back or say anything, only to keep walking, keep going.

'So,' the magician shouted after her, voice breaking the cold's grip, forcing her to turn against her will, 'what do you believe in now?'

He held up a scrap of paper tablecloth.

Mouth opening. Wanting flip or sarcastic or plain angry. And nothing there in mind or throat or mouth. Nothing but *what she had seen...*

'What was there to believe in, in Toledo?' Curry house door swinging shut. Torn paper moving in the breeze, knowing the cold had been real, it had dug deep into her shoulders, her hands, feet aching from it as much from so long walking, running from... *what she had seen*... The magician taking another stride towards her, pavement not seeming to give, bend: a solid pavement: but then, she had known the street was real, that pavement and all the others, the small bricks and stone sets and mortar between, that had pressed against her feet, bruising, making bones and muscles tired from running from *what she had seen*... Magician taking yet another stride, getting close enough that she could reach out and, if he was solid under her hand, know he was real, although she had known that, had felt, rather, that she was real, because of the cold, because of the exhaustion, because of the weight of the tasselled bag digging into her shoulder, the bag she had been carrying since leaving the boy and the bed and the house, bag so heavy after carrying it so long that it made it hard to think, shoulders sore and aching and feeling real, the ache had made her feel real, after *what she had seen*, and the city had been cold, bitter as the pale flush had spread across the horizon, strengthened as a new winter's day became a little firmer, a little more... real.

'What was in Toledo?'

Sounds of a car in the distance, another a little after that, sporadic, groggy in the pre-dawn. Empty street with one, two, three lights showing behind curtains or leaking out the crack between closed shutters, street still sleeping, still— But not her, she hadn't been dreaming. Numb. Cold. But numb because of, of shock and, through the numbness, very distant, there had been a desperation, the knowing that she had to find a place to get warm, get food, get sleep, but not dream, *what she had seen, if that*— but she knew, had known, she wasn't dreaming as she walked, so, so—

'What's in—'

'A castle.' Snapping and still sounding weak, Indian meal heavier in her gut, turning to acid. 'You should go. The old town's...' Vomit burning at the base of her throat, mind silent, refusing to voice the rest of the thought and knowing and hearing it anyway as she had hobbled: *She wasn't dreaming, not just* then, *not as she walked, but perhaps she had been* earlier *and, if she had been earlier, then perhaps, after all, she still* was. 'The old town's nice to walk through.'

Pushing the torn paper tablecloth closer to her face. 'Why write this?'

Everything had felt real. But it had felt real earlier, when she had seen... And she felt cold. But, stepping into the glow of the lanterns had felt warm, so what did that— It had looked familiar: sleeping street, parked cars, telegraph poles fading into the half-light, buildings, a bus stop—

'What's it matter?' Snatching at the doodle. Missing. Hand trembling, pulse sounding in her ears, sensations sharp and vivid and tangible and smelling spicy, air touched with musk. Wiping her nose on her thumb. Sniffing hard. Air too cold to smell of anything. Except memory, strong and concrete. 'No reason.' Making another grab. Missing, the magician moving his hand at the last instant. Scrap of paper flashing in the light from the nearest streetlamp, flash of white materialising another memory. Making her—

'Give me that fucking thing, I'm fucking sick—'

Making her stretch out her hand.

'What did you see in London?'

The magician holding the doodle behind his back.

Fingers outstretched.

'Nothing.'

Turning sharply away from him. Walking quickly. Hunching deeper into her jacket, hands fisted inside pockets, leather creaking, wheezing as she walked, heavy boot soles thumping against pavement, echoes hard-edged, aware of her memories—street transformed and warm light and the flash of falling masonry—boot soles thumping, echo doubling, thrusting through the edge of vision—

'What was there in Toledo?'

The magician keeping pace.

'I don't know.' She felt cold. Warm earlier. Acid spreading. All this familiar. Trying not to look at the magician, trying to concentrate, memories—

'So there was something?' The magician leaning forward so it was hard not to see him.

'No.' Hard to concentrate. Make this go away. Hand jerking from pocket, involuntary. Fingers spreading. 'Nothing. There wasn't anything.'

'But you saw something in London? Something we didn't expect? Something that came after the Working, something that manifested because of the Working?'

Fingers meeting nothing but cold air, darkness salted with damp and the wrong sort of light, street lights harsh, gritty, too white, not what she had in her head. 'How should I know?' Belief and memory and certainty and step lost in the double-footfall of rubber sole and leather, in questions and answers condensing on air that felt only superficially the same. 'Look, will you fuck off?' Trying to walk faster. Starting to limp. 'My stomach's killing me. I'm tired. I have to work tomorrow.'

'I thought it was a job interview. What was it in Toledo?'

Leeds growing sleepy. (Toledo had slept.) Dark, solid. (Dark, solid. It had waited.) Waiting. But solid.

'What's it to you?' Car engine (there had been a car engine, attenuated by brittle air, distance indeterminate) dank air smothering the sound, starter motor grinding (had whinged, sleepy and reluctant to wake). Car accelerating away, a street away. 'Just fuck off. I've had enough of this.'

Turning sharply. Stepping into the road without looking. (It had been deserted at that time of night.) The magician beside her each step. Taking an uncertain diagonal path across the road. Not sure (had not been sure) what (what to feel), where to go.

'Why are you hiding?'

Hand in front of her. Shivering growing worse, tremor forcing jaw tight, breath short and road wider than expected. Path weaving, fingers searching. 'Just fuck off.

I've had enough of this Moonie act of yours. I'm not your slave.' Vision blurring, beginning to draw in at the periphery. A shadow moving closer.

'I'm supposed—' catching toecap on kerb, stumbling onto the pavement, hand in front and fingers splayed, fingers searching and finding— 'I'm supposed to be your pupil.'

'Supposed?' The magician's voice low. 'Supposed?' Not harsh, not gentle. Not the voice. 'That's about right though, isn't it? Because you don't trust this, any of it, not what we're doing, not what I'm demonstrating. You don't trust that this is real magic, do you?'

Stopping. Turning so he had to step back. Hand outstretched. 'But that's just it.' Screaming. 'None of this is real.'

Stretching out a hand. Fingers splaying.

Meeting resistance. Brushing along the sandstone wall she was walking beside.

It ran, the wall, unbroken, for most of the length of the road, exterior wall of a building that was little more than a dark shape rising: a sense of mass against fading indigo, sky flushed to the east but still quite dark, night over but lingering on, lingering in the cold and the shadows and in the tiredness and the wall, wall real, as real as the laundrette window as the washing machines as the car engine as shivering as turning round sharply as the city sleeping as exhaustion as memories of the party and the café and the boy as the street, wall cold and rough, wall making her fingers throb as she bumped their tips along its face, face solid and cold and rough and as real as clammy palms as a road wider than expected as real as whispering and shadows tasting of musk as real as a sense of mass fading into indigo.

Minnette sniffed. Walked slowly down the road. One hand trailing along the wall. What she had seen a tremor, an insistence, a numbness, a blank. Pavement ahead sparkling faintly, air casting needles against her face. Shivering. Heel slipping, balance thrown but not lost. Wall guiding. Not minding how lost in thought she was, that one foot was blistered and ached more than the other, that she favoured that side, hand trailing. Sniffing. Not noticing the heavy wooden door inset into the wall, metal *snick* of a latch opening, until light winnowed out, drawing a line across the pavement.

Halting. 'Hello?' Realising she had spoken in French, struggling to recall the Spanish. Door opening a little wider. Hinges softly creaking and letting more light on to the pavement. Minnette calling again. Limping another step closer.

Swathe widening a fraction, light stronger. Door near to silent and opening by itself. Dismissing that as impossible. Too tired to disagree with herself and limping another step. Stopping again when the shadow blocked some of the light falling across the pavement.

Only someone approaching the light, coming closer to the doorway. Not able to see inside from where she was standing. Seeing only shadow, light making a wedge of pavement shine.

'Hello?' Voice deep, not harsh but gentle. 'Hello, are you there?' A soft bass, coming from the open doorway and speaking French without any trace of accent. Managing another step, too small a movement to let her see all of the door, opening hidden by the recess it stood in. Leaning forward, still seeing nothing as she tried to reply, nothing coming out because her throat was too dry, trying to swallow, finding no spit, and her attention drawn to the shadow across the pavement as the voice came again, closer, a little louder although there was no sound of footsteps.

'Hello, are you there?'

Shadow slewing, growing bigger because whoever was casting it was closer to the light, but bigger because this person, this man, was big: tall, well-built, broad shoulders blocking more light and so looking bigger. Shoulders broad. And head.

Mouth opening. No sound, words in any language forgotten as Minnette watched the shadow, broad shoulders, broad head expanding.

'Are you lost?' Voice sounding almost at the threshold, shadow large, head wide, spreading further. 'Can I help?'

Minnette turned and ran.

Why did you leave him?

Walking around Nivelles. Town invisible. Concentrating on each other.

You loved him, didn't you?

Turnings taken and forgotten. House- and shop-faces blanks. Never to be filled in.

This boy you lived with for so long.

Artist's face turned towards hers. Hand against her thigh. Warmth of hip against hip. A finger trailing across palm, hands intertwined. Face close. His breath touching her lips.

You loved him. Why did you leave him?

'He left me,' Minnette replied, taking the artist's hand, kissing him until questions were forgotten.

Where are you going?

Two middle-aged women in rayon suits tutting to each other. Man looking up from his croque-monsieur, dandruff on the wide lapels of his suit. Two young girls with Farrah Fawcett-Majors haircuts. Turning in their seats to watch. Or heads coming closer, tutting. Waiter coming out of the café and pretending nothing was happening.

Answer me!

Old lady hefting a bulging shopping bag, stepping out the *tabac* next door to the café and freezing. Watching.

Where are you going?

Ignoring everything but the figure striding away.

I've not finished, you hear? Not finished telling—

One hand rising, falling sharply.

Just piss off then, I don't want to talk to you anyway, never want, never, ever want to see—

Falling in dismissal.

Months passing after that. Staying in Paris. Cutting off every tie, every acquaintanceship, those few bonds that had felt like friendship, Yves gone a year ago, to New York or Berlin, his last phone call confused, no one left anyway, no one not tainted, shocked at how deeply his life had absorbed and shaped her. Finding a room, another job. Cut off from parents, sister: no going back there and no help likely anyway. So the boring job typing for a notary that at least paid. Staying in Paris even when it seemed like there was nothing left but to go back to home town and parents. No idea if he had tried to find her, to make contact. Assuming he hadn't. Half wishing he had and thinking, instead, of going back to university, 'though that seemed impossible, perhaps pointless. There was no going back. It felt like there was no going back.

She put all her books up for sale, boxed them and took them to a bookshop in Montmartre, not far from where her new flat was. Sick of magic. The occult nothing to do with her. A nonsense. Fraud. Delusion. It lead nowhere, offered nothing.

There was no going back.

The owner smiled when Minnette went in, ducked behind the brocaded curtain hanging over the doorway behind the counter, came back less than a minute later, I put it to one side, she told Minnette, I didn't think you were totally certain when you came in before. Nodding thanks, sure she was blushing as the woman opened the door, Minnette leaving the shop and lugging the box of books back to her apartment.

He waited at the end of the corridor, ignoring the other students as they left the day's final class, shoulder against the wall until he spotted her, standing upright, not waving or shouting, simply looking.

Minnette turned in the opposite direction. Pretended not to notice Guillaume was following her. Pretended not to be thinking about the dinner party last night, what he had said afterwards.

Joined the tail end of a bus queue, no idea were the next bus was going. Stepping out of the queue—on a whim, not because he was there at the edge of her vision—crossing the road. Turning sharply back towards the University buildings.

A glimpse.

Ducking her head. Staring only at the feet of the people in front. Walking more quickly. Straining to walk fast, almost running. Trying not to run. Urge a hand between shoulder blades, urge fingers stroking her neck, cradling skull.

'We'll have to talk eventually.'

No. No, they didn't. They could go on as they were. There was the dissertation, the degree to finish, post-graduate work to find, because Minnette wanted to continue her studies, she wanted that now, definitely, heart and mind set on post-graduate study, on having things go on as they were. Going to the old places where magic was still in the air? There was no need for that. No sense to it, that's what she meant. Minnette nodding, nodding harder, taking the next turning: a narrow side-street, almost empty of pedestrians, almost no place to hide.

'Minnette.' Guillaume's footfalls loud, suddenly loud and directly behind, startling at seeing him at her shoulder when he had been metres back, in another street, shying as he touched her shoulder, touch heavy, touch not enough to slow her much. She could pretend to be lost in thought, to think it was someone playing a joke, about to molest her. It will be something terrible, she thought, managing two more strides before he took her arm, snagging the strap of her shoulder bag, pulling it, bag dropping, almost tangling her legs.

Minnette looked at him without speaking, hauling the bag on to her shoulder, fingers knotting the strap.

'We can't leave this as it is.'

Yes we can.

'This place, it's wrong for us. We have to travel. Search out what we've dreamed of.' Guillaume reached forward to take her arms. Changed his mind, spreading his hands instead. 'What we want is out there. We owe it to ourselves, to each other, to experience it.'

Magic didn't have to be far away. It could be 'round a corner, or—

'We do, Minnette.' Taking her shoulders, looking at her intently as she continued to avoid meeting his gaze. Stopping her chain of thought running any further. Because there was nowhere for it to run. Stepping back, his arms extending, unwilling to let her go as she took another small step, body turning, tensing, about to walk, to start walking, to walk—

'You can't run forever.'

A second passing. Another. And another and another and another. Body tensing, ready to pull free. Head moving a fraction. Just enough to see him from the corner of her eye.

Jerking the bedsit's door shut and hurrying across the hall, eyes downcast and thoughts… First three stairs downwards, stairs creaking and eyes downcast. Almost bumping into the BT engineer climbing upstairs. Engineer standing still, watching. Balance lurched back to stand over him.

'Sorry.'

'Sorry.'

Get out of each other's way, edge past. Stepping to the same side of the staircase.

'Sorry.'

'Sorry.'

Hesitating. Not looking the man in the face. Frowning.

'Thanks for a lovely dance.'

Frown growing deeper.

The engineer coughed, said sorry again. 'Just a joke.'

Minnette tried to stop frowning, muscles refusing to relax. Not offended, by stand-off or joke. Uneasy, rather, because she was sure if she moved again this man would mirror her, that they were going to be trapped on these stairs, stepping to one side, then the other, one side, then the other, until—

"Ere—' the engineer pointed— 'you stand on the right and I'll go this way.'

She floundered out of his way. 'Sorry.'

'That's all right. Now you know what my job's like most of the time.' He laughed: a crumb of toast stuck to one tooth, a patch of stubble on his chin missed in that morning's shave, perhaps the day before, too. Minnette squeezed past, took three steps downwards.

'Oh, 'scuse me, love?' He turned on the stair. 'The payphone's been reported out of order. You haven't noticed anything, have you? The docket only says "out of order" and I was wondering if you knew more, maybe, "out of order" being—'

'I don't use it.' Shrugging, about to tell him sorry again and changing it to: 'I don't use it much, I haven't noticed anything.'

'Not to worry, it's probably—'

Pausing on the next floor. Sounds of tools clinking in the toolbox, humming, metal striking metal. Sounds of the engineer talking to himself.

it's probably...

He would find an explanation

it's probably a faulty connection
it's probably something out at the pole
it's probably a problem with the handset

and it would be the wrong explanation. Minnette knew this would be so, not needing to wait but heading down the last flight of stairs, feet heavy, pounding loudly, footfalls obscuring the clink of metal on metal, the engineer talking, unavoidably loud because Doc Marten's were cumbersome and—boots thumping—it was the only way of walking. Reaching the ground floor hallway, snatching at the latch on the front door, stepping out into the street. Almost. Almost before she heard anything. Walking. Quickly. Any direction. Original destination forgotten. Grabbing the lip of the first litter-bin she passed. It felt solid, and solid suggested real. But, she had been expecting it to feel solid. A lamp post. The edge of a bus shelter. Both solid. Both concrete, certain. But she wanted them to be solid. Stopping abruptly and turning never resulted in any change in the street, no slippage, no haziness as it quavered under her stare. Just as she hoped. Which proved nothing. Jostled by crowds. No choice but to slow. Streets growing busier. Constant in their state of flux. Constant despite their state of flux: traffic crawl-racing along the road, open shop-doorway flanked by speakers, music jangling, drums swallowed with a breath and continuing to thump under her ribs, car horn sounding, air brakes whispering, music funnelling, muttering along the gutter, litter clinging to the pavement, randomly, air tasting of diesel exhaust, petrol fumes crawling towards the pavement, slithering, fading into the acrid note of someone's cigarette. Spinning. Minnette spinning round. No change. Solid if she thought about it. Unchanging if not. But then, perhaps someone else was thinking about it. All these—jostled, stopping abruptly to let a woman with a toddler on reins and another child in a pram leave a shop, avoiding being bumped by a man in a greasy gaberdine mac, a sallow boy with a crest of green hair and acne and band names painted in white on his leather jacket mumbling sorry as he avoided someone else and almost walked into her, voices and cigarette smoke and perfume and sweat and moth-ball-aroma and body odour and the reek of soap and last night's dinner and this morning's breakfast on breath or chin or collar—all these people thinking this was solid and safe and that proved nothing nothing nothing nothing nothing nothing nothing nothing proved nothing all of it and none of it trustworthy or not trustworthy enough for there not to be a possibility or a chance at least a chance and that meant none of it proved anything no— A young Indian man in a sharp suit gave her a look. She had been thinking aloud. Mouth closed firmly, Minnette crossed the road, weaving through the traffic, nearly getting run over, reaching the opposite pavement, hesitating before striking off in one direction, changing her mind and going back the other, picking up pace, slowing with the effort of trying not to think. Seeing another junction ahead, crossing lights on green. Green man flashing. Speeding up again, wanting to get across the road before the red light, a few other people filled with the same need—which might have been significant—rushing towards the crossing from both sides of the road—which could have had some sort of hidden symbolism—Minnette reaching the drop-curb—which might have been proof that there was a subtle current of meaning to everything, suffusing all action, this life a mirror, but a solid mirror—and failing to notice the man striding across the black and white lines, almost at her side of the road, lost in thought, because not thinking implies thinking and the implication of an act is the same as performing the act itself which is the same as acting and not thinking about thinking is, after all, just another sort of thinking and once you start thinking there's no stopping the flow of thoughts and associations, which might be evidence of something—lost in thought and not noticing the man with the unreadable expression, the man striding towards her over the crossing but not looking at her, the man barging into Minnette as she reached the crossing's edge, impact forcing her back a step, man with the unreadable expression pushing between her and the other pedestrians on this side of the crossing, ploughing on before she had time to grunt *salaud*, signal turning to red. Leaving Minnette stranded.

Trying to spot him in the crowds. Finding no sign. Shoulder throbbing faintly from the impact. Rubbing the sore spot. Almost grateful because the pain at least silenced the obsessive voice in her head, gave her something else to think about. Made her feel real and present on the street. Registering how cold her hands were, how cold the morning was, the faint tint to the air that suggested spring might assert itself eventually. Which, she accepted, was a sign of sorts. Flexing her arm. Slipping hands into jacket pockets.

The note had not been there earlier, had not been there when she left the flat. The Punk? The Indian? Neither had come close enough.

Turning again. Searching the flow of pedestrians, nearby shop front in case he had ducked off the street and was watching. Crossing turning green. People moving past. No sign of the man with the unreadable expression. Looking at the note again. Sure he must have slipped it into her pocket. Unsure whether it might have got there some other way.

It was unsigned but she recognised the tiny, obsessively neat handwriting.

No trouble finding the multi-storey car park, sketch map at the bottom of the note very clear. No watch but she felt it had taken less than the half-hour he had given her. Bottom deck almost empty: a handful of cars parked with plenty of space between, vehicles wanting to stand by themselves, listen to the weight of concrete pillars and endless ramps stained with oil, tyre marks overlaid and tangled so there was no deciphering them. Deserted. No one here.

'I wasn't sure you would come.' The magician stepped out from behind a pillar.

Minnette nodded. There was nothing else to say and the magician beckoned, leading her. Up the nearest ramp. Along the empty deck above to the next ramp.

Upwards. Always upwards. A faded yellow Datsun Cherry watching them climb out of the mouth of the last ramp. Top deck capped by sky, clouds of scratched iron, low enough almost to touch. Cherry stirring in the wind, one gust dank, next prickling with rain. Minnette zipped up her jacket, pushed fists deep into jeans pocket. Trembling although she hardly noticed the cold, watching the magician stand by the parapet, wind jerking the tales of his long black crombie.

'What do you see?'

'Same as you.' Walking closer a few steps but pausing several metres behind him. Looking anywhere but where he was pointing. 'What do you want?'

'You to come here and tell me what you see.'

'I told you. You already know—' taking a step back, closer to the ramp, hesitating over a second. 'I came, didn't I? What is it you want?' Watching him from the corner of her eye as he leaned both elbows on the concrete, pushing forward on the balls of his feet, spitting, watching the spittle fall.

'Tell me.' His voice sounded as though he was beside her, murmuring in her ear. 'Tell me why you're holding back.'

'I'm not.'

It was the wind, some weird acoustic trick.

'You act like you don't understand or believe, like you think magic is impossible.'

Turning her head away sharply, neck craning, as if he was standing very close, face close beside hers. Fists straining, pockets feeling like handcuffs. 'No.'

'Then tell me what you see.'

Shutting her eyes. Telling herself she would not answer his next question, would walk away if he didn't get to the point.

'Tell me why you're holding back.'

'I'm not.' Words yanked from her.

'You're holding back and you don't see."

'I do.' Shout nearly smothered, body jerking with the effort as her head came up, eyes opening to reveal the magician, the parapet, the city squeezed under the sky. 'I only want to understand, to know what is true, what is—'

'Then tell me.' The magician spat over the side of the wall again. 'Tell me what is. What you believe to be true.'

Memories crowding. Body shaking. The magician spitting a third time. And the words *I believe* begging to be spoken.

'I want to know.' Minnette swallowing hard, trying again with more certainty: 'I want to know. Not believe.'

'They're the same.' One of his hands lifting until it seemed to be cupping a tower block in the distance. Holding it up.

'No.' He couldn't be holding up the tower. 'No. They can't be. There are some things which are true, exist regardless of our belief in them. They're there and they're true—' telling herself: *he can't be holding up the tower*— 'true always, no matter what.'

His hand steady. Tower standing firm. 'Then tell me what you know to be true.' Fingers tightening slowly. 'Tell me what you have seen and all you know and *then* tell me what you believe.'

The magician's hand jerked.

Minnette screamed.

But the tower block did not fall.

Instead, the dampness on the wind became a drizzle that promised to become rain, clouds grinding lower, threatening downpour.

'Tell me what you believe you know.'

Almost sprawling across the concrete deck as she backed away, watching the tower block, twitching, sure the first windows were about to crack, roof buckle, walls start to crack. And then the lightning would come.

He gestured again. Drizzle became rain, fat, ice-cold spots that sang as they struck the deck. Plastering hair to scalp and slithering down the back of her neck. 'I want to know.'

'Coincidence.' Word breath not sound, Minnette trying to take another step back and unable to move. 'This is coincidence. I don't, don't believe, I don't—'

'Really?' He moved his hand.

'Come back!'

Running. Clipping the wall, angle off the ramp sharp. Arms pumping. Willing herself to the mouth of the next ramp.

'Wait—'

His voice part of the wind cutting through the open sides of the car park.

'Where are you going?'

Nearly falling down the next ramp. Recovering. Making the deck below. Pelting rain gusting inwards. Pools and puddles forming on the concrete, surfaces silver-grey. Trembling. Boots slipping. Stumble headlong. Offering a glimpse of the magician, above and behind and running without effort.

'Wait—'

She hurled herself forward. Down the ramp, beyond. Wind inhaling. Breath held and, in the relative silence, his footfalls staccato, his shape spawning from a frame of concrete pillars, the magician running across the deck above.

Minnette lunged forward. Hitting the inner parapet wall, bruising knees, scraping shin, the heel of a hand as she scrambled over the edge, dropped to the level below. Heaving up. Running. Doing it again. Again.

She thought she saw the magician as she ran from the car park. Rain heavier, cloaking a shape peering down, three or four floors above. It might have been him. Sounds of rain, her ragged breathing, boots striking tarmac, hiding his shouts. Perhaps he had stopped shouting.

Snatching another glance over her shoulder. Shape gone.

A little over an hour later, Minnette was sitting on a bus. Heading out of Leeds. Heading out of the UK entirely.

'We keep running into each other.'

'No we don't. You keep finding me. Waiting until you get chance to irritate.'

'That's not how it seems to me.'

'You surprise me.'

'So, how's... What is it this week? New Age books? Vampire hunter novels?'

'Piss off, Guillaume.'

'No, Minnette, I'm interested. We meet so rarely—'

'A month ago. We met a month ago.'

'Six weeks, perhaps.'

'Whatever. Piss off.'

Shooing him away.

Feeling nothing. Nothing. Other than cross that he stayed.

In clusters. Never the same, exactly. Except the last and that only because its presence would eventually suffuse the shadows or sunlight turning to shadow, the feel of a step, or a word that could not be spoken, mouth working and the only sound the absence of a syllable and that syllable filled with its presence, presence becoming weightier, definite, until it appeared, heavy head bent towards her, brutish hand gentle, fingers and palm warm and soft as they rested against her shoulder, as she woke up. Gasping. Screaming. Tangled in bed sheets or shivering, sweat drying rapidly because the duvet had slipped away. Knowing this was waking and not sure this awareness could be trusted. But in the dreams before it came she began to notice qualities: the passage of air against the skin, a reflection slipping quickly from a mirror's frame, an emotion. In retrospect at first, piecing together fragments. Heart slowing, slowly. Pillow clutched tight. Bringing a little comfort. Less than she hoped, bedroom solid and familiar, scrutiny moving around the room. Aware of the extra-firm mattress against her buttocks, an ache in one elbow, stiff neck muscles, perhaps. The throb of her bad hip. Peripheral but familiar. Reassuring. Not feeling reassured. Unable to relax. Watching. Five minutes. Watching the clock expend another sixty seconds. Gaze moving. Hand, shaking, reaching out. Grasping mattress, bed frame. The edge of the bedside table. Trying not to remember *grabbing the lip of the first litter-bin she passed it felt solid and solid suggested real but she had been expecting it to feel solid a lamp post the edge of a bus shelter both solid both concrete certain but she wanted* let the dream return. Prodding. Interrogating. Beginning to relax after twenty minutes. Or half an hour. Suspicion of unreality lingering. Fading. Returning more frequently the longer the dreams continued. Putting it down to fatigue or the boredom of the bookshop on the Rue St Jacques, the lingering resentment that, no matter its appearance, the shop survived primarily on that expensive selection of vintage smut in its upstairs room. There was almost a nostalgia for the running dreams. Although that passed. As she recognised the feel of the dreams. As she recognised what was coming.

A train and bus strike, a dozen minor details overlooked in Guillaume's initial burst of enthusiasm on the night of the dinner party, each one listed in a notebook she bought especially, underlined or ticked off, depending how difficult they proved, listing the days afterwards, of course, the days after the dinner party, listing those as check marks in the corner of the first page, because each one added freight that needed to be accounted for, everything had to be accounted for, yet, sometime during the wait, the Israel Regardie book left its stand, was replaced a few hours later by a pile of notes and coins, a handwritten bill of sale, and that appeared nowhere in her accounts, might never have happened, although without it there would have been no flight, no train rides, no days listed in the notebook, entries growing sparse by the end of the first week, second week evaporating into the third, which seemed to come apart like gossamer so the only memories that stayed with her were confused impressions of sunlight off impossibly blue water; old towns encrusted with signs for 7 Up and Orangina; bus rides that were like hours in a jolting oven; hillsides of white rock and spiky vegetation; the smell of wild oregano mingling with dope as the sun set; another evening when they scored acid off a group of American kids who talked about hitting the hippy trail one day but seemed more interested in staying in parents' houses in Barcelona or Rome; being hung-over in a hostel, staggering outside and throwing up; impressions of towns becoming villages becoming hamlets; of wondering where the time was going; of trying not to care; of surprising herself, by the fourth week, that she didn't care.

Which was when they found the dilapidated farmhouse in the hills above a village that, itself, was little more than a cluster of farmhouses.

'It's perfect.'

The sun had baked the roof, corrugated metal beginning to curl and fray. Walls white, afternoon making one side blaze. Shutters covered the windows. Front door rattling faintly in the breeze. Breeze setting the weeds hissing.

'It's perfect,' he said again, running around the deserted building.

They moved in. No one in the tiny village that itself was little more than a cluster of farmhouses seemed to mind.

She watched the sun come up next morning, an Aegean sun that peeked over the lip of the horizon at her in a way the sun in Paris never had, shadows becoming visible, harder-edged, air cold and dry and smelling of tamarind, cedar tree on the hillside above the farmhouse beginning to stand out against the sky. And the sky—

Looking directly upwards and seeing stars, more than she had seen filling the skies over Paris or the sky above her parent's house; a smear of white arcing, catching her eye, moments passing before she realised this was the Milky Way, the galaxy's centre seen edge-on, millions of stars hanging over her head beyond a sky clear and deep and near-to-bottomless, sky turning a fragile shade of blue.

The sun reached out, taking her face in its hands, wanting her attention.

'What do you think?'

She couldn't turn away from the sun. 'Yes.' Voice soft, all attention otherwise fixed on the sunrise. 'Yes.'

There was no need to say anything more.

They began preparing for the ritual.

Sun moving, shadows chasing, day swelling, gravid in a way, a bee lingering over nodding sage, nodding rosemary, a bird's song, a voice, sun moving, shadows chasing clouds chasing a breeze chasing a bee, a poppy bowing, pages turning, a clump of weeds torn free, a bird's flight, voices murmuring, stones reluctant, stones willing, voices, a bird, a bee, a breeze, cloud sculpting the mountains in the distance, sculpting a dog's bark, dog bark forgotten in the hiss of feet through grass, hiss of breath let out, hiss of the sun moving, shadows settling, day waning, air cooling, bee gone, birds silent, a voice, breath regular, shallow, sun absent but still moving, moving still...

Sun moved, lingering beneath the horizon, new day faint, a blush silhouetting mountains, hills, a lone cedar, sky a bottomless blue, a glimmering, shores turning pink, touching orange. Air tasting of the night just leaving. Air cold turning into cool into neither chill nor close. Into a foretaste: of the hours ahead, of heat. Wind light-footed, lingering under the branches of the lone cedar on the hill overlooking the two-room farmhouse, meandering over the hillside, brushing the half-open shutters, murmurs bringing out no one, no one home to talk to. Turning. Skimming over the track through the long grass, long grass set to gyring, copse rattling, branches falling still. Wind falling still. Last stars hanging bright and cold and distant and mute and secretive and watching impassively: shadows clinging to their feet, swallowing voices raised to the stars, the new day's sun, shadows ebbing, swelling a last time in the candlelight, the guttering bonfire on the lee side of the hill away from the village that seemed to have no name...

She woke later to find a lizard pausing on her chest. She could not decide if this was a sign. He said he would have to think about it.

There was one shelf in the two-room farmhouse. Little by little, they put things here: herbs picked from outside the door; mushrooms, their identities memorised long before they came here; a little food; more wine; shards of crystal; a knife, symbols scratched on its blade with a rock; a dish bought from the world outside, along with incense, a mirror; a chord, knotted, red rag woven through the knots: little-by-little, they put things on that shelf.

They sat in discussion. They sat in contemplation. They fasted, thirst and hunger sitting beside her as she sat beside him in the shade of the two-room farmhouse.

There was the wine. There was weed. There were pills he said would help, scored by walking into the village with no name, walking through the village to a bus stop on a steep incline, a four-hour bus ride, a change of bus after that, the destination—streets with cars, pavements with tourists, transistor radios playing, newspapers written in Greek, written in German, French, Spanish, written in tongues, signs that lit up, the air filled with the smell of food, of perfume or diesel exhaust, with hundreds, thousands of voices all talking at once—the destination more frightening and strange each visit. There were trackless, plastic times afterwards, that might have been mere seconds or eons, there was no telling, but in those times the hillside and the stars and the wind and the shadows and the smell of tamarind and oregano and bay and wild olives began to run and twist, to suggest… but she was never sure what they suggested and he said it was too early to say for certain.

She counted the coins that were all that was left of the money they had brought with them.

He cleared more of the shallow, flat stretch of land beyond the curve of the hillside and the trees: the place he had chosen, that she had agreed was perfect, for the Working.

She helped him, moving around the ragged circle of fresh ash and cinder at the centre. A hand around a clock. Smelling fresh char, thinking of the next propitiation. Thinking of nothing but the feel of the sun on her back.

They fasted, hunger and thirst sitting beside her in the shade of the olive trees that watched the two-room farmhouse from beyond the weeds that were all that was left of what had once been a farmyard.

She sat meditating, hours running, hours motionless, shutters closed as best they could, sunlight finding plenty of cracks to slip through, insects talking in tongues; trying to loose her body, let it fall away, wanting to find a core of quietude; wanting to cease to exist.

They set out rocks, scratched dirt, outer circle almost complete, inner circle beginning to arc, its circumference measured from its northern axis, its circumference measured from anywhere, line endless once it was finished and its start beginning to arc, turning around inside the outer circle, turning around her as she knelt on the cleared ground, as the circle turned, turned.

He talked to her.

There were mushrooms. There was wine. There were pills.

He talked to her. Incessantly. Going over each detail. Each hope, each expectation. She heard his voice but not the words, not always the words. She listened to the insects, the weeds talking, the house creaking, the sound of the sunlight moving around the house, the shadows in the corners of the room.

They made love. He told her all of this was an act of love. She told him all of this was an act of love. So they made love, made love, and he offered the energy of their passion to the Working.

She made a little money in the village, watching a flock of goats. She made a little money in the next village down the road, walking along an olive grove nipping insects off the branches with her fingernails. She felt the villagers watching her. The insects pausing as she made her way slowly down the length of the grove. The goats' rectangular eyes resting on her. Slipping away.

He worked each day round on the ritual.

They performed rites preparatory, rites incantatory, rites of evocation.

The stars... the wind... a mushroom... the hunger... a mouthful of wine... to sleep only to wake and begin again...

'This is going to work.'

Sun bringing another dawn. Sitting outside the circle. The latest ritual of propitiation, meant to open the way for the angel Hanael, over an hour or more ago.

She looked at the sky, not noticing the cold.

'Yes, Guillaume,' was all she said.

There was no need to say anything more.

The notebook lay forgotten under the shelf.

They waited. The time had to be just right. He watched the stars each evening, each midnight, each morning. The time had to be exact. They waited, watching. She stood listening to him talk, listening to his silence. Hunched over his calculations and horoscopes, checking, re-checking, numbers and symbols not making much sense, sometimes, looking like nothing more than numbers and symbols and random marks on the page, but they had to be right, had to have meaning, she knew that was so, knew they must and did, and so looked at the pages of pencil marks and said that the day was definitely in five days time, and the time—

Her watch had stopped long ago, so time was—

'Sunrise,' he told her, 'when the Gates of Heaven open.'

'Yes... the Fourth Sephirot...' and she nodded understanding, any doubt this was the right thing to say erased when he, too, nodded:

'Yes, of course, I'd forgotten: when the Fourth Sephirot's Archangel brings a balance.'

'Yes, yes, that's it.' Nodding also, smiling her agreement. 'I remember reading it in... in...' No memory of reading it, no intention of admitting this, not when all their work and preparation and sacrifice was about to be rewarded.

'Yes,' she said, 'you're right: we finish at sunrise.'

There was waiting. There was meditation. There was fasting, ritual cleansing. There was ritual love making and ritual abstinence. There were the stars, the wind, the weed, the wine, the voices of the shadows and the insects. And there was expectation. That most of all. Sun moving. Shadows chasing, day chasing wind. Heat opening its mouth. A lizard skittering. A village watching the road watching the hillside watching sun moving watching insects and shadows wine weed wind stars abstinence love making cleansing fasting meditation waiting and expectation and expectation, that most of all

so there was already an energy pervading the shallow, flat area cupped by the hillside as they followed the path out of the copse, walking slowly, steps measured and timed, although there was no need to walk with such formality yet, unable to help themselves or break step. She felt it, could smell the energy on the edge of the dusk, on the wind as it brushed against the rosemary bushes. It was a prickling in the air as she closed the circle. It was a tension inside making the hairs on the back of her neck stand, her breath short.

They sang at first, as night strengthened around the circle, as the sky emptied of all but a trace of cloud, stars growing brighter as the singing became chanting, both of them swaying beside the fire kindled in the makeshift brazier in front of the low altar made of rocks, sun-bleached planks. She put everything into each word, all breath, all expectation, words drawing out as they left her, leaving a vibration that shimmered in her diaphragm, made nerves tingle, made the next breath spark, made the next breath sparkle against lips and tongue and throat as chanting became dancing and she turned and turned and turned around the circle, around the altar at its middle, turned around him as he recited long, sinuous poetry as she turned and turned and turned around the circle, around the altar, around him reciting lines of words, lines of words as woven and threaded as her steps around him, altar, circle.

He paused. Taking her hands. Stilling the dance. Pressing another sliver of mushroom between her dry lips, feeding a gulp of wine from a cracked bowl, letting her dance again, dance because standing still was impossible, because the evening was resonant in her chest, in her nostrils, at the edge of each half-closed eye and the tip of each outstretched finger, because the air was tangled with sweet threads of sandalwood and bergamot and myrrh and patchouli and resinous weed, the burr of woodsmoke, of olive wood smouldering. But there was an undercurrent she caught every few breaths, felt as a tingling against the nostrils, a pressure between her eyes. Beyond the firelight there was almost nothing, an inkiness that made the air solid as it erased everything else, everything except the sky, the stars cold and secretive. She felt sweat run down her back, breath catching each time she glanced beyond circle and firelight, each glimpse spinning away because she could not stop dancing, because his words were a thrum in her chest, because there was something out there.

She was certain, certain, certain something was coming.

Time dissolved. Even when she tripped over her feet, laughing, giddy, literally giddy with joy and the sheer thrill of the power they were gathering inside the circle, even as she staggered, fell, rolled to face him, arms lifting, even as he knelt, time could gain no grip, none at all, moments and instants cascading into the firelight, their lovemaking frantic and slippery and lasting longer than any Age or Eternity, their lovemaking over too soon, over in a moment or an instant that had no duration, their cries mingling, pressing through the solid black beyond the circle, calling to the stars, to somewhere beyond the stars, or to just beside them, a single step but an entire Universe away.

She lay back. Watching as he called again, invoking the angel Hanael. Mouth forming the words he spoke, or so it seemed, entreating the Power to manifest.

In the darkness beyond the fire... there was shape and form again. Vague, no more than patches of dark grey in a darkness that itself was beginning to turn grey, air grainy as shadows made impressions of rocks, a bush, a tree, sky no longer flawless indigo but waning towards blue, pink leaching into one horizon, giving depth and mass to the hillside, levelled ground and circle scratched into cold earth. Ritual fire dwindling, becoming smoke and embers.

A cold bit through skin and bone. Exhaustion a spirit descending, taking possession. Head disjointed. Thoughts ending. Unfinished. An edge to each breath and each movement foreshadowing coming down although, for now, weed and mushrooms and sex and dancing and wine lent her a sense of hovering just above the flesh, ebbing sensations lingering, strengthened by a transcendent rush of elation.

She could feel the power they had gathered. Knew it was there as she stifled laughter, clambered to her feet, swaying, legs giving way as she knelt beside him at the altar. She felt the Power they had called down coming closer.

As the sun edged over the hillside, they began the final stage of the ritual. In silence, like—and the words appeared in her mind as if put there by some one or some thing else—like a breath held.

A wind appeared. Air placid one moment, moving swiftly the next. Next gust stronger. One after eddying around the circle; its moan surely more than the random passage of air.

A rumble of thunder. Distant but unmistakeable.

She listened, straining. The thunder did not repeat but she was sure she could hear a dog bark, once, in the village, that the birds were not singing but talking, language secret but at the very edge of understanding.

The wind roused and fell back, hillside becalmed.

She opened her mouth, ready to speak the last part of the closing ritual. But he stood, arms thrown wide as he intoned:

'It is done.'

The shutters were thrown wide.

'They were closed.' Feeling him just behind and still reluctant to cross the threshold. Peering through the open front door, ajar where it had been latched. Shadows coiled aside, thickened and restive in the morning light falling through the rear door, door that had been jammed. Shadows denser in spite of the extra light. 'This door, all of them, closed.'

'It has come.' His voice low, almost intoning. 'It has come.'

Nothing inside seemed different. Pausing, one hand lifted to touch the air, other palm up, weighing the shadows. Breath held. Let out slowly, before drawing in another breath. Finding a trace of incense, woodsmoke beginning to loose its tang. Air feeling different, somehow, against both hands. Turning sharply. Deciding it was shade and shapes and nothing after all. Neck taught, shoulders tight. Next breath juddering a little, conscious of trying not to make noise, attract attention, conscious of a trace on this breath, a musk beyond the earthiness of the mostly dirt floor.

'It will come again.' He nodded, features thrown into relief by the sunlight streaming through the open rear door.

Awake. Groggy, hungover. Unsure of the time, quite where she was. Staring at the shafts of sunlight through the half-closed shutters. Guessing time as mid-afternoon; remembering place, night before. Sitting up on the mattress, bedding—old blankets and oddments of clothing—tangling around her midriff.

He lay beside her, naked, snoring gently.

Wind vanished. Silence. But for his breathing, the rustle of her own movements. Bird calls, the click-clicking of grasshoppers: too familiar to be noticed.

Palms dry against cheeks, the moist, velvet hollows of her eyes. Rubbing her face again, thinking about something to drink, or relieving her bladder first. Deciding to lie a while longer, a little while longer, back arched, relaxing, about to settle—

There was a shape.

Dark. Unformed.

A something beyond the light reaching across the room.

Exhaustion blunting adrenaline surge as hand rose to shade eyes. Straining forward. Seeing a mass within the gloom in the opposite corner, an intimation of solidity where there should be nothing.

Fear keening, driving from stomach to skull.

She blinked.

Nothing. Only the empty corner.

Nothing there when she finally managed to creep close enough to look.

After looking over the whole house, she sat, listening to his gentle snoring, the insects, a bird, a silence on the point of being broken, mind moving to a different rhythm. Until she couldn't put off eating any longer.

No food left in the farmhouse.

Dregs of the day left by the time she returned, hangover sour and weariness a sediment chafing between skin and bone. Looking up. Looking twice at the next bend in the narrow track. Memory scuffling over the last seconds.

There had been a shape. In the bushes, standing in the dusk. Tall. Heavyset. Shoulders broad and head— reminding her of Toledo: the open door, light spilling across the pavement, shadow... Shuffling closer to the edge of the track. And suspecting that would make it easier, a rustle of undergrowth her only warning before— Back crawling. Scalp tight. Unwilling to move and managing a step closer to the bend. Thinking she must tell him, of this manifestation, visitation, this contact, tell him what had appeared in the bushes, in the dusk at the bend in the track, tell him. If this wouldn't also mean speaking about Toledo, attempting to explain why she'd said nothing before. Easier to will herself into the bushes, ignore the crawling of spine and shoulder blade as she searched further and deeper, easier to shrink from the expectation of a hand coming out of the darkness.

The shutters bursting open jolted them awake. Both doors banging. As if something were desperate to get in.

She hugged herself tightly as he stumbled to the window.

The wind howled, notes long and drawn from far away. Grit pattered against the roof. A second handful crackling. She made herself rise to her knees and peer outside.

Dust spun around the house.

The wind moaned again, next gust making the metal roof flex and beat, flex and beat, flex, beat, rising towards crescendo, cowering, tin sheets about to be ripped away—

Stillness.

His bound towards the front door, his shout calling for her to come and look, finding her frozen, unable to understand. Coming back, dragging her off the bed, pointing—'Look'—pointing to the ground in front of the farmhouse, instructing again: 'Look!'

A layer of dust blurred the scuffs left by their feet, coating almost enough to smooth away the shallower footprints.

'Those marks.'

She knelt, clinging to the doorframe. The wind had stirred patterns across what it had kicked up and let fall. 'I don't see…'

He knelt, tracing in the air. 'Here, here, this—' Eyes following his finger, back and forth, trying to see as he began naming letters and signs.

'Don't you see?' More gently this time, holding her shoulder, guiding her eyes with his outstretched finger. 'It's Enochian. Isn't it Enochian? It has to be. They can't be random marks. Don't you think? I think so. I know. It's Enochian writing. It has to be…'

'Yes…' Head moving, side to side, nod uncertain as he repeated how sure he was, nod becoming firmer until she clapped her hands together—'Oh, god, yes!'—sure she was seeing what he was seeing. 'Yes, it is, isn't it? Enochian…'

The language of the Angels.

The shelf collapsed that night, spilling its contents across the room.

While she laughed at her own fright, he rebalanced the length of wood on its brackets, both of them picking up spillage, shards of broken glass.

He gave a grunt. 'This book's just lying open.' Bending to pick it up. Straightening as if startled by a noise.

'What is it? What's wrong?'

Before she could reach the book, he scooped it off the floor, holding it so he could read in the light from the gas lantern.

'This is...' Brandishing the book, finger keeping place. 'It's a message.'

Confused as he tilted the page to the light, reading:

'... *until a bloom returned and, curtain drawn, the room grew still. He noticed neither, listening to the stars slow...*' Looking up. 'Don't you see? Don't you see the significance?'

She didn't. Not at first. Listening as he re-read the passage, reading further, going back over the whole page, teasing understanding from her, his excitement and conviction mounting as she stumbled, misinterpreted, as he pointed out connections she had missed as he recited the passage again, she began to see the significance of what Guillaume was saying, came to understand.

They had been contacted by the angel Hanael, given wisdom from another plane of existence. The ritual was a success.

Stirring, not exactly awake, conscious of duvet's weight and warmth, light making a silhouette of the blinds over the bedroom window, feeling something was missing, gap shaped like that much-thumbed copy of *Airport*, a little like the box and the photograph of them at the Eiffel Tower, eyes closing and seeing a living room, a dowdy flat with something missing, smelling scrambled eggs and fresh bread, a kettle huffing, a cheery, tuneless whistling coming from the kitchen, door ajar, not exactly dreaming nor remembering Düsseldorf but drifting, part dream, part memory—I hope you have slept well? I did not have any heart for moving you, my dear, I hope the chair was not uncomfortable, I hope you have slept well—German guiding her into the kitchen, the sound of voices on the radio, the German turning it down as he indicated she should sit at the table, two places set, coffee, jam, eggs steaming partly a memory, perhaps partly a dream—Did we talk? Last night, I remember—part of a dream of sipping coffee, spreading jam, not hungry, a dream memory of being hungry—I remember talking, did we talk?—sipping again, another slice of bread—No, you were so very tired, very tired, I'm afraid we didn't speak at all, you slept, my dear—another mouthful of eggs—I thought—the German smiling, spooning bacon on to her plate—No, you were very tired, you slept—and the memory skipping as she tasted the bacon, dream, if this was a dream, presenting a memory of the bus station, telling him there was no need to walk with her, to wait at the stop, the German insisting—Are you sure?—it was no trouble, memory of the dream, dream-memory hovering, an undertow—It's kind of you, but—uneasy, unwilling to check her watch, wanting, wanting something, a gap in memory, dream turning to face him—but I have to keep searching—the German's face unreadable—Such a shame you won't reconsider—as she says again that she has to go, keep—Sometimes it is better to stand, see what comes—keep searching—than go looking for what might be on its way—feeling something missing, a silhouette of the blinds, duvet's weight and warmth, conscious, not exactly stirring.

Getting up in darkness. As usual. Guillaume still asleep, snoring gently. As usual. Bedroom cold, thoughts sluggish. Sound of rain spatting against the bedroom window making her shiver, long for bed, blearily hugging a shawl to shoulders and neck. Remembering white rocks, white sunshine, heat making her skin tingle, memory making her nostalgic, rain finding strength, last summer distant, peppered with hail between the raindrops. Foot tangling in a piece of discarded clothing, edging around towards the door. Minnette remembering only once she reached the hallway that she had to go back and turn off the alarm before it rang.

There had been talk of finishing her degree. August becoming October. Guillaume thinking it was something to aim for, picking up where she had left off. Minnette said yes. Said probably. Thought about it a little, October becoming the Christmas run-up. Sitting on the bus on the way to the factory that made trays for aeroplane meals where she did clerical work, filling in as the general manager's PA more and more. Work easier than studying. In some ways. But picking up where she had left off. Yes. She might do that. Was doing that, New Year becoming a dank January, in a way.

The general manager asked if she could work late that night.

Minnette phoned the flat during her lunch break, later in the afternoon, again just after six. No reply.

It had turned eight when she got home. No sign of Guillaume.

This flat was smaller than the one they had had before the Aegean. Which wasn't a bad thing. They agreed. They needed only a little. Their small collections of books, some clothes. Everything else had been sold or pawned when they got back.

Founding the community was more important than possessions.

Guillaume worked harder than she did. Minnette told everyone that.

She woke up, neck bent awkwardly and arm numb from the way she had been lying on the rickety sofa. Confused that the clock read nine-forty.

Still evening.

Guillaume not back yet.

She wanted a bath and knew there would be no hot water at this time of night.

Founding the community was worth the sacrifice. To live in the Aegean sun, a place where they could study, work magic, help others do the same. It was worth the tiredness, the long days. Worth not having a bath.

Nine forty-six. Guillaume still not back yet.

Most mornings he wrote. Horoscopes for magazines, a few newspapers. Articles, book reviews. A lot of people were interested in the occult these days and, even if they weren't into paying much to have that interest satisfied, there were opportunities. In the afternoons, he gave talks wherever he could. Little bookshops and conscious-raising groups in the city on weekdays, scruffy counter-cultural co-ops in the suburbs at weekends. Talking to anyone willing to listen, willing to pay a little more than travelling expenses. Evenings were when his real work began. Lecturing about the community to fringe meetings, talks he organised himself, going back, trying new places, getting out the message of what they hoped and offered. They already had a handful of students (Guillaume hated the word 'followers') and numbers were growing, slowly, the money they donated a help. Minnette, usually working overtime and too tired anyway to make most of these talks, worked on the community's accounts, or wrote letters seeking support, seeking interest, seeking funds. It wasn't much but it was a contribution. As she told everyone, Guillaume worked harder than she.

As she told everyone, magic was everything in her life.

He was drunk when he came in.

'Kept me talkin'.' Guillaume almost falling across the bed as he tried kneeling on it to kiss her. 'After th' talk.' Minnette crushed against pillow, headboard, as he threw an arm across her, embrace becoming a collapse. 'Café. Entire audience, after. Nothin' I could do, was there?'

'I have to sleep.' Craning away from his flaccid, insistent kisses. 'I have to get up early, remember?'

'Got to get up, too...' Fumbling at her nightdress. Pausing. 'New student. New... Wouldn't let me...'

Slumping across her stomach, ribs, mumbles—'Great talk...'—becoming a soft gentle snoring.

After she had rolled him away, tugged off boots, wrestled his dead weight out of his suede jacket, Minnette gave up any thought of undressing him properly. Throwing a blanket over Guillaume. Checking the alarm clock was set before getting back into bed. Knowing she would be awake before it had chance to go off.

They spoke of the Aegean.

She believed in the community.

They talked about how the ritual had confirmed all of their hopes.

The community would be a wonderful, vital thing.

The ritual last summer had been proof positive.

She told everyone how much she was proud of Guillaume, how proud she was to be a part of it all.

The ritual showed that Guillaume had been right to leave university that winter after they had first met, strike out on his own. They agree on that, too, agreed his doubts when he came back had been wrong, that he—that they—could touch the numinous.

She told everyone. She believed.

She believed.

When winter started to give way, Minnette told herself the longer days and warmer weather had made everything different. She attended more of Guillaume's meetings, sure she had been losing herself in the day-to-day as she had at University.

Finding that evening's venue was harder than she expected. A métro ride and several buses brought her to a district she didn't know, address scribbled on a slip of paper seeming to match nothing around her, shops closed and no one around to ask. If she had left work on time, she wouldn't have had to feel this anxious.

Wandering. Muttering. Swearing at the anonymous buildings, at work, at the clock for running out of control. Shaking as she looked at her watch again. Almost denying it when an old man, pink scalp bracketed by a hazing of thin white hair, appeared at a ground floor window, asked if she was lost.

The meeting was about to start when she pushed open the door to the long, narrow, upstairs room. Some hippies and younger people, mostly students from the look of them, a couple of Guillaume's friends, some of the community's students, a scattering of older people sitting along the rows of folding metal chairs. Minnette gave Guillaume a quick kiss and sat at the back. Listening to his voice, words familiar, talk a variation of one he had given before, words losing their grip, attention turning inwards, rousing when the audience began to clap, joining in, settling back before understanding this was the end of the talk.

Minnette fetched a tray of cheap wine and fruit juice from a table at the side. A group clustered around Guillaume, Guillaume smiling, animated as he explained, listened politely to more questions. Unwilling to interrupt just yet, feeling a sense of pride and purpose.

He tilted his head, laughing, hand resting briefly on the upper arm of one of the people standing beside him.

Minnette's smile became waxen.

She was a girl, nineteen or twenty, the person who had made him laugh.

On his other side, another girl, only a little closer to Minnette's age, leaned in, touching his arm, wanting Guillaume's attention.

One of his students hovered close. A man in his thirties, beard already showing white in a few places, asked a question. As Guillaume began to answer, the student interrupted, her joke making everyone laugh, ensured Guillaume noticed her.

She was twenty-six or twenty-seven.

Guillaume glanced up, noticed Minnette watching him. He smiled.

She turned away.

In 1588, Florian Rudolphus Dippel published *Numinosity in the Darkness*. Long and discursive, illustrated by engravings that are as exquisite as they are bizarre as they are largely impossible to interpret, the core of the book is the assertion that humanity and the entirety of Creation are no more than an epiphenomenon of something greater and more mysterious. Although he never quite says what this larger mystery might be, Dippel does promise to have answers soon.

He never gave those answers, bankruptcy driving him from his home and into obscurity.

Yet the rumours persist: Dippel staged his disappearance. Dippel had found something, a hidden truth more fundamental and important than books, notoriety. Dippel had been anything but a crank.

Spring. Boulevards, parks awash with blossom. Sun more direct, days warmer. Big-brimmed hats and short-sleeved dresses the fashion that season. Minnette told the other secretaries at the factory she couldn't spare the money. Told Guillaume's friends she was sensitive to sunlight. It wasn't uncomfortable wearing long-sleeved sweaters. Or keeping the sleeves of her blouses buttoned even indoors. Really, she repeated. She was fine.

Sometimes she woke screaming. Not every night. Enough for Guillaume to notice. She said she never remembered any of her dreams. This was almost true. Told him it was nothing. This might have been true. It might.

Guillaume had a phone installed. Handset modish and angular and seeming out of place among the flat's mend-and-make-do. Minnette stared at the phone as he put an arm around her. I can keep in touch with students, potential students more easily, he was saying. And jobs. He told her something like that, squeezing her shoulders. Speaking engagements, I told you I missed a last-minute thing last week?

Minnette nodded.

He had told her.

She stared at the pale green trim phone as Guillaume squeezed her shoulders again, looking at the phone but judging the tension in his chest and upper arms, looking for meaning in the splay of fingers, pitch of voice as he said something again, something like: This is going to be so much help so much help—

Minnette took a breath. 'I'm not— I mean, are we sure we can afford...?'

Guillaume lifted his other arm, embracing her, fingers stroking the back of her neck, head close so she could feel the vibration of air in his chest. Oh, I was worried about that, too. He said. Something like it, saying: It's a legitimate expense, isn't it? So I can pay. Through students' fees, he went on, more or less, students' fees and contributions, Guillaume pressing Minnette's forehead against his chest. Questioning flex, intonation, the fingers stroking the back of her neck.

I can pay, Guillaume said.

Minnette nodded.

Sometimes she slept so deeply she slept through the alarm. Not every morning. Enough for Guillaume to get annoyed, push her out of bed. 'This is for both of us,' he mumbled from under the pillow he dragged over his head. And this was true. She thought.

In the gloom of a staff toilet stall, the scratches looked almost colourless although the flesh was raised and fevered to the touch and lifting each forearm in search of direct light revealed angry pink weals, edges ragged, the freshest still crowned by half-moons of skin gouged by nails skipping as they dug.

Minnette rolled down her sleeves and flushed the toilet.

We never make love these days, Guillaume only a little drunk, gone eleven when he came in, bedside lamp flicked off as the latch key turned, pretend sleep disturbed as he turned on the overhead light and dropped on to the bed, we never do, Guillaume's weight shifting, trousers still on, belt buckle poking uncomfortably into her waist as he wriggled closer, chin on her shoulder, beer or something stronger on his breath, saying we never make love these days as she turned her face into the arm she had tucked under her head.

'We did it last week.'

That's like never, and I've had a disappointing evening, a student… Trying not to show anything, weighing the hesitation that followed, pretending not to resist as he tried to slip the bedclothes from her breasts. Wondering if the hesitation was nothing other than the struggle with bedclothes as Guillaume amended: An almost-student, I thought we had another ready to join but… unsure if he faltered before adding: he didn't, before trying to slip a hand over her breasts.

'I'm very tired. Work. Sorry.'

But a little… Guillaume stopping, guessing from the tension in his body that he must be frowning.

'Why are you always wearing these ugly nightdresses these days? The long sleeves make you look like a bloody maiden aunt.'

The phone's trill pushed her awake. Guillaume was already out of bed, hunched over the phone by the time she tottered to the doorway, voice hushed, furtive.

Minnette shook her head. Looked again: Guillaume still half-asleep, yes, so unable to straighten up, hunching because of sleep, yes, voice husky because he had yet to wake up completely, huskiness misleading, creating furtiveness where there was—

Thank you, yes, Guillaume reaching for Biro, diary, and not noticing her in the bedroom doorway and not changing his mind because she was watching. Saying into the phone something like thank you, again, something like that, without any inflection, saying thank you into the phone in a way anyone would expect him to say it, assuming this was a business phone call, someone wanting him to do a talk, saying thank you and putting down the phone.

You go back to bed if you like.

Hearing the words. Searching beneath and between them. 'Who was that? Speaking engagement?'

Yes, Guillaume reaching for the diary again.

'It's very early, isn't it?'

Hmm? Changing his mind about the diary, nodding distractedly, She, er, he jogs, early. He forgot the time.

Taking a spare pen from the shelf, holding it out. 'Here.'

Oh, I'll write it down later. I might phone him back, double-check the time. Yeah. Maybe later.

All very innocent. Reminding herself of this as she calmly closed bathroom door, sat on the edge of the toilet bowl. All innocent. Insisting. Rolling up the sleeves of her nightdress and reminding herself it was wrong to think otherwise as she unscrewed Guillaume's razor and began cutting a fresh, uneven line along her forearm.

She was wrong. That's what she had to remember.

The general manager asked her to come into his office, said he was sorry to have to say anything, said he thought she was usually very good at her job, he had no complaints, usually had no complaints. Minnette stopped listening. Apologised. Apologised again, manager talking as she apologised, stopping only after he repeated the question another time. 'My husband's gone away,' Minnette admitted after a pause, watching the general manager from the corner of her eye. 'Business,' she added, 'a lecture tour.'

How did your day go? Guillaume was home when she got back. Minnette smiled. Asked him if he had eaten. Watched the corner of his mouth. The tension in the muscles around his eyes, whatever he was saying unimportant. Truth lay under the surface of everything. In the unspoken. 'I had a fine day.' Minnette smiling.

Watching. Pausing. Not speaking. Asking him: How was yours?

A fortnight. Of days, nights. A night. Late. So late she hadn't been able to stay awake, was asleep, noise of him startling, her body convulsing. One hand knocking draft letters to the floor from the edge of the mattress, torso upsetting the community's accounts book from her chest.
 Sorry. Voice a hiss, escaping breath. Didn't mean to…
 Guillaume dropping awkwardly on the edge of the bed, fear chasing at the dregs of whatever she had been dreaming, making her frown, making it hard to judge inflexion and tone. ''S okay.' Wondering if this was the right thing to say. Perhaps anger. Perhaps concern. 'You're late.'
 Time got away from us. Sorry. And a hesitation after that. Time for her to blink. See his shirt almost unbuttoned, his upper body turned awkwardly half-away, suspicious that his belt was undone, that he had been in the bedroom longer than she had thought, that the dream had been him, had been the sound of Guillaume coming in, beginning to undress. Bedside light off on his side of the bed, hers throwing shadows.
 It was great great you would have loved it Minnette you know real enthusiasm and desire for the community for what we're trying to build commitment you know and a desire to learn it was great great you would have loved—
 The words were only there to both carry and hide meaning. In themselves, they weren't so important and she focused on cadence, pause, silence as meaningful as sound, because it was the way Guillaume spoke that gave true meaning to the messages interwoven through his words like secrets carried in an alchemical text.
 'Who was there?' Voice light, her meaning hidden. She could do that. 'Seems so long since I was able to come—' talk like this was as innocent as it could be— 'to a meeting.'

Oh yeah yeah right that's sad but you're doing so much for us working and looking after the accounts and doing —

She knew when he would reach the end of this, finding the pause where she expected: 'So who was there?'

Oh the usual you know.

More words followed and Guillaume stood and Minnette watched as he finished taking off his shirt, listening, partly listening to him speak, what he was saying not an evasion, no, but he turned away from her as he spoke, bedside lamp on her side of the bed throwing shadows, hollowing out an eye socket, light crawling across brow, nose, slipping off cheek bone without gaining purchase just as it failed to reveal anything of torso.

'That's good, that they're committed, so enthusiastic, the new...' she pretended to be on the verge of sneezing, trying to hide the hesitation, the tell-tale pause before she could continue: 'students. Who was there?'

Oh... Guillaume slipping out of his shirt, wadding it as he crossed to the bathroom. You remember Jean and Gérard of course and— and his voice dropped, a whisper, it was late, the time of night people whisper, unless they're angry, rowing, don't care about the neighbours, the weight of the clock, the smallness of the hour— and you know Yves hasn't been for ages and— and he walked to the bathroom.

'I don't know Nils-Bertil.'

Yes you do, the bathroom door closing a little behind him, blurring intonation, joined us in March, you've met him.

'I have?'

Only yes. Only the rustle of clothing.

'I have?'

Guillaume came out of the bathroom. Unconsciously, Minnette adjusted the long sleeves of her nightdress. You've met him, Guillaume told her, sitting on the bed, sitting in clean underpants and T-shirt, sitting close enough she could see them to be fresh-on, smell washing powder, prompting him to go on, face straight because her expression might say what her voice should not, that he often slept nude, often slept in underwear, almost never in a T-shirt.

René. Raymond. Giles. Jean-Paul. François...

All male. Except, perhaps... Had he stumbled a little over the last, given it a male pronunciation?

René. Raymond. Giles. Jean-Paul. Françoise...

It's so late. Guillaume gave her a kiss, turned over, back towards her. Saying good night. Or something like that.

She lay for a long time. Listening. Sure he was still awake. Listening to his breathing. Trying to sense when he relaxed, slept, without touching him or moving closer. Wanting to be sure before she dared go to the bathroom to look at his shirt, to examine his underwear.

I don't want to be like this.

Flat empty when she came home from work.

I could spend the evening reading. I could study. I could.

Guillaume would be home later. Sometime.

I could think something else.

Guillaume was out. He would be home. Later.

'I'm not thinking this any more,' Minnette told the empty apartment as she began systematically going through Guillaume's drawers, boxes of notes, old diaries.

Giulio Schifano was reputed to be the most adept seer and fortune-teller in 17th Century Rome, famed for using a black mirror of ground volcanic glass. It was with this mirror that he was said to have translated part of a certain book, written in an alien language and claimed to be more profound and important than the writings of the hermeticist, Giodarno Bruno, or any of the greatest grimoires then in circulation. The claims were made by a Swiss physician who said that he had corresponded with Schifano on the contents of the mysterious book for over three years. Concerned when the letters stopped, the physician said that he had travelled to Rome but could find no trace of the fortune-teller despite an exhaustive search.

The story lay forgotten until it was resurrected, first in an unfinished novel by the writer and occultist, Edward Bulwer-Lytton, later in the writings and correspondence of Samuel Liddell 'MacGregor' Mathers, who styled himself the Comte de Glenstrae and had co-founded the Golden Dawn. From there, Schifano's remarkable powers and his work on the mysterious book entered into wider currency, appearing as an incidental detail in Dennis Wheatley's *Strange Conflict* and in a short story fragment by the great fantasy writer, H.P. Lovecraft, which later inspired works by artists as diverse as Thomas Ligotti and Nurse With Wound. Eventually, Schifano's discoveries and the bizarre cosmogony described by the Swiss physician worked their way back into mainstream esoteric lore, their retelling in numerous popular books on the subject ultimately helping them gain a niche in the work of a dozen modern-day occult societies.

In 1998, a researcher based in Minneapolis proved, as conclusively as is possible, that the Swiss physician had fabricated the whole story. It seemed that Schifano had not even existed. Yet tales of his book and his black mirror continue to circulate and are quoted frequently in on-line journals, pamphlets and magazines. Several popular books discussing the 'secret and true nature' of world history have mentioned Schifano's discoveries in a way that would leave the casual reader in no doubt of their authenticity.

Stories have an inertia, as has often been observed.

It probably means nothing then that, three years ago, a highly respected collector of occult artefacts, with well-established connections with several museums and academic institutions, announced that he had located Schifano's mirror and was close to securing its purchase. A silence followed the announcement and it was thought that, in all likelihood, the collector had been mistaken or the deal had fallen through. And yet, two months ago, the collector announced that he was on the trail of Schifano's book.

Guillaume wasn't giving the young blonde woman any more attention than anyone else at the meeting. Back room at a café, posters in the corridor advertising Maoist discussion groups and spiritual consciousness-raising encounters. Narrow window in the door.
Guillaume not giving the young blonde girl any more attention than anyone else at the meeting. Fifteen, twenty people. Talking. Enthused. It had looked like a good talk. Hard to tell. In the corridor, door closed, having to duck out the side exit when anyone came near, but Guillaume had looked impressive. And the audience were talking, clustered around him, around René, Raymond, Giles, Jean-Paul, François, Nils-Bertil, around Guillaume, Guillaume gesturing and animated and lapping up the attention, obviously enjoying this, call it a triumph, the words hardly mattered.
He was carefully not giving the little blonde any more attention than anyone else at the meeting. The truth was framed behind scratched glass, lit with a halogen strip-light. It was in the flexing of a hand or a shoulder or a turn of his head as he nodded, as he laughed, as he adopted an earnest expression, as he pretended not to be so very aware of the blonde, eighteen or nineteen or twenty at most, the girl framed behind scratched glass, window in the door giving an unbreakable view of a nod or the angle between one torso, the mass of another.
Minnette slipped out of the side exit.

Minnette stood on the bus, searching the faces of the people walking along the pavement.
Minnette watched Guillaume sleep, muscles twitch, grow still.
Minnette stared at the words of a half-finished letter, paper bent around the typewriter's roller, scanning the spaces between sentences, the blank lines between paragraphs.

Minnette sniffed at Guillaume's shirts, fished from the laundry hamper, searching for hints of perfume.

Minnette asked herself if she might be seeing what wasn't there.

Minnette never asked herself if she might be seeing what wasn't there.

Following him. Waiting a count of nine, of nineteen. Until the sound of footsteps had just faded. Corridor outside the apartment deserted. Wanting to run down the stairs and holding, holding back. Searching for his shape along the pavement ahead, weaving between other people whose only purpose was to obstruct, to give a temporary hiding place. Breaking off only when the pressure of thoughts about being late for work grew too much. Those thoughts becoming less urgent, promises to the general manager that she would be early or on time from now on slipping, fading, freeing her to follow Guillaume for longer, longer.

Talks and meetings most nights now. Standing outside bookshop, meeting hall, sometimes someone's apartment, watching people in ones and twos or threes milling, searching or going directly in, looking at their faces from across the street. Searching.

If she couldn't make it home before him, and some nights the urge to know and understand transfixed her past the point when the voices of caution told her she had to get back to make everything appear normal, on those nights she had the chance of overtime, had to work late on a rush job, catch up before the quarterly audit, the semi-annual stocktake, smiling and sighing and repeating that the money will come in handy and asking again how was your evening, did the meeting go well, how do you feel about progress, and feeling no doubt that for now, for always, she would never have to tell him she had been sacked from the factory, instead watching him as he walked, rode the métro, watching Guillaume in cafés, bookshops, meeting halls, waiting outside someone's apartment, watching closely, until the young blonde girl appeared.

Minnette waited across the street, merging deeper into the stone of the doorway. An old woman walking a dog, dog reluctant to be led, wanting to linger in the doorway, sniff, cock one leg. An Algerian man standing on the edge of the doorway, talking, angry there was no reply, wanting to know why, swearing and muttering when he finally gave up. Conscious of time passing. Not worried about that. A slight anxiety, perhaps. Night unseasonably hot. Sweat running, finding paths of its own. Leaving thirst. Conscious of stone, of time.

The young blonde woman-girl-slut. Head down. Arse wiggling to the clouds and the last face of the moon. Night hot, smelling of the bins overflowing at the gutterside, the waiters pausing as they hosed down the pavement, watching the young blonde woman-girl-slut, arse wiggling under the last face of the moon.

Arse wiggling until it stopped.

Next morning no cooler and the café reeking of carbolic and the nattering of a race commentator on the radio, waitress pretending she didn't exist even when, finally, she indicated that she had finished with this coffee, would like another after all.

The young blonde woman-girl-slut, caught in the art nouveau curlicues of the café's name on the window, pushing the door to the tiny apartment house shut before a lorry crossed between them, hiding her.

Minnette almost forgot to leave any money.

She followed her everywhere. To the boutique where she fiddled and tinkered with the window displays two days a week. The university lectures on three mornings, the tutorials on two afternoons. To cafés, bookshops, the cinema, meetings.

Guillaume was clever, never standing too close, never giving too much attention at the expense of others. The slut stared at him and drooled and cooed and simpered. But she never tried to touch him.

He walked her to the nearest bus stop.

Two others from the meeting walked with them.

He embraced her, met her at an afternoon talk at a room over a vegan café.

Three other followers were with him.

Guillaume was cunning. But she had seen the truth, knew that it lay, interwoven if hidden, beneath the surface of all this.

Minnette walked closer behind the young blond slut in the street. Sat at most two tables away in cafés. The same row in the cinema. She called the pay phone in the lobby of the slut's apartment house. Minnette waited, knowing what she would see eventually.

Guillaume and the blonde thing. Sitting. Together. A little table in the corner, partially hidden by a potted plant, bistro busy but not so much this corner at the back didn't seem romantic, didn't feel intimate.

No surprise when the blonde thing rounded in the street, turning a corner and finding her waiting.

'I…'

Wanting to get in first, say something damaging, scouring, and unable, despite how oddly inevitable this felt, to think of anything. Silence. Neither of them moving. Until Minnette began to smile.

'I've done nothing wrong.' An edge of tears to her voice.

Minnette smiled.

'Nothing.' Frustration and anger. But, was that the anger of innocence or the anger of guilt?

Minnette smiled and the blonde thing began to shake, stammered that nothing was going on, nothing wrong. Blurting she and Guillaume were friends, she respected, looked up to him.

Minnette smiled. Tried to look the thing in the eye. Kept trying although the other one looked away, looked away, grew more red faced and louder voiced.

'He came to me. Guillaume. I went, okay, at first, I went with friends, curiosity, you've got to understand this isn't, I mean, there's nothing, there's nothing— you've got a right, I guess, I mean, to be fair and that, I see that, that you're upset, I do, but please, can't you, can't you please—'

Minnette smiled.

Tears now. Just in time. And snot. That was to be expected. And the hands, reaching, falling away. Still no eye contact, though. And that was also to be expected.

'— you need to talk to, I mean, you don't understand, you don't—please, he came to me, Guillaume came to me, saying, you know, that I have potential and and and I was flattered, okay, of course, but he meant it, means it, you see, Guillaume came up to me and asked if there was something wrong, if he could help.'

Minnette stopped smiling.

No point in listening.

'It's your fault. You did this.'

Me?

He would repeat it again. She knew. Knew he would tell her again that her going in search of the truth was wrong, that she had found the wrong truth.

I'm not doing this, not now. I'm too, too—

Guilty. But there was no time to say it. Guillaume wrenched open the front door.

A head appeared across the hall, attracted by their voices, neighbour ducking back as she glowered, as the neighbour caught the look on Guillaume's face.

Self-conscious.

Guilty.

I can't do this now. Go back.

She knew he was going to say that, too. Something of the sort. Both of them walking downstairs. Pace increasing. Almost running.

I'll talk to you later, Minnette, I'm too angry now, too angry to, to— I can't believe what you—

'Liar.' Word filling her mouth like bile, or vomit, or grease heated to blood temperature and dribbling between her lips. 'Liar.'

Me? Me? I didn't lie about going to work every day, about—

'Liar.' Grabbing the street door as he tried to slam it in her face. 'Going to her now, are you?'

He walked away, stride lengthening, quickening. So she almost had to run to keep pace. So she knew what he was hiding was the truth.

'Eh? Liar? Was she another unhappy searcher you could reach out to, offer to help, offer—'

It's nothing like that.

But then, he had to say that.

She has tremendous potential, power, maybe, that's—

That was exactly what she expected him to say.

'Liar.'

Stop saying that, it's nothing like that, I can't believe you could think, that you could do what you've— 'what have you done, Minnette?'

Guillaume stopped abruptly and it was hard not to crash into him, to avoid his hands reaching, spreading towards her. Pleading. No. In false sincerity. That was the truth.

She could make a great high priestess. Don't you see? She has the need, the potential, and, okay, 'yes, that wasn't what I thought, not the first thing I—'

Taking a step out of reach. Searching for that smile, the one she had used on the blonde creature, the one she needed to complete this moment. Because this, this scene, this moment, was what she had been thinking of. Something like this.

I saw potential in her, Minnette and, yes, I know we 'talked about you being the community's high priestess and you'll always, always' be my priestess, you know that, but this girl, 'you have to understand—'

It was clever, the way he mixed truths and lies, truths with other kinds of truth. Minnette laughed. Ignoring passers-by staring, the look on his face, which seemed frightened, and angry. But she expected him to be angry.

'Stop this, Minnette, stop this—'

'Liar.' Yelling. It felt good to yell, release it all, all the pressure that had been building since he'd placed her in this impossible position. Since he had come back, claimed to have wanted her all along. 'Liar.'

And he turned his back, strode away. As he was supposed to.

And she followed. Finding breath to run and shout, legs hitting the pavement hard, almost running because he was almost running. Which was hard to account for because, in the truth as she had thought of it, turning away at this point was what she should have done. Not run until she was ahead of him so that it was he who was chasing her, words exchanged, goading, or encouraging, there was no saying, only letting him take the lead, following him, swapping again, again, until there was no saying, no telling who was chasing whom, what either of them hoped for. Except to run, to shout. Until they passed a café with two middle-aged women in rayon suits tutting, a man with dandruff on the lapels of his suit, teenagers with Farrah Fawcett-Majors haircuts.

'Answer me!'

Old lady hefting a bulging shopping bag, stepping out of a *tabac*, freezing, watching.

'Where are you going?'

Walking quickly. Crossing the road and avoiding traffic more by luck than instinct. Emotions adding fuel to muscles, lengthening stride, making it hard to breathe, hard to see through the tears, hard to know who was running away from whom.

It was in 1628 that the hermeticist Albrecht Claes agreed to manufacture the Philosopher's Stone, the *calculus albis*, for a very wealthy patron. Claes' spectacular failure resulted in a spell in prison, after which he dropped out of history completely. His name has become a by-word in popular books on fringe science and the folly of alchemy: here was a man who had believed in nonsense and been justly rewarded for his hubris and stupidity. And if rumours continue to circulate, it proves only that the truth can never get in the way of a good story. Because only the most fanatical, a True Believer, would accept anything in the notion that he had failed deliberately, that he had been hounded, threatened by this patron, placed under intolerable pressure until, unable to say 'no', Claes had gone ahead with the Great Work, knowing that the best way to hide his secrets was to be publicly humiliated. And yet, in the last, there is no proof, none at all one way or the other, although surely the rational explanation—Claes as hubristic fraud—makes the most sense, doesn't it? Closing the book, book sinking into shadows, shadows sinking into darkness. Doesn't it? she asked again and she might ask again and get no answer, silence a different answer each time she asked, huge shape keeping pace, black on blacker so it stood out enough for her to see the heft and width of shoulders and neck, the weight of its angular head, its horns, its eyes slow-blinking and never leaving her, never, leaving her blinking, staring at the light through the curtains, disoriented, not sure if this was Düsseldorf or Paris of the 1970s or whether, or whether...

There was no going back to sleep. Hip complaining bitterly, Minnette managed to swing her legs out of bed, eyes gritty, the corner of one caked with gunge, broken night chafing at the inside of her skull, making her bones and sinews ache. Foot catching the edge of *Airport*, knocking it aside without noticing, box of photographs forgotten. Dumping muesli into a bowl, holding on to the edge of the kitchen counter. She would clean this place, the kitchen at least, clean it when she got back tonight. Looking at the crumbs scattered across the counter-top. Like stars. Like dots to be connected.

Like crumbs. Which she would clean up tonight.

Besides, she would feel better by this evening, Minnette nodded to herself as she sniffed the first open carton of milk, moved on to the second lodged in the fridge door. Bad night, exhausted before the day had chance to begin. But once it got going... And, either way, this place, the kitchen at least, was due a clean and she was going to do that tonight. Slopping milk over cereal, taking comfort in what she was thinking even if she knew it wasn't true, wasn't very likely, anyway, because it was that or wish she had enough saved to throw it all in and go somewhere hot and sunny and simpler and gently roast until there was no moisture left and she was perfectly preserved after sitting in the sun for so long without moving. Wandering into the living room, chewing unenthusiastically at the next mouthful of muesli, happy with the thought of baking in the sun even if it was nonsense because the thought of sitting and doing nothing was worse than the thought of going to the bookshop each day, each day no different from the last, which was a terrible thought, as terrible as—

Minnette watched the iMac's screen change colour, fan and disk drive spinning up. Not finishing that line of thought. Staring out the window instead, not thinking of anything, except, perhaps, cleaning the kitchen tonight, which was a decision of sorts. Another mouthful of muesli. Or—and she hesitated to think this, turning towards computer, paper piled haphazardly around it, yellow sticky notes peeling off the iMac's purple shell.

Another mouthful of muesli.

Or giving up.

'There. Said it.'

Her mouth full.

'Or giving up.'

Words blurred by milk, cereals, a raisin stuck to one tooth. The usual morning sounds from the building, outside. But nothing dramatic.

The iMac hummed.

'And cleaning the kitchen. Tonight.'

Taking comfort from this even if she knew it wasn't true, wasn't very likely, anyway. Bowl in one hand, using the other to turn M. Jacotey's piece of paper, launch a browser, tap in URL and login details, wincing as she flexed her bad hip, watching the progress bar. Standing still as the podcast began to play, Guillaume Boucaya's voice coming out of the iMac's speakers.

Business was slow that day. When someone did come into the shop, Minnette straightened, relaxing when she saw it was not M. Jacotey. Few of the customers lingered. She slouched on the high stool behind the till. Staring at the books, the shelves that needed dusting or reordering. Not thinking of anything.

There was a man on the métro. About forty, dark hair streaked with grey, clothes baggy, clean if cheap-looking. Anonymous. He sat, hunched over a book, writing. A page-a-day diary, probably open at today's date, page half-full, words getting smaller the further he went down the page, trying to get everything in. The train bucked into motion, diary almost slipping free, giving a glimpse of a phrase or two before he caught hold, began writing again. His day. He was writing about his day. Trying to make sense.

Minnette caught sight of her reflection backed by the smears and shadows of the tunnel wall.
He had betrayed her. It made no sense but it was the truth. And his voice on the podcast had been slick and insinuating and he had said the sorts of things a charlatan would say. It made sense but it was the truth. And she had spent her life...

Minnette looked away from her reflection.

Her reflection tried to catch her eye.
A third eye over the squat's front door—
Her reflection was no longer that woman.
You keep saying you want to get more into it, so I thought—
Her reflection was not the woman Nicholas had been trying to please.
The years had marked him, turned hair from dark brown to granite and his eyes—
Her reflection tried to catch her eye, wanting to frame itself in the window, entrance lobby in total darkness behind the glass.

Minnette ignored it, grunting as she opened the front door, urgency making her fumble all the more as she searched the walls for the light switch.

Not that there was any reason to be afraid of the dark. And that was the truth.

The second hand moved inexorably, no matter how much concentration, how hard she stared, willed it forward.

When the time of M. Jacotey's meeting passed, Minnette relaxed.

No point getting involved, getting up hope. Anything, everything else was futile.

No point getting involved, getting up hope. Anything, everything else was futile.

No point getting involved, getting up hope. Anything, everything else was futile.

Minnette smiled at herself in the mirror.

And the smile, that was true, too.

Still she hesitated. Flustered, taxi ride adding to a mounting anxiety that it would be nice to explain away.

No answer when she pressed the intercom. Of course. Resisting the urge to check the time again.

A buzz, and the sound of the lock releasing.

Minnette looking at the open door.

And still she hesitated.

They were not what she had expected. It didn't matter. This was still a stupid thing to do.

The woman greeted her on the stairs, smiled, led her upwards, to this apartment, her apartment, the woman speaking, in a way meant to put Minnette in an inferior position, that's how it sounded, only the woman smiled as she led Minnette up the spiralling staircase and it was hard to find conviction that a put-down was what she had intended, Minnette trying to cling onto this interpretation as the woman showed her through the door, told her she should, she must make herself at home, as the woman introduced Minnette to the people sitting around the living room, offering her something to drink, eat, as M.

Jacotey nodded to her from the other side of the wide living room, half rising in his seat, looking incongruous in his rumpled canvas jacket, jogging bottoms, room unostentatious but confident, paintings on the walls deeply metaphysical, but only on the third or fourth glance, M. Jacotey's round dreamer's face and diffident stoop looking out of place amongst restrained Scandinavian design and what looked to be quietly valuable antiques and Guillaume, eight or nine other people in the room beside them, and Guillaume, everyone seated in a rough circle of chairs and two sofas and Guillaume in jeans and casual shirt and jumper draped across his shoulders, not the blazer and cravat from London she hated, no sign of the monocle she hated, little outward sign of the man she hated from book covers and talks and from good reason, the man she had been sniping with and defaming for the past fifteen or so years, that man replaced by this, apparently more reserved man, not sitting at the centre of attention, as she had imagined, sitting to one side on a footstool, a cup of tea steaming beside him on the floor, and M. Jacotey half-rising as the woman who had met her introduced Minnette, and Guillaume standing as the woman who had met her introduced Minnette, and the others around the room, Minnette glancing at them, mumbling, a greeting or a thank you for their hospitality, the sound more important than the words and the sound didn't matter so much, each one of them welcoming and pleasant, open expressions, so far as she could tell in a glance, expecting and imagining hostility and unable not to look back at Guillaume, away almost at once to M. Jacotey, dreamer's round face seeming incongruent as he bobbed her a half-bow of greeting, as the people on the sofas nodded and greeted her arrival, warmly although she searched for what she wanted and expected in them, mumbling something as her gaze skimmed over them, toward M. Jacotey, not taking them in properly but seeing they were older than she had expected, none under fifty when she had presumed, wanted, imagined that Guillaume would be surrounding himself with cranks and kids and crackpots and overt signs of having finally succumbed to madness, which would, might, could have been a comfort of sorts, M. Jacotey bobbing a little bow and sitting again, taking up his glass of what appeared to be fizzing orangeade, Guillaume's expression one she wasn't able to interpret, starting for the vacant chair the woman who had showed her in was indicating, the others in the room turning in their seats to watch, room big and wide and comfortable in a way that suggested a confidence, that came from having no money worries or from somewhere else, these people older than she had imagined, hoped, to be honest, and some of them looking, at a glance, as affluent as this apartment, which she instantly hated, which made her try to keep her eyes down, unable to resist a second glance, her face becoming warm because they were watching her and because, frankly, this was a stupid thing to do, another glance for signs they were laughing, that this was a joke, a bored lark, M. Jacotey in canvas jacket and jogging trousers and dreamer's face, looking away from Guillaume, still standing, still watching her, still with an expression she didn't want to interpret, not while looking at him, easier with eye averted when she could think what she liked, M. Jacotey sitting, patting the chair beside his, asking the man sitting there if he wouldn't mind…? man willingly, happily giving up his seat, perhaps happily, because she wanted to believe otherwise, because she was self-conscious and wanted, expected, this to be a disaster, better if it were, man standing to one side, indicating Minnette should sit, offering to get her a drink, a plate of something, Minnette finding it hard to meet his eye, mumbling something like: Thank you, or something like: I'm sorry, I'm interrupting your meeting, and M. Jacotey gently taking her hand, patting her hand as she sat, his presence incongruous, mannerisms just as she remembered from the shop but this wasn't that M. Jacotey offering her something from his plate of nibbles while her drink came, not quite the bumbler and dreamer, more present, less distracted, less trying to distract unwanted attention, which was

disconcerting, all of this was disconcerting as the man whose seat she had taken handed her a glass of wine, taking a large mouthful of wine to cover confusion, to find the strength to go on hating these people, because they hated her, they didn't want her here, not now, not late, flush on her face deepening as she noticed Guillaume, still standing, still with that expression she couldn't interpret, Guillaume saying horrible things in a snide voice, Guillaume smiling, encouraging further murmurs of welcome from the people around the room as he introduced Minnette to them again, subtly castigating her for being late, reassuring her they had hardly started, that she had come at the best time, M. Jacotey squeezing her arm to underline how unwelcome she was, M. Jacotey squeezing her hand in a companionable sort of way, Guillaume nodding to her, saying they should continue, Guillaume—
This was not what she had imagined. It didn't matter. It would still be a stupid thing to do.

And she tried. Tried to find fault and distrust and animosity. She knew it was there. She wanted it to be there.

But the words, the voices. Speaking of their researches and theories. Serious, sincere. No bluster. None of the wild credulity she expected, repudiated, had come to mock and reject, a wild and final and cataclysmic rejection so she could be done with all this.

She tried. To find fault. To conjure ridicule, make something to be scorned. She knew those things were here. She wanted them to be here.

When M. Jacotey cleared his throat, she knew she had what she wanted, the drivel, the nonsense, the impracticality, the ridiculous. He cleared his throat and spoke and Minnette leaned forward, seeing Guillaume from the corner of her eye, pretending to see only M.

Jacotey, ready to have provocation at last, remaining poised as he spoke because surprise would not release her, the eccentric, obsessive meanderings he babbled in the shop stripped away to leave the concepts that had been hidden, in plain sight, amongst the verbiage all along.

And still she tried and still she was suspicious and still she refused to accept. She knew what she was listening to. She knew what was here.

But she could rely on Guillaume. On Svengali. The Charlatan. As the others spoke he would never be able to stop himself from wading in, taking control, spouting crap, slick and superficially convincing but lies at heart, all of it lies. As they spoke, he said very little, seeming to listen, and when he spoke it was mostly to encourage, to prod, spur, twist, voice strident, voice soft, dominating, drawing out the others and making it easier for them to speculate, make leaps of intuition, that he derailed, corrupted to make it seem like it was his idea all along, satisfied that each one of them had contributed, created something. Of his making alone. Something they had all shared in.

She tried, because that was why she had come. To find the spur and reason, the dramatic end. Or something like that. All this being wrong. All this being a waste of a life. All this jarring, galling because it should be easy to reconcile the truth with what she was seeing and hearing, outside events matching inside fact. She knew what she was seeing. And she tried. And she tried hard.

Minnette listened to the discussion around the room, knowing the truth was here.
    Somewhere.

Guillaume held out a glass of brandy.
    The formal meeting was over, group fragmenting into clusters that in turn fragmented and recombined,

discussion not over yet. Minnette watching from a corner of the room, pain in her hip bad after sitting so long. Pain in her hip beside the point.

'You look like you could do with this.'

She took the glass without a word, sipping without tasting.

'Is this...?'

Looking at him over the rim of the glass. Looking away and taking another sip, another breath.

'Is it?'

Guillaume tilted his head to one side and she wanted to see mockery in that.

'I'm not sure— Oh, I think I see...'

She could convince herself it was mockery.

'Yes.' Guillaume nodded. 'Yes. Very. For us. Completely.'

Real.

Minnette took another sip, glass slick against her palm. No, other way round, both hands moist, cold, shaky. She was trembling.

She bit her lip.

'I hate you,' she told Guillaume, looking away. Making herself look him in the eye. 'I hate you.'

'I know.' He sipped from his own glass.

'But I want this.'

'Yes.' Another sip, deeper. 'You can't have it.'

Tone too soft to be the slap across the face it should have been. It should have been a blow, the final provocation. Minnette swallowed most of her brandy. Trembling. Hands cold. Head no less tight as the brandy went down hard. 'I thought so... I hate you.'

'I know. But you still want this.'

Not a question.

'No.'

Not a choice.

'Yes.'

'I'm sorry—'

'Really?' Something of the anger she wanted to load into that word. And gone as she looked at him, into

Guillaume's eyes, the tension of muscles that betrayed the truth within. 'Sorry.' Raising her glass, knowing it was empty. 'I've decided to give in. Give up. All of this. There's no—'

'There's an alternative. If you want it. Genuinely.' He put down his glass. 'If you genuinely want, there is somewhere you could, somewhere you might want to go, Minnette.'

Silence. Nothing. Hope was not something she could feel. I'm going to give up, I've had enough, there's no point: that was the truth she had come to find. That was what she wanted to make true.

'If you want it, the chance is there, Minnette, a chance of maybe finding what you're searching for.'

It was.

Traffic pours along this stretch of road, endless, fractious. There is no time here. Only motion. Endless. Mindless. There is no time here. No breath. The trees lining one side of this road are black, branches spikes. They stand over the footpath, trembling in the slight breeze, straining with an impossible desire to join in, uproot themselves, run with the traffic: the footpath is broken by the flexing of their roots. They want to be away from here as much as any of these racing drivers.

The wall rising to face the trees is sallow, worn by the slow, slow passage of years. Some of the trees reach across the footpath to chafe and prod. The wall remains unresponsive. The trees were planted long after the wall was raised, the traffic has dashed and quibbled for even less time. Neither is worthy of notice. The wall faces the street without betraying anything.

She glances up at its face as she walks along the cracked footpath beneath the trees. The wall is long, featureless for most of its length, anonymous. Yet there is time and space here. Enough for her bad hip to make her limp worse. Enough for anxiety to make her slow, stop as the traffic continues.

Careful not to trip over the roots and fissures, she goes to the wall, lays a hand flat against its stones, finger tips trailing as she takes the hand away.

She looks at her palm, feeling the roughness of the wall on her skin, seeing dust and tiny crystals on palm, fingers. She stops herself wiping them away on her thigh, remembering she is wearing her best suit: a pale green, woollen suit she has not worn in possibly ten years, her low-heeled shoes turning white from the dust on the pavement, ruining the shine she diligently worked into them before leaving the apartment. Thinking this was like a job interview. Laughing at the thought. Cutting off the laugh because there was an edge of hysteria, a reminder of how scared she was. How scared she still is.

Taking a handkerchief from her sleeve, she wipes at the grit. Hands shaking. Sweating. Trembling spreading, growing as she resumes walking.

The door is inset into a shallow archway, its wood dark, almost black. She lifts a hand. Lets it fall. There is a bell pull, metal loop no less blackened than the door. Cold against her fingers. Biting her bottom lip, weight shifting. Bad hip protesting.

Her knuckles strike the wood without conscious volition. They seem to make no sound, not enough sound, wood old, dense, traffic endlessly noisy.

She knocks again. Once more with greater force, wincing at the pain in her fingers. The blow still sounds flat, shallow: too little.

Standing back, becoming self-conscious, she does not knock again. Seconds pass to the accompaniment of engines revving, horns snarling, the thud of car stereos, the no-less-aggressive soughing of the trees, branches creaking as they rub together.

No one will answer. They have not heard. And she feels reprieve, that it is better this way. But she knows what she feels the most.

She hesitates, reluctant to use the bell, thinking that, perhaps, yes, after everything, there being no answer is answer enough. A fitting end to it all: the kind of end she had come to expect.

She turns, ignoring hip, taking one stride over the cracked footpath, a second, not feeling, refusing to feel, and almost missing the sound of a lock turning, of the door opening, silently, opening almost silently, and almost —almost—walking on this time instead of stopping, going back, standing on the threshold for a moment, two, no more than three, before, at last, going inside.

Afterword

I don't wish to say very much about the origins and inspirations for this novel; self-effacement aside, this story found me, not the other way around. I do feel I should say, in deference to both the general reader and those who may come to this story because of its subject matter, that I've largely and very deliberately invented the majority of occult lore on display here. Although I did a lot of research during the writing of the novel, on top of years already spent reading in and around the subject, I didn't feel an approach heavily indebted to its source materials fitted in with Minnette's obsessive, enclosed world. If you like, as I was blurring the boundaries between the literary and the fantastique, so I wanted to blur the boundaries between what exists in the external world and what is true within the confines of the imagination... and the pages of this book. I hope, however, leavened as they are with the occasional snippet of documented lore, that the systems and worldviews I've created for Minnette are largely true in spirit to the concepts and practices of real magicians and occultists, if otherwise fictional in detail or their ultimate conclusions about our universe.

A couple of thank yous are in order. First of all, many thanks to Ian Gregson, who cheerfully read several drafts of this book and whose advice was just right in getting me to the final shape of this story—I'm only sorry this hasn't turned out as *The Unbearable Lightness of Being* for the occult, Ian, but maybe next time...

Secondly, I must thank Jan Fortune, who is much more than my editor and publisher. That you believe in this book is all the validation it needs. That you believe in me is a constant surprise. It is for this and much more that this novel is dedicated to you.

Finally, I extend a big thank you to the unknown woman I noticed on the streets of Paris one September day in 2014. You don't know it, *madame*, but it's thanks to you